# WITHOUT A TRACE

SHADOWS OF LONDON #5

ARIANA NASH

Without a Trace, Shadows of London #5

**Ariana Nash** ~ *Dark Fantasy Author*

Subscribe to Ariana's mailing list & get the exclusive story 'Sealed with a Kiss' free.

Join the Ariana Nash Facebook group for all the news, as it happens.

Copyright © 2022 Ariana Nash.

Edited by No Stone Unturned Editing.

Proofread by Marked and Read.

Cover design by Natasha Snow.

Edited in US English but retains some UK spelling as part of the character of the work.

Version 1 - August 2022

www.ariananashbooks.com

# Alexander

Everything had to be perfect.

Dinner out. Our first official excursion from the cottage.

In the six months since our apparent deaths, John and I had traversed Scottish lochs and mapped every gorse bush and patch of heather in a five-mile radius of the cottage. I'd read the limited collection of books three times and John had fixed the cottage's old plumbing, while teaching himself how to summon and control the source.

It was time for Phase Two: living our new lives in public. Me, as Harvey Lloyd, and John as Christopher Jennings. Harvey and Chris. The names were taking some getting used to. Nobody knew us, besides the intrepid postman and grocery delivery driver. Alone, we were still very much Alex and John. But that had to change if our new identities were going to stick.

Dinner out was the beginning of Phase Two.

John rode in the passenger seat of the Range Rover I'd recently bought using Harvey Lloyd's healthy bank balance. His gaze tracked over the rolling Scottish Highlands. He'd grown his hair out, allowing its loose waves to lick the bottom of his jaw. It suited him and gave me something satisfying to grip when I bent him under me. I'd grown a hint of a beard—not too long, the itch was unbearable. Just enough to scrub the notion from anyone we met that I might be the clean-cut Alexander Kempthorne who had died in an unfortunate accident.

"You all right?" he asked.

"Yes." He'd seen me glancing over. "I was wondering whether to shave off the beard."

His smirk was enough to cut me off and then his gaze turned sly, and the delicious kind of hungry. "That would be a bloody shame."

If he liked it, then so did I. I chuckled, now a victim of his scrutiny, and pulled the Range Rover into the restaurant's parking lot, on the outskirts of Fort William. During mid-tourist season, the parking lot was almost full, and tonight was no exception. We'd have no trouble blending into the crowd. Two unknown faces from out of town wouldn't raise any eyebrows.

John climbed from the Range Rover. I met him on his side of the car, spotting his thumbs tucked into his trouser pockets and the quizzical look on his face. "What is this?" he asked.

I'd only told him we were going out for the evening, not where. "Dinner."

His smile ticced. "Is that a good idea?"

"We certainly can't stay isolated forever."

"You sure it's been long enough?"

"We're about to find out."

His smile was the good, relaxed kind. "Lead on, Harv."

"Harvey," I corrected, walking up the little winding path to the restaurant's front door. Chatter and laughter bubbled from inside, sounds neither of us had heard in months. John Domenici and Alexander Kempthorne were dead and buried. This was Chris and Harvey's first genuine test.

"Whatever you say, Harv."

He was impossible. And I loved him for it. As I opened the door, a blast of noise hit us. I hesitated, then held the door open for John and met his smirk with my own. He knew how to tease, and he knew how it drove me wild. If he continued with those salacious glances all evening, we wouldn't make it back to the cottage before I made sure he paid for them, against the Range's Rover's front grille, my hand on his erection, just out of public sight, and risky enough to be exhilarating.

"What has you smirking?" he whispered.

"Nothing suitable for public conversation."

I'd booked us a table near the windows, with a view of the inky loch and twilight sky nestled between distant mountains.

"So," John said once we'd settled in our seats. The server handed us both menus and poured the wine I'd pre-ordered. "Finally, this is the dinner you promised me?"

"Sorry it's a few months late."

He lifted his glass. "To new beginnings."

"New beginnings."

We chinked our glasses, ordered, ate, drank wine, and chatted, and the restaurant could have been a McDonalds for all the attention I gave it. John was all I cared to admire. He talked about the time he'd gotten caught stealing pens from the school supplies and selling them to the kids on the playground. He'd been twelve and had only been caught because a friend had grassed him up. I'd heard the story before—we'd shared a great deal from our pasts during the quiet times in the cottage—but let him tell it again, enjoying the timbre of his voice and the way his eyes sparkled with mischief.

"You going to tell me what happened at that theater, where you got Tasered?"

I chuckled. The dessert arrived. Two chocolate and truffle cheesecake ensembles that had heart attack written all over them. John tucked in, fork prying the dessert apart, then sliding it between his lips.

"It's not nearly as exciting as I've made it out to be."

"Try me." He teased the dessert with his fork, picking up delicate pieces and eating them seductively, not needing to say a word. He knew I was his. All he had to do was crook a finger, and I'd be on my knees.

I cleared my throat and shifted in the chair, then told him about the disastrous theater trip, my recall trailing off whenever he licked his fork.

He laughed at the story, his demeanor so relaxed, I never wanted this night to end.

"So what's all this really about?" he asked, carefully dissecting the final piece of cheesecake.

I blinked, ambushed. "What do you mean?"

He shrugged and scooped a tiny morsel onto his fork. "You're nervous."

"No, I'm not."

He laughed, devoured the bite of cheesecake, and pointed the fork at me. "That, Mister Lloyd, is a lie."

I picked up my wine, took a gulp, and slowed the second he grinned, knowing me too well. "I'm excited to be here—that we're here. Together. Like you said, new beginnings."

His right eyebrow arched. He still smiled, so I wasn't yet in trouble, just skirting the edges. There had been a time he wouldn't have been able to read me. Nobody had broken through my barriers. I'd made sure of it. But I couldn't keep John Domenici out of my head, even if I'd wanted to. He'd witnessed too much, and the rest I'd shared.

Hm, no. *That* was a lie. And touched on the one thing he needed to know. The one thing I'd tried and failed to tell him a hundred times in the cottage. The last secret between us, like an unseen thorn in my side.

But that wasn't what I'd brought him here for.

He was right. I *was* nervous. And it had nothing to do with the dinner, or venturing out in public.

His smile cracked. "Al—Harvey?"

He'd seen something on my face, some nervous little twitch had slipped through. Bloody hell. I laughed him off with a dismissive wave and refilled our glasses from the wine bottle. "It's nothing."

"Which, from you, means it's definitely something." He set his fork down and peered through his lashes.

Leaning back in the chair, I smiled into my glass. "Drink your wine."

"You're going to end up with this wine all over that nice shirt if you don't spill whatever it is that has your heart racing, *Harv*. I don't need to hear it. I can feel your trick churning."

That last part he said low and quiet, then leaned forward on the table and narrowed his eyes.

"It's not important." An absolute lie, and I averted my gaze, unable to withstand his scrutiny a second longer. It might have been the most important thing I'd ever had to say. But my heart was racing, nerves ratcheting up. Because it wasn't as simple as just saying the words.

"The fuck it isn't." The teasing tone had vanished, and when I looked, his smile was long gone. "What's going on? It's something bad, isn't it."

"No."

"What aren't you telling me?"

"Chris," I hissed. "Keep your voice down."

Shaking his head, he sighed and then downed his glass of wine. "I'm not doing this." He stood and threw down his napkin. "You promised me. No more lies."

I had said that. I recalled having him wrapped in my arms, naked and slick, breathing hard, and I'd told him those exact words. Perhaps the dinner hadn't been such a great idea, perhaps this was all too soon. Perhaps I was a

fool for getting this far. "And I meant it. If you'd calm down—"

"This could be great." He threw his arms wide. "You and me, we're fuckin' awesome."

A few heads turned our way. I was going to have to stop him, and fast.

"But you can't help keeping those secrets." His eyes flashed, excess trick simmering inside him. "You have to stop—"

"Will you marry me?"

Oh good lord. It was out there. I'd said it. I couldn't take it back, not that I'd want to, but now I'd said it, it was real, and not an insane idea I hadn't been able to get out of my head for the past six months.

My heart stopped. I was definitely having a heart attack brought on by the deadly dessert, or it might have been the beginnings of a panic attack, because John stared, his mouth open, and it seemed as though the entire restaurant had fallen silent. My heart thudded in my ears, behind my ribs, everywhere. I hadn't heard of any latent spiraling from asking one question, but there was always a first time for everything.

"Fuck," John said.

"Well, that is not the answer I was expecting."

He raked a hand through his hair and stepped back from the table. "Fuck."

Again. Not entirely a reply. I hadn't exactly done this before, and I'd planned for it to go slightly different, such as on my knee, with a ring I'd walked seven miles into Fort William for and then back again, to pick up without him knowing. *The ring!* I fumbled in my pocket, grateful I didn't have to see his wrecked expression and wonder why, if we were so great together, as he'd just suggested, he looked as though I'd just punched him in the chest and torn out his heart, not offered him mine.

I pulled the velvet box free. John saw it, recoiled, and couldn't have fled the restaurant any faster if he'd sprinted off a start line.

Jilted, I slumped back in my chair. No, that definitely had not gone as I'd imagined. He'd fled our table like a crime scene. "Hm."

"Er... Mister Harvey, would you like the bill?" The server had seen and heard all of it and had no idea where to look.

I tucked the velvet box back into my pocket and cleared my throat. "Yes, I think that's probably a good idea."

## 2

# D<sup>om</sup>

*Fuck.*

I...

*Fuck.*

I paced in front of the Range Rover, then braced against the hood. "Fuck." Christ, my heart was going to explode or stop, or thump through my ribs. I pushed off the car and paced some more.

Happy noises continued to spill from inside the restaurant, people laughing, joking, having a great time. Alex was in there. He'd... He'd asked me—*me*?!—to marry him?

I pressed a hand over my chest and tried to remember how to breathe. He'd asked me... and what had I done?

I'd lost it, that was what I'd done. I'd lost my shit and left him there.

"Fuck!"

Gravel crunched under my boots. Oh Christ. He'd asked, so I had to answer, right? That was how these things worked. Only, I couldn't. How? How was I supposed to answer that? He could have warned me. But no, he'd gone and dropped that bombshell with no notice, no warning. Six months we'd been in that cottage, six months and he hadn't even hinted that he...

I'd known he was nervous. He'd been nervous all day. Maybe all week. Kinda shady, sometimes quiet, damn jumpy... I'd known something had been up with him, but not *that*.

A car pulled into a spot in the lot and a smiley couple climbed out, glancing over. I braced against the Range Rover's hood again, threw them a fake smile and a nod, so they didn't see me teeter on the verge of having some kind of latent breakdown, and the second they looked the other way I groaned and bowed my head between my arms to stare at the ground.

Oh god.

We'd been doing just fine, why had he asked—I lifted my head, and blinked.

A brown, A4 sized envelope had been tucked under the right windshield wiper. No name. None of the other parked cars had one. Desperate for the distraction so I could think and breathe again and pretend I hadn't just run away from my boyfriend's fucking marriage proposal —I grabbed the envelope, tore it open, and pulled out several sheets of what appeared to be bank statements.

The Kempthorne Enterprises logo had been stamped in the top right-hand corner. Alex's family business, I figured. It took me too long to realize the fact it was there, tucked in an envelope, on our Range Rover windshield, meant someone knew who we were and where we were. And that was very, very bad.

I whirled, scanning the shadowy bushes for any suspicious movement. The noises from the restaurant no longer seemed so jovial and the night no longer harmless. Nobody was obviously lurking nearby, but someone had been here and left the envelope. I examined the sheets of paper again. Bank accounts, for sure. Several six-figure sums of money had been ringed, amounts leaving the Kempthorne accounts for something called *Blackwater*.

What the fuck was Blackwater?

Alex needed to know. But that meant going back inside the restaurant, and as right as that idea was, I also really did not want to walk back in there and see the awful look on his face when he thought something ridiculous, like I didn't want him. It wasn't that. It could never be that. I just…

The restaurant door opened and Alexander Kempthorne jogged down the steps, jacket flaring, face cold. When he marched to the car, he made sure to avoid me. He unlocked the car with a blip of the alarm and climbed behind the wheel.

Oh man, I'd messed up. I'd messed *us* up. I'd messed the dinner up, fucked all his plans, ruined everything, and he was pissed. And now I had to show him that someone was onto us? Maybe it would be better to wait a few hours, until he'd cooled off, so we didn't accidentally trigger some kind of spiraling episode.

I folded the envelope, tucked it into my back pocket, opened the Range Rover door, and got in. He put the car into gear and pulled out of the parking lot. Nobody followed us, I made sure to watch the mirrors. We were so far out in the sticks that there was no way someone could tail us for miles without being spotted.

When we got home, the cottage fire had burned down to embers. Alex threw on a few logs and stoked it back to life, while I loitered in the kitchen area, stuck between wanting to go to him and having to explain why I'd bolted, but also knowing that whatever I had tucked against my back was going to upset everything I hadn't already, and I didn't want that. We'd been fine. Him and me. It had been perfect.

We should never have gone to fucking dinner.

"I'm going to bed." He started up the small iron spiral staircase.

"Alex?"

He stopped halfway, frozen, and still didn't look over.

I had to say something. What if I just said yes? Would that fix everything? But what if I didn't want that? I did... At least, I thought I did. I loved him. More than anything. I just... I wasn't for marrying. That shit didn't happen to me. "G'night."

He climbed the rest of the way in silence.

"Fuck," I whispered and slumped against the kitchen counter. Why was I made like this? Why did I have to go and fuck everything good up?

I needed Gina. She'd have told it to me straight, made

everything sound easy. But she wasn't here, and she could never be here. That life was over. John Domenici. Cecil Court. Gone. This was a fresh start. I could be anyone, I was Chris now, and Chris did not have to be a knob.

After rummaging through the cupboards, I found the stash of whiskey, poured a glass, and sat at the little kitchen table, then spread the bank statements out to get a better picture of what I was seeing. Over two million pounds had been sent to *Blackwater* in a two-week period. Whoever had left the envelope expected Blackwater to mean something.

I grabbed my phone, Googled it and, sipping the whiskey, scrolled through the results. Name of an indie rock band—they didn't sound much like a Kempthorne investment. Some romantic vampire novel; again, not really a Kempthorne Enterprises interest. Blackwater: A privately owned military force. "Hello..." I sat up, clicked, and brought up a fancy webpage for Blackwater Military Research. Apparently, among other things, Blackwater had funded the creation of venom or Ink, as the Americans knew it, the drug that turned latent soldiers into well-behaved murder machines. Kempthorne Enterprises had donated millions to Blackwater. Christ... Did Alex know? It probably didn't mean anything. The bank statements showed countless outgoing payments to other companies. Blackwater was just another way to move money. This kind of financial juggling was automated anyway, wasn't it? Handled by fund managers or some shit?

The dates were from the previous year. I'd been working at Kempthorne & Co Artifact Retrieval Agency during that time. Not that it mattered. Alex wasn't his company. He ran Kempthorne & Co to protect latents... Didn't he?

I'd known he had connections to the military. He'd bought me, for fuck's sake. He'd admitted as much months ago. We'd gotten past all that. He'd bought me to keep me safe, to keep me out of the hands of people who would use my apparently special latent power for all the wrong reasons.

But, according to Kage—back when we'd been on talking terms—Alex had also known, or suspected, I was a lot more of a unique latent than everyone had told me. Our trip to America had revealed how I could *make* more latents. And recently, we'd figured out I could summon the source—although I had no idea what I was supposed to do with it, other than being bathed in trick and kinda able to feel connected to all the latents through it. Maybe. We were still figuring it out.

Blackwater was private military research.

Blackwater bankrolled ink.

Kempthorne Enterprises bankrolled Blackwater.

If there was more to it, I wasn't going to get it from the statements. I'd ask Alex in the morning, when he wasn't pissed off.

I grabbed a patterned throw, sprawled on the sofa by the fireplace, and finished off the bottle of whiskey as the fire died down.

## 3

Dom

The smell of coffee and sound of sizzling bacon woke me. Alex was pottering about the kitchen. I stretched, winced at a jab from a looming headache, and glared at the empty bottle of whiskey by the sofa. With Alex's back turned, I hurried upstairs, showered, and shaved, getting in front of the impending hangover, then breezed back into the kitchen to find breakfast waiting on the little table. I spotted Alex outside, through the window, sipping coffee on the deck overlooking miles of crisp, morning forest and in the distance, the peak of Ben Nevis. With his watch glinting on his wrist, the whole scene could have been straight out of a posh TV ad for expensive shit. He looked the part, having that perfectly rugged chic down to an art.

I should apologize for the previous clusterfuck that had been our dinner, but I also needed to bring up Blackwater. He'd moved the documents to the end of the counter, so he'd seen them. Did he know what they meant? It was time for some questions...

I grabbed a piece of toast, threw a strip of bacon inside, picked up my coffee, and joined him on the deck. The air smelled of wet pine and moss. "Hey..."

"Morning." Finally, his blue eyes met mine and he smiled his soft morning smile. I hadn't realized how much I'd needed to see that smile until that moment. Whatever happened, whatever all this meant, we were going to be okay.

"So... about last night—"

"Where did the documents come from?" he asked.

Okay. We were starting there. I leaned against the rickety timber rail. "Someone left it on the Range Rover. I was going to tell you—"

He waved the explanation away. "It's done." His hand dove into his trouser pocket and for a few seconds, I thought he was going for the ring box again, and that I might make everything a hundred times worse if he did, but he took out a small black plastic rectangular box instead and set it down on the rail between us.

A tracker. The implications of it being here were dire.

"I found it under the wheel arch." He didn't sound alarmed, just mildly irritated.

Bollocks, I should have known last night to check for anything but hadn't exactly been thinking clearly. I scanned the nearby tree line. Our location had been compromised. Everything was compromised. We had to leave.

"The shotgun is behind the door," Alex added. "But I haven't seen any signs of movement."

"How long have you been out here?"

"Since dawn."

While I'd slept on the sofa, like an idiot. "I should have told you as soon as I opened it."

"Hm."

"We should pack up and leave. If we can get out before they—"

"We aren't going anywhere."

"Whoever it is knows who we are. Our whole identities are fucked."

"They will come to us."

He was handling this a lot better than me. He didn't even look ruffled; he just leaned against the rail, sipping his coffee, as though nothing had changed. I chewed on my bacon toasted sandwich, feeling foolish in more ways than one. I'd jumped to all the wrong conclusions last night, called him a liar, and all he'd been doing was trying to make everything perfect for the Big Question... What did that say about me? I should have trusted him more. And now this tracker, and the bank statements, and I hadn't told him when I should have. If I'd told him, he'd have known to search for the tracker and our location would be safe. Now, we were sitting ducks in the middle of nowhere.

"It's all right." His mouth quirked in that small, sideways smile again.

I sighed, needing to hear that.

"What did you make of the bank statements?"

"Blackwater is private military research," I recalled. "Your company donated to it, like it donates to half a dozen other businesses. Blackwater also bankrolled Ink. That's about as far as I got. Does it mean anything to you?"

"Yes, I'm afraid it does." He squinted toward the woods. "It means Kage Mitchell will not let this rest."

"Kage? What's he got to do with anything?"

Alex tapped the tracker. "American-issued. Private, not military."

Shit. "LOA?"

"No. He's working alone."

"Kage? You're sure? Or it could just be the LOA—" Alex gave me the arched eyebrow. "Yeah, okay." When it came to Kage Mitchell, I had a blind spot a mile wide. Kage had fucked us over to try to save his brother, then I'd killed his brother to save Alex, so there was *that*. He'd also tried to hand us both over to his buddies at the LOA. He'd been known to be good, depending on what day of the week it was, just enough to keep us all guessing. But he'd drugged me, readily executed latents, and all things considered, he was a dick. "He's alive then?" I hadn't been sure after the helicopter incident at the weird bunker house.

"Oh, he's alive." Alex spoke as though he knew for certain this was all Kage's doing. But how could he know that? From one tracker and a few bank statements?

"Okay. So, let's say it's him. How'd he find us?" I set my empty coffee cup down and joined Alex back at the deck's wobbly rail again.

"He's resourceful and determined."

"How come he doesn't believe we're dead like everyone else?"

"Because he knows a lie, John. This has Kage Mitchell written all over it."

I was trusting Alex, right? So I trusted him in this, even if he was holding something back, like always. "I'm just going to say this once, but you're right. When it comes to Kage, my judgement is fucked, but so is yours. You hate him. You've always hated him. It could be you're seeing him in this because you want to?"

"It's possible." He finished his coffee, set the cup down on the little bistro table, vanished inside, and returned a moment later with the shotgun cocked under his arm. "It could also be, I'm right."

To be fair, he *was* usually right.

At least if this was Kage, then our identities and new life could still be salvaged.

Alex rested the gun against the rail. A rifle would have been better in this terrain, but shotguns were easier to explain a need for to the local firearms officer than a sniper rifle. "If he's leaving us cryptic envelopes, maybe he just wants a chat?"

Alex gazed at the trees, his cheek flickering. "You killed his brother."

"Yeah but..." I hadn't meant to. Mostly. It had been the heat of a moment thing. Greyson Mitchell had had his own agenda, and that involved killing Alex and maybe me. He had to go down. Although, Kage probably hadn't seen it that way.

Alex looked over. Weariness softened his eyes, but not

in weakness. Like weathered steel. "He wants you dead, John."

"Fuck." I sighed.

"He'll come here, we'll deal with him, and he won't be found. This will all be over." He gazed at the trees, willing his words to be true.

If I'd learned anything in the past few years, it was that when it came to Kage, nothing was simple. "So, the plan is to wait?"

"For now."

We'd been waiting for six months, what were a few more weeks? "Right." We both fell quiet. Grasshoppers buried in the grass did that weird hissing thing—that, as a city boy, I'd tried not to think too hard about—and a soft breeze disturbed the distant trees. And the seconds dragged into long, painful minutes.

"So, about last night—"

"Forget I said anything." He straightened and his smile painted over the cracks. "It didn't happen."

"Okay." If that was what he wanted. I didn't get to be disappointed after acting like a dick. "Sure." We could forget the dinner and carry on as normal, apart from the vengeful American hunting us down. "I mean... After six months, it was about time someone tried to kill us, right?"

He laughed. "Long overdue, if we're honest." He stepped closer and eased an arm around my waist, drawing me tight against him. I molded myself close, the two of us fitting so perfectly together. I knew his body like my own, but that didn't lessen the rush touching him gave me. The fact I was even *allowed* to touch him. Alexander Kempthorne. All fucking mine. I folded an arm around his warm neck, making it clear he had no escape. The smile on his lips melted the ice in his eyes.

"I don't believe—" he murmured against my lips, "—we've fucked on this part of the deck."

How to make me weak but also *hard* with just a few words. In the last few months, I'd learned Alex had a control kink, which shouldn't have been a surprise, considering everything I'd known about him before we'd hooked up. We'd switch it up, especially if he was looking for something slow and kinda emotional, but he liked to be the one holding my wrists. A part of me wondered if he was pissed at me still. When he fucked, he didn't go easy, and I was a fool for it. For him.

"I dunno... There was that time, right over there, when I had you on your knees—" His mouth scorched mine, stealing whatever I'd been about to say and had already forgotten because his hands were fighting with my shirt, trying to get inside. Reeling from the onslaught, I'd barely wrapped my head around the fact we were doing this now, with everything else going on, when he tore open my fly and his hot fingers grabbed my rapidly hardening dick.

I groaned or gasped, breaking free of the kiss, and his mouth dropped to my neck, rough whiskers burning. Oh Christ, yes. If there was anyone in the trees, they were about to have a front row seat to one hell of a show.

## 4

Alexander

I'd always known I wasn't a good man. Never enough of a talent for parents who forever wanted more, too much of a talent to be around others, and when it came down to it, a killer for all the wrong reasons. And now, with John writhing in my hands, moaning under my tongue, I suspected some part of me was doing this for more of those wrong reasons, such as distracting him from asking questions about Blackwater.

When I'd seen those bank statements on the kitchen table, I'd almost burned them, but John had obviously seen them too, just as Kage Mitchell had hoped he would. I couldn't escape the truth. It was coming for me, even here, with a new life, a new name.

I turned John in my arms, facing him away, pinned his muscular body to the wobbling timber rail, and kissed his neck, then his shoulder. Hard for him—he had no choice but to feel how hard where my hips trapped his arse under me. If John ever learned what I'd done, Kage was right, he'd probably kill me. At the very least, he'd wish it.

I should never have asked him to marry me. His reaction had been the correct one. Six months in the cottage and I'd forgotten who I was. Changing my name didn't change me.

He shifted, trying to find a more comfortable position. I caught him by the neck, holding him still, and brought my lips to his ear. "Do not move. If you want this to stop, tell me it's raining."

He exhaled. "Fuck, don't stop."

That was all I needed to hear. I'd already loosened his trousers and tugged them down over his hips with a few powerful jerks, exposing his backside. I didn't have lubricant and was too far gone to contemplate trying to find some. As practical as ever, John slipped a small bottle of clear gel from his pocket and handed it back. With a few quick adjustments, I freed my erection, pressed between his cheeks, and flicked my tongue over his ear. "Need to be in you."

"Do it."

Not yet. He liked it fast and rough, but he liked it even more when he was denied those things. I dropped my hand, wrapped my fingers around his dick, and swept up just enough pre-cum to grease things up.

His hand locked on the rail, knuckles whitening. "Christ, Alex. Do me."

"Be still."

He froze. I collected myself again, my own dick weeping, and pressed against his slick hole, spreading him just enough for the pressure to be an infuriating tease. He attempted to push back, but my hold on his neck and arse held. Sweet, mind-numbing pleasure shivered though me, radiating from the tight clamp of his muscles. Resisting was as much my torture as his. I eased off, heard him groan, saw his knuckles whiten, and pushed in again. Just enough to widen him, no more, despite the almost overriding urge to thrust.

"Fucking tease," John growled.

I switched my grip from his neck to his shoulder. Ragged breaths shook him. We were both dressed, making the anticipation all the more devastating. The tree line caught my eye. If Kage was out there, let him see how John Domenici *was mine*. My mouth at his ear again, I said, "Beg me to fuck you, John."

He gurgled a half growl, half moan. "Beg you?" As he turned his head, I caught his jittering smile laced with lust and a touch of uncertainty.

"You want it, then demand it."

"I want your cock in me now and if you keep fuckin' teasin' me I'll make you pay."

He could too. His trick had become powerful, he had become powerful, but to have him in my hands, panting for my touch, there was no other rush like it. Slowly, an inch in, an inch out, opening him, easing off, opening him, sliding my swollen, slick head through his tight, wet ring. Deeper, each time.

It still felt wrong. Not what we were doing, but *why* we were doing it. Why I'd chosen now to fuck him, with the threat of Blackwater at the back of my mind. I was a bastard. He'd hate me, if he knew. But damn, it felt too good not to.

"You're killing me." He shuddered. "Alex, please."

And there was the begging. I reached around his hip and caught his erect dick again. He jolted from the sudden contact, and I slid myself in deeper, his body slick and accepting.

"Fuck... yes. Right there."

I pumped, feeling his quiver and tremor. I held back as much as I could, but even my steadfast will began to fail.

"Shit!" John bucked, shuddered, and that was my cue. I thrust deep. He gulped, gasping and groaning. And now, when I got my hands on both his hips, I fucked him hard, pumping into him, hips slapping his bare arse. With the tree line in my sights and John under me, I took him. Anyone out there watching would see how he was mine, and mine alone. That thought tipped me over the edge, and with a snarl, I climaxed, jerking in staccato beats.

John levered himself up and managed to half-twist to plant a messy kiss on my lips.

In all the times we'd been together—the times we'd fucked, made love, fooled around—none had made me feel guilty. Until now.

The day passed slowly with no sign we were being observed. When night fell, we took shifts watching for trouble. I stood on guard, with the cottage lights off, while John slept, and vice versa. The next day passed in similar fashion, with John growing ever more uneasy. He'd taken the news that Kage wanted him dead rather well, but I also knew the more time he had to think on something, the more it would bother him.

Day three, and it was clear things couldn't stay as they were. John paced from room to room, and when he wasn't pacing, he was shuffling his deck of tattered cards— replenished since he'd used most of them in the States. They weren't as potent as his last deck, he'd told me, but in time, the psychic burn would leak into those new cards.

Mid-afternoon, he rose abruptly from the chair by the fireplace. "I'm going to the stones."

We'd usually go to the stones, where he tested his growing strength, together, but his words suggested I wasn't invited. "Be careful."

"I've got this." He threw on his jacket and boots and stalked outside. I watched from the window as he marched up the path we'd worn in the grass toward higher ground behind the cottage where the early season heather painted the landscape purple.

His silhouette disappeared and concern set in. I should have gone with him. And taken the shotgun. The gun was back in its spot behind the kitchen door. I picked it up, strode outside, and walked down the track. Clouds covered the sun, only letting it peek through fleetingly.

The air was cold for late summer but the Highlands rarely basked in sunshine.

Waiting for Kage to make his move wasn't working.

He had to know where we were, so why hadn't he shown his face?

Because he didn't want me. He wanted John. He wanted to tell John everything, destroying him, and then he'd kill him. Because Kage Mitchell and I were alike. We'd burn it all down to prove a point. It just so happened, his point was wrong.

I had to get to him before he got to John.

I tossed the shotgun into the Range Rover's trunk and climbed behind the wheel. I'd be back before John knew I'd left.

---

Only a few cars dotted the restaurant parking lot. I pulled up, cut the engine, and climbed out. Kage had known enough to find us here and leave his bloody envelope. But after pacing the lot, nothing seemed suspicious or out of place, and there were certainly no obvious traces of the American, although I hadn't truly known what to look for.

I left the restaurant on foot and walked the road into Fort William. Dozens of shops sold cheap Scotland keychains and T-shirts alongside the more typical store brands, but I was more interested in watching the people. John had suggested the LOA might be behind the tracker, and I hadn't ruled it out. There was a chance both Kage and the LOA were trying to find us. We hadn't left US soil on the best of terms.

After purchasing a take-away coffee, I meandered down the length of the town's main street, found a bench, and waited there. A local newsagent displayed the front-page news. *Local Latent Spirals: Kills Five. Neighborhood Plans for Latent Separation to Go Ahead. All Latents to be Tracked.* Someone had scrawled LUL on a nearby bin. Lock up latents. While John and I had been tucked away from the world, the hate for our kind had grown worse. Instances of latents spiraling had increased too. The future was a terrifying place.

Blackwater reared its ugly head in my mind. And my part in its ventures. Things had been different then...

I snarled those thoughts away, downed my coffee, and tossed the cup into the trash.

A figure in a long black coat moved through the nearby crowd of tourists, his back to me, his gait familiar. Dark hair pulled into a stumpy ponytail. Kage. It had to be. I got to my feet and jogged closer but lost him in the fray. When the crowd bumbled away, I was left standing at the edge of the pavement, with a high street bank to my left and a fishing tackle shop on my right. Neither likely targets for Kage.

This game of cat and mouse was beginning to wear thin.

With no leads and John due back at the cottage soon, I hurried back to the Range Rover outside the restaurant.

The wind teased a slip of paper pinched under the wiper. I snatched it free and unfolded it.

*Fuck you, Kempthorne.*

Maybe he had been watching from the woods, after all.

Good. Let him hate me. If he was emotional, he'd make mistakes. All I had to do was get to him before John did and Kage Mitchell would no longer be a problem.

5

D<sup>om</sup>

The standing stones were a mini-Stonehenge. Half as tall as me, each stone was lost in the gorse until the path we'd trampled led me right to them. Hundreds of years ago, they'd been positioned in a rough circle. Alex and his sister had visited regularly. Alex often brought me here, we'd picnic in the grass, among other things, and I'd throw my trick around. It had become a safe place, somewhere I could be myself.

Most times I visited with Alex. But not today. The gloomy sky suited my mood.

The stones weren't necessary to control my trick, Alex had told me. They just helped provide a visual boundary. Now, I stood at their center, flicked out my hands, and breathed, silencing the endless chatter in my head. It took a while, longer than usual, but eventually the latent part of me unfurled, and once that happened, trick simmered at my fingertips. Next, came the source. The part that was new and terrifying. Alex had been made to be powerful, to connect to the source, but I was a direct conduit. Like a faucet, able to turn the source on and off.

It thrummed deep below my feet, like an underground river of power I could dip my hands into and heave to the surface. I tried it now. The source stirred, inexplicably responding to a nobody. I had no idea why the source thought I was the one latent it wanted to reach out to. Did it even think at all?

Every latent borrowed their trick from the source, but we knew almost nothing about it. Just that it was a part of us from birth, and it vanished when we died—unless you became a shadow. Then the trick kind of animated you after death. I didn't pretend to understand it. I just knew I could touch it, and when I did, it felt as though I could do *anything*. Level mountains, bury cities, touch a million lives. That kind of power shouldn't be in human hands, and definitely not mine, but here it was. John Domenici was the fucking latent messiah. Except, what the fuck should I do with that?

I opened my eyes and golden light shimmered all around. A few weeks ago, I'd sent that wave out, to see what happened, and scorched a few hundred yards of heather in every direction. It would have been more had the ground not been soaked with rain. Other times, like now, I built a barrier, keeping everything outside from crashing in. This was the barrier I'd thrown up when I'd grabbed Alex from the helicopter. The source seemed to know what I needed, even when I didn't.

If I took a card from my pocket and launched it into the sky, it would fork like lightning, blasting anything it hit into a million pieces. Which was great, I figured, but what was I supposed to do with all that? Was I even meant to do anything? I was one of the most powerful latents—maybe the most powerful—and all I'd managed to do was run away.

Wasn't I supposed to do important shit with all this power?

I dropped my hands and the golden barrier fizzled away, dissipating back into the ground. Maybe there had been a mistake and this gift had been meant for someone else? Someone better than an East End street thug with blood on his hands.

Using the trick, summoning the source, usually left me feeling buzzed, but not today. I just felt empty, and maybe a bit lost, in the middle of fucking Scotland with a boyfriend who had wanted to spend the rest of his life with me and then changed his mind, having realized he'd dodged a bullet.

A huge stag stood outside the stone circle.

I blinked, expecting it to vanish, but it stayed, head up, forked antlers three foot long. Deer didn't kill people, right? Even big bastards? Wasn't it mostly the other way around, and folks shot deer? It didn't look pissed that I'd lit its backyard up, but it wasn't chilled either.

"Hey," I croaked.

The stag bolted.

Such a fucking city boy. Who the fuck says hello to a

stag? Alex would probably have shot it and baked it into a pie for dinner. I snorted, figured the answers I searched for weren't among the stones, and trudged back along the trampled path.

Kage had said Alex had known I was *special*, that was the reason he'd brought me from the military, to keep me safe. Alex hadn't denied it, and he'd brought me up here, to the stones, and showed me what I could do. Because he already knew more about my trick than I did. Had he been waiting for me to figure it out, all this time?

What if that was all he'd been waiting for and he just wanted me for my lit trick?

No, couldn't think that. I knew him. He did love me and it wasn't for my trick. But sometimes he made it impossible to figure out what was going on in that brilliant head of his. He'd have ten thoughts to my one, always be one step ahead, always had a backup plan. So what had been my backup plan? The ex-military latent who had joined Kempthorne & Co with nothing but the clothes on his back and a tattered deck of artifact cards in his pocket. Alex had bought some latent guy who could blow shit up. Why? Because he knew I could connect to the source? Why was that important to him?

We needed to talk, a *real* talk, not one of those conversations where he answered every question and it wasn't until later I realized he hadn't answered a bloody thing.

I made it back to the cottage moments after the heavy skies began to drizzle all over me and caught sight of the Range Rover headlights sweeping up the lane. Propping my arse against the cottage wall, I waited for him to park and climb out. He gifted me with a quick smile.

"Weather's closing in," he said, passing me by and climbing the steps to the front door. "All okay here?"

"Sure. Where were you?"

He unlocked the door and pushed inside. "Fort William. I went back to the restaurant to see if there was any sign of Kage."

I followed him inside. "Was there?"

"No."

He flicked on the lights, breezing through each of the rooms, and tugged off his coat in the lounge, as though in a hurry to do everything at once and *not* look at me.

"Hey," I said.

"Hm?"

"We need to talk."

"About what?" He hung up his coat on a stand, then strode across the front room and into the kitchen to fill the kettle.

Still following, I said, "About you, the military, about me, and what I can do. And how you knew about it."

He leaned a hip against the counter and folded his arms. "I don't know what I can tell you that I haven't already."

"Make us some coffees and let's find out. It's not as though we have much else to do."

"We need to keep watch. Kage is close, he could—"

His gaze flicked to the window, its glass now fogged with condensation. "I thought you said he wasn't in Fort William?"

"No, I said he wasn't at the restaurant."

I frowned and huffed a short laugh. "See, this is what you do."

"What do I do?"

"You let me think you've said everything you know, but you hold half the information back. And it was okay before. It's who you are, I get it." I stopped at the counter too, putting him in front of me with nowhere to run to. "But I'm getting pretty fucking tired of always being told the minimum to get by, just enough to shut me up."

He shook his head, smiling to make light of it. "No, that's not—"

"You need to start fucking talking, Alex. Right now."

His icy gaze locked on me. "And what am I to say? What is it you think I'm hiding from you?"

"It's not..." He made it sound as though I didn't trust him. "I *do* trust you. But the point is, I don't know what you're hiding. But you don't need to keep all your cards close to your chest anymore, right? You can let me see. Isn't that what being together is about? I can help you. I want to, but you shut me out."

"When have I shut you out, John?"

I shrugged and leaned against the counter. "How about right now? You've locked down. The second you got out of the car, I saw it. Something happened and you don't want me knowing."

He waved a hand and grabbed two mugs from a cupboard. "Because it's hardly worth mentioning."

"Why don't you mention it and I'll judge whether it's worth it or not for once?"

He huffed, poured hot water into the mugs, then dumped my sugar in, clanging the spoon against the side. "It *was* nothing. I went into the town and thought I saw

Kage. It may not have been. I tried to follow, but he disappeared."

This would normally have been where I'd back off, thinking he'd told me all of it, but he never did. He always had to keep some information back. "Is that it?"

He sighed, plucked a piece of paper from his jacket pocket, and handed it over.

I unfolded it. *Fuck you, Kempthorne.*

I knew Kage's handwriting. "Shit." He really was in Scotland.

"It seems my suspicions are correct."

I held up the note. "You told me he wasn't there, you said it was nothing, and then you give me this? This isn't *nothing*. This is Kage Mitchell fucking with you and if I hadn't bloody pushed, you never would have told me." I flung the note into the sink and marched into the living area. Why did he have to be like this? "Why can't you just trust me?"

"John, please, I do. It's not—it's not you, it's me."

Jesus Christ, that old chestnut. "Don't." I paced in front of the window. "What else have you *half*-told me, huh?"

His shoulders sloped. A muscle fluttered in his jaw as he ground his teeth. "I know I'm difficult. I just... I don't want to lose you."

Christ, he looked as beaten as I'd ever seen him. But fierce too, angry even. I'd gotten better at reading him, but at times like this, it almost felt as though he was two different people. The thoughtful, caring, a bit possessive, charming, bloody scary bastard I loved, and some deeper, darker part, who even I couldn't touch. The Alex who kept his secrets and only revealed them when it suited him. The Alex who had killed Renick and would absolutely kill Kage Mitchell.

"You can't kill Kage."

He laughed. "Don't be ridiculous. Of course I can."

"You can't just fucking kill people you don't agree with." Kage was a dick. He'd done terrible things. And he was pissed off, but murder?

"John," Alex snapped. "He will kill you, and if you think for one second I'm going to allow that to happen, then you certainly have no idea who I really am."

I took a step toward him, and in the next breath, the whole world lurched sideways. I hit a wall or it hit me. Heat and white light and a thousand cuts burned my side, and then I was on the floor, pushing up, because I needed to move, to get away. Licks of fire climbed the cottage curtains in front of a window that had lost its glass. My ears rang. Shattered glass sparkled all around and rained off me as I pushed upright.

Alex rushed in, hooked me by the arm, and hauled me to my feet. "We have to go. *Now*." He had the shotgun in his other hand, and when he opened the battered front door, he raised the gun, pointing it toward the front yard.

Where the Range Rover had been moments ago, a burning wreck remained. Black smoke bellowed skyward. My blood chilled. Alex had driven that car home. He could have been killed.

I plucked my cards from my pocket, charged them up with trick, and scanned the tree line. "Come on then!" I wasn't thinking. "Here we fucking are, Kage!" Alex grabbed my arm and pulled, and I yanked free. "Fucking coward! You come at him, you come for me!" Rage and fear scorched my heart. "I killed your brother, you dick. I'll kill you!"

"John!" Alex barked. "Now!"

It was the fear in his eyes that snapped me out of the rage, and if he was afraid, then I needed to be too. I ran with him, vaulted over a fence, and we kept right on running, until there was nothing but misty rain and heather in every direction.

I pulled Alex down into a divot, using a gorse bush as cover. We laid on our fronts and watched the moorland, waiting for Kage to stalk through the fog. Eventually, my racing breaths and my heart slowed.

Alex touched my forehead. His fingers came away wet with blood. "Are you all right?"

"Just a few scrapes. You?"

He flopped onto his back and closed his eyes. "I was driving that Range Rover."

"Yeah," I croaked. Couldn't think about that. About what Kage had almost done.

"Still want to keep him alive?" Alex blinked.

I didn't hesitate. "No."

## 6

Alexander

Harvey Lloyd and Christopher Jennings checked into a quaint B&B in the tiny village of Fort Augustus at the southwestern point of Loch Ness, and a ten-mile walk from the cottage. Mismatch furniture dotted the room, and a musty smell permeated the air, but we had an en-suite bathroom and the free packet of custard creams improved John's mood. We'd stopped at a stream to clean up, but there was no washing off the grass stains and smell of diesel. We could only hope the B&B owner didn't talk about the two men who had appeared from the glen, shrouded in mist and smoke.

Until the explosion, I hadn't been sure Kage had it in him to carry out his threats. At least now, John under-stood who we were dealing with. Kage wasn't the same man I'd saved in Cecil Court's kitchen. During his life, he'd spent years thinking he'd killed his brother, he'd tried to make it right, then learned Greyson wasn't dead and his father had lied, loading the blame onto Kage. Kage had wanted John, hated me, lost his job, and now lost his brother for a second time. He blamed John and me for all his misfortunes and saw wicked intent where there was none. He probably thought himself the hero in all of this.

John and I cleaned up as best we could, then left the B&B and strolled through the village, getting the lay of the land. John's mind likely worked on escape routes for every eventuality, while I contemplated the best place to bury a body. We didn't speak about the argument Kage's explosion had interrupted, although it was coming. He wasn't going to give up on this, not this time. I'd gotten away with telling him half-truths. It was how I did things, how I lived and breathed, but he was right. If I wanted to make us work, he needed to know it all.

And I'd lose him as soon as he did.

Perhaps that was for the best.

And maybe I'd take every precious moment I could get with him before that happened.

A canal ran through the middle of Fort Augustus, feeding from Loch Ness. We walked its banks, past quaint little cottage gardens, admiring the black-and-white lock gates that adjusted the water level for passing canal boats. Despite the gloomy mist, the picture-postcard village was rather atmospheric and had been a favorite of my sister's.

"We've been through some shit," John mused. He walked alongside me, thumbs tucked into his new jeans pockets. His *I Heart Nessie* grey and green T-shirt with a cartoon Nessie looked a little ridiculous, and was a size too small, but it made me smile every time I glanced over. He'd tried to convince me to buy shorts and flip-flops, but one of us had to draw the line somewhere. I'd opted for a more reserved black, hooded sweater with a small stag motif on the left breast. With my scruffy beard and his daft T-shirt, we were perfectly mismatched.

"Yes, we have," I agreed.

"Do you think it's because we're like we are, or is it some cosmic two-fingers to us?" His hair stuck out at odd, ruffled angles, and some scratches from the explosion peppered his cheek. He appeared pensive, deep in thought, which could be dangerous, but also a delight to watch.

"I think... we make our own luck, and sometimes when we try and do the right thing, it comes with a price."

His eyebrows lifted. "Okay. So we are doing the right thing then?"

"What do you mean?"

"I dunno." He stopped at the canal's edge and peered into the water. "I've been given this power and I'm the worst person for it."

Good Heavens, he was so very wrong. "What makes you say that?"

He shrugged. "Everything."

He was absolutely the best person for it. Despite his commitment to thinking he was bad, he was good to his core. The world had dumped him into terrible situations time and time again, but he always came out of them swinging. If I'd had half the strength he did, I might have been able to salvage something of my humanity.

Before the mood soured or I said something to upset him, I brushed my thumb against the corner of his mouth and softly kissed his lips. I was still trying to understand what good I'd done for fate or destiny or some cosmic being to give John to me. He kissed me back, just as gently, too softly for him and my heart ached, so bloody afraid that I was going to ruin us. The kiss ended, but I stepped close, cradled his face, and wished I'd done more for him.

"You were always the best candidate."

His eyes narrowed. "What?"

"I just mean, nobody else would be able to bear the weight of such a responsibility. You can *make* latents. You're remarkable."

"Yeah, well... I dunno." He stepped away. "We should get back."

"You go. I'll be right behind you."

He nodded and walked back alongside the canal. I frowned after him. Nothing had changed between us. So why did I feel as though I was falling with no way of stopping?

My phone pinged.

*Incoming AirDrop. Accept. Decline?*

I glanced around. Of the few people wandering along the canal, nobody seemed interested in me. But an AirDrop had to be close.

I hit *Accept.*

Multiple images opened on my phone, cascading onto the screen. Up-close photos of a man, his hands bound, mouth gagged, eyes wide and pleading. I lifted my gaze, searching again for the sender among the paths and canalboats, and seeing nobody. Then the last image landed. My heart dropped. A piercing, panicked whine drowned out all other sounds.

Jordan.

On his side, blood leaking from the bullet hole in his forehead. He'd been executed.

I knew how Kage had found us.

And I knew, when I found him, I'd tear him apart.

## 7

D<sup>om</sup>

I paced our little B&B room. Alex hadn't returned. He'd said he'd be right behind me, but he wasn't, which might have been a good thing. Because something he'd said had set all kinds of alarm bells ringing.

*You were the best candidate.*

What. The. Fuck.

That wasn't an "Oh, hey, you're a great person." That had been an "I know this because I planned it."

*Candidate.* Kind of a heavy word, that. And Alex was careful with words. Tired, pissed off, he'd let that one slip.

I didn't want to think like this.

I didn't want to go back to how things had been

before, with Alex moving all the chess pieces while I sat in the dark, trying to blindly feel my way.

If he came back to our room now, I'd lose my shit with him, and I didn't want that... Didn't want to argue after Kage had almost blown him to bits, didn't want to lose him, but I was also so fucking close to pushing him away. There was more to all of this, more he wasn't telling me. And I was *so* done with that shit.

I left the B&B, kept my head down, and veered into the pub next door. A few tourists ate hearty pie and chips at the window tables, and some locals sat at the bar, drinking beer. I needed to be around people, real life, normal things, before I bounced off the walls and leaked trick all over the place. I needed... to breathe.

Candidate.

Maybe it was nothing. It was probably nothing. I'd know for certain if it was something... if he fucking talked to me.

No. Wasn't thinking that. I needed to cool down, take a breath, get my head on straight and not ruin everything we had by being a suspicious dick.

I ordered a beer and watched a rugby game on the TV hung on the far wall. For a while, all the drama faded to the back of my mind. I forgot who I was and wasn't. I could be just a guy in the bar, drinking a beer and watching rugby. There was nothing special about me.

Then some twat poked a gun in my back and said in an American accent, "Don't react. Turn around, nice an' slow. If you so much as summon a spark, I will shoot the barman between the eyes."

"You absolute cunt." I turned, slowly, just like he'd

said, and got a good long look at a new Kage Mitchell. He'd lost weight, making his face leaner, sharper. Where humor had once sparkled in his eyes, they now seemed dull and lifeless, like the eyes of a shark. My anger short-circuited. I hadn't wanted this for him, for any of us.

One-handed—he still had a gun poked in my side—he reached inside his long duster coat and withdrew more papers, then slid them across the bar.

"No." I peered into those cool eyes, searching for a shred of humanity.

"You're going to want to look."

"I'm not playing your game. Shoot me, if you want."

He snarled and snatched at the top sheet, them jabbed a finger at it. "Look, Dom."

"You need to get out of here."

"Look at it. Look at what he's done to you!"

"You need to get off that stool, walk out that door, and you need to keep right on walking, because the second I catch up with you I am going to turn your bones to ash. Do you hear me, Kage Mitchell? *You nearly fucking killed Alex.*"

He snorted. "If I'd wanted him dead, he would be. Look at the document, Dom, and find out exactly who you're letting fuck you."

I didn't know this man. Not anymore. Somewhere in all of this he'd crossed a line. Maybe he'd changed, or maybe he'd always been like this and I was only now seeing it. I'd been so blind. He had used me from the first moment we'd met.

"Tell me you trust him," he said, peering into my eyes.

"Tell me right now you absolutely trust Alexander Kempthorne and I'll walk away."

I swallowed. I did trust him. Most of him.

"You're smart, Dom. You know he's lying to you." Kage tapped the papers again. "Look."

If I looked down, my gut told me it would be bad, and did I really need to know? Yeah... I did. I scanned the sheet of paper with the Kempthorne Enterprises logo in the corner and what appeared to be a purchase receipt for fifty human embryos. The date was dated in the late nineties. What was any of that supposed to mean?

Kage grabbed the second sheet and slid it over the first. This document was more recent, showing a Blackwater progress report for something called: C32. Mention of Syria stood out and my Psy Ops unit number.

"I don't understand," I mumbled.

Kage grabbed the third sheet, again a progress report, this one five years ago, and signed in pen by Alexander Kempthorne's swirling penmanship.

Five years ago. Before I'd joined Kempthorne & Co, but close enough that he should have told me.

Kage grabbed the final sheet and placed it in front of me.

*Adoption Order. C32. To Domenici from Blackwater.*

*Wait...*

"No."

"It's all a lie," Kage said.

"This isn't... That's not me. They're not talking about me."

"You're not a Domenici. You're a lab experiment, Dom. One of fifty. Number Thirty-Two."

"No, that doesn't make any sense. This is bollocks." Some folks glanced over. I lowered my voice. "Look, I get what you're trying to do here. But I told you about my shithead of a father, right? Why would he buy a latent kid and then hate on it?"

"Because he didn't buy you, your mom did." Kage pointed to the name on the adoption documents. Janine Domenici. My mum.

"Maybe she wanted something that was hers," he said. "I don't know. But it's there, in black and white. And after she bought you, Blackwater paid her to raise you. Blackwater fucks up latents. It's what they're good at. And Kempthorne's company pays for Blackwater. Without Kempthorne Enterprises, you wouldn't exist."

None of that made any sense. It didn't relate to me. It couldn't. "Kempthorne Enterprises was his parents' company, not his. He wouldn't have anything to do with this—and there's nothing in there that proves I'm this..." *candidate*. The word stuck in my throat.

Kage grabbed the papers in his fist and waved them in front of my face. "His name is on the fucking documents, Dom. He signed it. It's right there." He flung the papers down and grabbed me by the shoulder, fingers digging deep. "Your whole fucking life is a lie, because of him. When are you going to realize this is all his game? When will you see—"

"Get the fuck off me—" I launched a messy right hook and mostly missed, just clipping his chin. He must have seen something dangerous on my face because he raised the gun, in plain view of everyone, and the whole place lost its shit. People bolted for the doors like rats when the lights go on. I raised my hands and Kage backed up.

"I'm doing you a favor, Dom. You should thank me." Then Kage ran too, heading through a door at the back of the bar.

I almost chased him but shock had rooted me to the floor. The strewn pile of papers lured my attention back. Nothing made any sense. Blackwater, Domenici, Candidate Thirty-Two. Janine Domenici had bought a Blackwater baby, a latent child fucking made in a test tube somewhere. It wasn't bad luck, me being a latent. It had been planned that way; my whole fucking life was a game... and Alex had known.

No, no, no... He'd have told me.

The pub's music throbbed too loudly. Or maybe that was my heart in my head.

This was all a misunderstanding... Kage was fucking with me. He'd made it all up. Except for that one word: *Candidate*. I choked on something like a sob. I wasn't even a fucking Domenici? I'd tried to be everything my shithead of a dad had wanted and I was never going to succeed? Was that why he'd hated me?

Everything was unraveling. I was coming apart.

The bar door flung open and there he was, Alexander Kempthorne. "John, there you are." He dashed forward. "It's Jordan—"

I grabbed him by the neck, swung him around, and slammed him facedown against the bar top. "Candidate Thirty-Two?"

His face fell. And right there, that was the truth. "John," he choked out. "Let me explain."

My whole world was on fire, and there I was in the middle of the inferno, as cold as ice. I tightened my hold on his neck. Alex plucked at my fingers. His eyes glistened, too wide, too bright. Trick sizzled down my arm, lighting me up. I welcomed it. It felt good, felt right. Just like the artifact knife in my hand had felt right when I'd killed Max, like it had felt good when I'd finally snuffed out my dad's life.

Alex brought his hand up, and a blast of trick hit my chest, throwing me off. I reeled, stumbling against a table, knocking over its chair.

Trick burned in a loop around Alex's arm, coiled, ready to thrash my way. "Don't." He raised his other hand, the one with a phone in it. "Please, John—don't. Just… stop? Listen—"

"I don't know what's real around you."

"It's not… It's not what you think. Some of it is, probably. I don't know. I should have told you, yes. Can we talk about it now? Will you let me explain?"

Christ, it hurt. Who was I if I wasn't John Domenici? And this man I loved, he'd known all this time, through everything, that I was the biggest lie of all? How could I ever trust him?

"You had your chance." I walked past him, glad he didn't grab for me, and I kept right on walking down the road, out of the village. I walked for what felt like hours, deep into the night. And when the driver of a passing car offered me a ride, I took it all the way to Inverness bus station. And from there, I bought a ticket to London.

8

lexander

John would come back.

He'd told me before that he'd never leave. So he'd come back. Probably in the morning, when he'd cooled down. We'd talk and I'd tell him everything I should have told him months ago. Of course, he'd be furious. As had been clear from the bar. But we'd be all right. We had to be. He was all I had...

But the bed stayed empty, and the morning came and went. Lunchtime rolled around, into the afternoon, and then the sun set again and the woman who owned the B&B asked if I was staying another night.

John wasn't coming back.

I'd known this would happen. I'd seen it coming. My fears had come true. And I deserved it.

I sat at the bar where he'd lashed out and downed too many glasses of Scotch, hoping John would storm back in, rage at me, tell me I was a fucking prick, a lying bastard, and everything I knew to be true, but he'd stay. Because he'd said he always would.

But nobody I loved ever stayed. So... why was I waiting? He shouldn't come back. Why would he? I'd lied to him, manipulated him. I did not deserve him.

More whiskey went down.

"Hey, you look kinda familiar?" I barely heard the young woman speak, and only noticed her when she planted herself on the barstool next to mine.

"I'm waiting for someone," I slurred. Acutely intoxicated and decisively uncaring.

"Wait, I'll get it..." She stared, two inches inside my personal space.

"Do you mind?"

"Wait a second." Her lipstick-coated lips screwed up and her painted eyelids narrowed. "Aren't you that famous rich guy? Came out as latent *and* gay. TikTok went nuts over it."

"Oh good, you're a fan."

"I thought you—"

"Died? Yes, very good." I shooed her away. "Move along now please."

"Holy shit." She grabbed a phone from her bag and before I could snarl at her, the phone was in my face, flash blinding.

"Excuse me—"

"Oh my God." She typed at-speed into her phone while I contemplated snatching the device from her hand and dropping it in my whiskey. Would that be assault?

"If you upload that photo online the financial repercussions will be—"

She grinned and showed me her phone's screen, with a very clear picture of me—I'd had better days—uploaded to Facebook with the caption: *Alexander Kempthorne is NOT DEAD.* As I blinked at my bearded, red-eyed self, the likes and hearts and angry faces floated up. Someone was writing a comment... *Where is this?*—popped up in the comments section—*Is that really him? —Looks like a hobo—No way!—Get his autograph.*

"Hey, lassie," the barman grunted. "Leave the guy alone, eh?"

She wasn't listening to him either. After typing some more, probably answering those comments, she giggled, held up the phone again to take another picture. I grabbed it, turned it to ash in my hand, and dropped its remains on the bar.

She squealed an intolerably high sound and threatened to call the police, by which time I was on my feet and staggering toward the door.

The fact Alexander Kempthorne was alive was a very bad thing. But I couldn't bring myself to care. Because I'd lost the one thing I'd lived for, and if he was gone, then what was the point in me?

---

Doors slamming outside the window jolted me from a heavy, dreamless sleep. I winced into daylight, dragged myself from the bed, and showered. When the sound of rapid voices sailed through the closed drapes, I snuck a peek outside.

Five local news vans parked alongside the canal.

"Oh dear."

I grabbed my phone, opened the news app, and sat on the bed, the results churning my stomach.

*KEMPTHORNE ALIVE!*

*ALEXANDER KEMPTHORNE HIDING IN HIGHLANDS*

*BILLIONARE RESURFACES*

*IS IT REALLY KEMPTHORNE?*

That wretched photograph was going to haunt me forever. I dashed for the bathroom, hacked the beard off, and shaved clean, hesitating when I remembered John had liked the scruffiness. But it had to go. *Goodbye Harvey Lloyd.* It had been nice living your pretend life for all of six months. But all dreams ended, and I couldn't hide from who I was.

"Are you leaving us today, Mister... er... Lloyd?" The lovely lady owner of the B&B smiled politely from behind her reception desk, which was really just a table with a cloth draped over it and a bowl of toffees for guests.

I handed her cash. "I think we both know that's not my name."

Her smile softened. "I'm sorry, Mister Kempthorne. I kept them all outside but I can't tell them to move along."

She was kind. "I appreciate it, thank you."

I'd barely turned toward the door when she added,

"Remember to leave us a five-star review on Trip Advisor."

"Of course."

With my hand on the door handle, I hesitated. The moment I stepped outside, the lie would be over. I'd be plunged back into my old life like a baptism of fire. I'd just wanted to be free, to be someone else, to have John and a good life, and not be the gay latent billionaire Alexander Kempthorne, who everyone had an opinion on, as though they all somehow owned a small piece of me.

Maybe it was as John had said. The universe had decided I didn't deserve it. And now everything had turned full circle. I had a target on my back and I'd never been more alone.

I let go of the handle and took a step back. "Is there, perhaps, a back exit?"

"Oh yes, dear. Right this way."

## 9

**D**om

Janine Domenici lived in a cute semi-detached house with a tiny garden, tucked into a sprawling but well-kept housing estate on the outskirts of Rickmansworth, in northwest London. She joined running club every Wednesday, visited book club on the first Friday of every month, and was part of the area's Neighborhood Watch—which meant anyone who came and went, she knew about. But she wasn't Janine Domenici, East-End mob boss's wife, to those people. She was just Joan Craven, the friendly neighbor with one cat and pretty flower boxes in her manicured garden.

I wasn't supposed to be here.

The last time I'd seen her, in Rickmansworth Costa,

I'd been freaked out by Kempthorne dying on me at Wordsworth.

Today, I needed to see her, to know if Kage's documents were real. I needed to know if Blackwater had paid her to raise me, or if she'd bought me, however the fuck it all worked. *I had to know.*

Christ, I wasn't even Italian. Renick with his D tattoo, trying so hard to be part of the family, had been more Italian than me. The fucking irony.

Hood up, I sauntered across the road and knocked on Mum's front door.

A rotund late-sixties woman with early-onset silver hair opened the door. "No fanks, mate. I don' want whateva' you're sellin'."

Wow. "Mum, it's me."

"John?" She squinted, then her eyes widened and her mouth opened in a perfect 'O'.

She'd thought me dead. They'd probably had a funeral. And here I was, standing on her doorstep. It had to be a shock.

The shock vanished. She stuck her head out of the door and glanced down the street, then pulled on my sleeve. "Bloody 'ell. Get in 'ere, before Karen sees yah." She shoved me into the tiny entrance porch and slammed the door.

"Hi, Mum."

"Wanna cuppa, luv? Did yah take the bus? I was talkin' to June jus' the other day 'bout how those bloody busses are makin' a right mess..."

She waffled about busses, hurrying down the cramped hallway to the kitchen at the back of the house, while I grinned after her. It was as though I'd never left. She chatted and I wandered into her living room with its soft carpets, cream-painted walls, weird gnome figurine things, and air plants. The second she'd gone into witness protection, years ago, she'd gone all the way off the gangsta rails into suburbia and I wasn't at all jealous. I'd always known where she was. She'd told me. Not a big one for rules, was Mum.

Still chatting, she found me in the front room and shoved a mug of tea into my hand. "What happened to you, luv? You look like you've seen a ghost. Are you gettin' enough protein? When you get over a certain age, your body needs more a that protein, like chicken. Do you cook your own dinners? I've got some pasta in the fridge. I can pack you a lunch."

I dropped into the comfy chair by the window and let her waffle roll over me. It was nice, as if I was fifteen again and she was more interested in if I'd eaten dinner than my bloody-knuckles and split lip.

"I knew you weren't dead. A muvah knows these things."

But she wasn't my mother, was she? Christ, I couldn't say it. It didn't feel right, as though I was disrespecting her to even think it. I didn't want to know. What if Kage was right about it all? If I asked her, and she told me I wasn't her son, what was I supposed to do with that?

"John?"

"Yeah."

Her warm, wrinkled face pouted. "You can stay 'owever long you like, luv."

"That's okay, thanks." I couldn't risk exposing her to

the Business. They didn't know I was alive, but it wasn't worth the risk. If they knew where Domenici's wife was holed up, all this would be over. She'd been due to testify against him. She was a grass. And snitches got stitches. They'd probably burn her little house down, just because.

"'ow's that nice man o' yours?"

I sighed and put my tea down on the table beside my chair.

"There's a coaster right there."

"Right. Sorry." Coaster shoved under my tea, I finally looked her in the eyes. "So, if you knew I wasn't dead, I guess you kinda figured Kempthorne weren't dead, either?" I hadn't told her it was Kempthorne I was seeing, but she knew where I'd worked, she'd have seen us in news reports, she'd have figured it out.

"Plane crash?" She snorted. "Nah, I weren't buyin' it. He's lookin' a bit rough these days. Did you two 'ave a fight?"

"What do you mean he's rough? You've seen him?"

"That picture of 'im in some Scotland pub?"

"Huh?"

"It's been on the news? Don't you watch the news?"

"No. I've been..." He was in the news? "Shit, everyone knows he's alive?"

"Yeah, big hoo-hah. Was it tax evasion?"

"Eh?"

"The reason you two faked your deaths? I always figured people like 'im never pay the right amount of taxes. They squirrel it away offshore while the rest of us get taxed up to the tits—"

"Mum, you literally laundered hundreds of thousands for Dad."

"Well, that was then," she huffed, caught out. "So what's the rich geezer dragged you into, eh? Do you wan' me to 'ave a word with him?"

Oh my god. "No, Mum." I almost laughed. *'ave a word* with Kempthorne? That would be entertaining.

"Good. Nasty business. But I'll tell 'im, if he's not treatin' you right. Just because you're gay don't mean you 'ave to take it up the arse—"

"Okay. Look, Mum. I have to ask you something, and I really need you to be straight with me."

She settled, hands on her knees. "Ask me, luv. Anyfing."

"Blackwater."

She blinked, and she was good at hiding her feelings, she'd made a career out of it when she'd stood beside Dad, but her right eye ticced and her lips thinned, pressed so tightly together they turned almost white.

"Yeah, okay." I sighed. "So it's true?"

Her shoulders deflated, and her whole body tensed. "I just... I wanted someone. And he..." She looked away, and the fierceness in her took over, shuttering her face and hiding her expression. "There are things you don't know, John. About what your father did. Before you were around, he... There was an accident."

There weren't any bloody accidents. "He hit you."

"I was in hospital for almost two months."

He hadn't just hit her then, he'd nearly killed her. Not for the first time, I was glad I'd cut his throat.

She smoothed her skirt over her thighs. "After that, well, I couldn't 'ave kids."

I nodded and slumped in the chair. It was true. All of it. I wasn't a Domenici. "Did you know Kempthorne was in on it?"

"Eh? The toff?"

"Yeah, the toff."

"What's 'e got to do with it?"

"His company invests in Blackwater. Blackwater is where I come from, right?"

"Huh. I didn't know that. So your boyfriend runs the company that oversees the company that er... paid me to look after you?"

"Yeah."

"Is that what you argued about, luv?"

"Mostly."

"John..." She shuffled forward to the edge of her chair. "Look at me, luv. Please..."

I gulped and met the gaze of the woman who had raised me. The only good thing in my life. A woman who had lied to me since I was old enough to remember her face.

"You were my everythin'," she said. "You were my sunshine. You're my boy, an' nothin' will change that or take it away from us. You didn't come from me an' your dad, but you know what? That's probably a good thing. Nothin' good ever came from that bastard. I love you so much. I loved you more because I couldn't 'ave kids. I tried to do the best for you, I really did. I didn't want... Well, your dad, he hated me and then 'e hated you, the man was made of hate. I'm glad you did what you had to —What I should have done."

Shit, she knew I'd killed him? I swallowed, my voice long gone.

"One of us 'ad to and I wasn't brave enough, and for that I'm sorry."

"Jesus, Mum. It's all right."

"Do you 'ate me?"

"No, I'd never... No." I shrugged. "You're me mum."

"Good." She smiled. "Want some cake? I've got Vicky sponge? None of that Tesco crap. I bought it at the cake sale last Sunday. You can never 'ave enuf cake."

"Yeah, okay. Have you got any custard creams?"

She laughed. "Always, luv."

She left me alone to stew in my thoughts. I'd had a lot of time to think since walking out of Fort Augustus. Kage had dropped a bomb on me—things Kempthorne should have told me long ago—and I'd reacted badly. But I'd had a right to be pissed off, didn't I? So, I wasn't a Domenici. What did that change right then? Nothing. My mum was still my mum. I was still me.

The TV in the corner caught my eye. Mum always left the news on with the sound down. Old habits, to see if any of dad's exploits had made us all famous. A news ticket ran along the bottom of the screen. *Alexander Kempthorne's assets seized by IRL. Kempthorne family valet found dead.*

Oh fuck.

Jordan was dead?

Alex had blurted Jordan's name when he'd entered the pub, his face fraught, right before I'd lost my shit with him. Jesus Christ, I'd been so out of it, I hadn't listened. Jordan was dead, and I'd abandoned Alex in Scotland to deal with that? I needed to find him. "Mum?"

"Yeah, luv?" she called from the kitchen.

"Is it safe to use your phone?" Mine had died hours ago.

"Yeah, withheld number."

I picked up her landline phone and dialed Alex's new mobile number. It rang out with no answer service. He probably wouldn't answer a withheld number, thinking it was a journalist.

A picture flashed on screen, of Alex looking like death warmed up in the Scottish pub bar I'd left him in.

"Oh, there he is. Man of the hour," Mum said, handing me a side plate of cake. "Hasn't he let himself go." She tsked. "What a shame. He's always been so 'and-some. An' you reckon he 'as something to do with Blackwater?"

"Something, yeah." I hung up the call, unable to connect. "But it wasn't his agency that invested in it, just his parents' company, Kempthorne Enterprises. And his parents were fucking dicks."

"Language." She tutted, then frowned at the awful picture of Alex on TV. His hair was mussed, as though he'd been dragged through a bush. His eyes were all red, his beard scruffy. "I can tell. He 'as that look about him. Haunted, you know? Poor man. The press will never leave 'im alone now. That's what you get for tax evasion."

"It wasn't tax evasion."

"It's always tax evasion with that posh lot. Unless he's

in the Business? Is he? He'd better not drag you back into—"

"No, he's not in the Business, he's just... a guy caught up in all his parents' latent shit from years ago." I hoped. We really needed to talk.

Wherever he was, he'd be hurting. I was still bloody pissed at him, but I had to get to him, and fast. And I knew exactly who to contact to make that happen.

I wolfed down the cake and started for the door. "Thanks, Mum, you're a legend."

"John Domenici, you aren't going to leave without giving your mum a kiss, are you?"

"No." I kissed her on the forehead, then wrapped her in a hug.

"You an' the Alex boy, you always 'ave a place here. Both of you." Her eyes gleamed. "All this... the house and book clubs. It don't mean shit when family are in trouble."

"Thanks, Mum."

I flipped my hood up and left Mum's tiny house, my heart pounding faster with every step. I had to get to him fast or something bad was going to happen. I could feel it. Or maybe it was being back in London with the source rushing deep beneath my feet that had me restless. Whatever the reason, my next stop was Gina.

## 10

D <sup>om</sup>

Cecil Court's big windows had been boarded up and a bright yellow No Entry notice had been posted on the door. I hurried by, boots sloshing in puddles, keeping my head down. If the world knew Kempthorne was alive, the world likely assumed I was too, and before our fake deaths, we'd had a shit-ton of enemies breathing down our necks. Not to mention the fuzz. Was faking your own death illegal? Probably for latents.

I headed toward Soho, where I might find Gina. If she wasn't there, then she had family up north, but I had no idea where. She *had* to be in Soho. It was still early, and most of the bars were closed. But Big Rick's was open; he liked to get in early and grab the alcoholic commuters before they thought about going home. I couldn't just hang around inside. He'd notice me. And these old haunts of mine were obvious places to find me, should any government agencies be looking.

I bounced around the parks, wasting a few hours in the rain, and headed back to Soho as soon as the streetlights blinked on. The bars were Friday-night lively. I didn't even know what fucking day of the week it was. I'd spent way too long on busses, had only slept in snatches, and hadn't showered since the highland B&B, which felt like a lifetime ago. Running on empty, I *really* needed Gina to show.

Slinking into the bar, I skirted to the fringes of the crowd, avoiding anyone who might recognize me. Gina was always hard to miss with her purple coat and bouncy hair, but tonight, she hadn't yet turned up.

Propping myself against the wall in a shady corner, I kept my head down. Hopefully, nobody would notice the weirdo in a Nessie T-shirt not buying drinks.

Pink—Cas to everyone else, I called her Pink due to her crazy hair—showed up just after nine, all swagger in her big boots, hacked-at tops, and half-shaved bright pink hair. Cas believed I was dead. Or had done. Unless she'd seen the news recently.

She headed for the bar and ordered a drink. The shifting crowd blocked my view every few seconds. There was no way I could get to her without being seen. Maybe if I stared hard enough, she'd turn around.

"Hey, mate, you got a problem?"

I scowled at the prick who'd taken a disliking to me for no reason. "Yeah, you." It was out before I'd engaged my brain.

He puffed out his chest. "Wad you say?"

I flashed a smile. "Nothin', mate. It's all good."

"Oh, there you are, Boytoy!" Pink flew in, threw an arm around my shoulder, and scooted me away from the fight about to happen. She grinned, offered her knuckles, and bumped with mine. Relief made my head spin. I needed something to go right.

"Dom, dude, you look like you've escaped from the psych ward. Again."

Her digs usually rolled right off me but smiling back was a struggle. "Can we get out of here? Have you seen Gina?"

"Yeah, yeah." She play-punched me in the chest and guided me out of the bar, back on the pavement, and into the sporadic flow of Friday night revelers. "Not so dead, huh? Shit. I knew, of course."

"You knew?"

"Gina told me."

"She what?"

"Dom?!" The screech barreled down the street. Gina stood up ahead next to a cab, her purple coat like a flare. Her mouth fell open. "Oh my god!" She ran at me— almost knocking me off my feet—and wrapped me in a full-body hug.

"Hey," I croaked, trying and failing not to choke up.

"Fuck." She shoved me away at arm's length and frowned. "You're not supposed to be here."

"You weren't supposed to tell anyone." I thumbed at Cas.

"Oh. I just—" Her gaze darted, flicking to me, to Cas, and back again.

Cas slunk from my side to Gina's and tucked her close. The pair slotted together, hip to hip. Oh right. Why hadn't I seen it before? They were a thing, like me and Alex were a thing, but hopefully fewer death threats and drama. "Cool."

Gina shrugged. "She kinda knows everything, so..."

"Awesome." I eyed Cas. "You hurt her, you die."

She chuckled. "Yeah, from you lot, that's actually a legit threat, so... I don't plan to."

Gina whirled and waved at her taxicab to stay. "Get in. We can't stay here. We'll head back to our flat."

We all slid into the back of the cab and Gina reeled off an address not far from Soho.

The second we got underway, and before Gina could ambush me with a thousand questions, I said, "G, I need you to call Alex."

"He's not with you?"

"No. We er... We had a fight."

"Like an actual fight, with fists?" Cas asked.

I winced, remembering how I'd pinned him to the bar. "Yeah. I left him in Scotland."

"Oh my God." Gina sighed. "Why can't you just take the happy ever after?" She grabbed her phone and dialed, I assumed, Alex's new number. Alex had made sure she'd had it, for dire emergencies. "He's not answering." She tapped out a text message. "You are both on my shit-list. What's going on with you? You had the good life. What's he done this time?"

"Yeah, it's a lot. Can it wait until we get wherever we're going?"

"Yeah." She glowered. "And you can shower too. Just sayin'."

"Thanks."

Her glower softened. "Are you okay though?"

"Better now I'm back in London." Better now I had her in my corner. Everything was always better with Gina. Cas I wasn't a hundred percent sure about, more like eighty percent, but if Gina cared for her, then she was tight.

"You in danger?" Cas asked. "Whatever was after you in the States, is it still after you here?"

"Probably. And Kage, America—what happened there—it was bad. Kage has lost the plot, gone fuckin' nuts. He blew up Kempthorne's Range Rover and I think he maybe killed Jordan."

"Jordan's dead?" Gina gasped. "Oh no, he was like Alfred was to Batman, but with Kempthorne, and more awesome."

And that hadn't even touched on the whole I-was-the-latent-messiah-and-made-in-a-lab-somewhere news. "All of us are going to need to lay low for a while."

"Yeah, but the boss man is all over the TV," Cas said. "That cat is out the bag and 'alf way to Hackney."

"Yeah, that's probably my fault. I shouldn't have left him." I'd said I'd never leave him and I'd... *walked away*. I hadn't technically walked away from him, more like *everything*. Shit, the way his mind worked, he'd think I'd left for good. Alex could take a lot, but he was also really, really vulnerable, like toughened glass. One wrong hit, and the whole lot shattered. "I need to talk to Alex."

Gina tried to call him again and shook her head when

it rang out. What did it mean if he wasn't even picking up for her?

Wherever he was, he was in trouble. And he thought he was alone. I might have been super powerful, but Alex was a top level latent too. If he spiraled—because of Jordan, because of me—there'd be no coming back.

lexander

"Mister Kempthorne, right this way, please." The young woman I followed down a thick-carpeted hallway was the first person not to stare when she'd seen my name on the visitor form for Blackwater Industries.

She escorted me into a generic meeting room with blue fabric office chairs around a fake-beech table, handed me a cup of tea and little biscuit with a polite smile, and left.

Blackwater Research & Development.

Many decisions had been made in my past, for me and by me. None I regretted more than the decision regarding Candidate Thirty-Two.

I tapped my finger on the desk and watched the TV

on the wall pan through glossy photographs of smiling scientists laughing at test tubes.

In the late 70s, my parents had invested in a small military research start-up, helping it find its feet in the new frontier of latent experimentation. The Kempthornes had a long history of latent research. And Blackwater had offered something they hadn't seen before. A way to make the latent issue *go away*. Potentially. It required money, and time, both of which they had. And fifty suspected-latent embryos. They had invested in multiple latent ventures. For the longest time, Blackwater had just been another company name on an end-of-year spreadsheet.

After their deaths, I'd inherited everything. Including Kempthorne Enterprises and the contract with Blackwater.

"Ah, Mister Kempthorne!"

A dashing well-dressed man entered the conference room, a few decades older than me but with a similar well-practiced boardroom smile and intelligent gleam in his eyes. I vaguely recalled meeting him a few times over the years.

"I'm Sean McGovern. I oversee shareholders' interests, such as yourself. I hope you don't mind me saying, you've been having a tough time of things lately."

I smiled, mirroring his. "All a bizarre misunderstanding. You know how the press are. Rumors become fact unless nipped in the bud. My solicitors are gradually clawing back control of my assets."

"Of course. Well, little has changed at our end. Your estate, as it were, continued investing, for which we are of course very grateful." He sat at the table, unbuttoned his jacket, and flicked it open, the epitome of sophisticated control. It was rather like looking at myself, twenty years from now. And I wasn't sure I liked the view. "Your return requires no more from us than a few signatures to reassert your shares." He placed a tablet on the table, swiped the screen, and pushed it toward me with an electronic pen.

I scanned it, pretending to read. "Yes, well. There's been something of a change of plans."

"Oh?"

"Candidate Thirty-Two."

He blinked, stayed silent, waited. To him, the name likely didn't mean a thing.

"You are to discontinue all involvement," I added.

"I'm sorry? 'Discontinue'?" He spluttered a laugh. "Wasn't it you who pursued that project personally?"

"Yes, well." I unbuttoned my jacket. "He is no longer your concern."

McGovern's smile turned to steel. "I'm afraid it doesn't work like that, Mr Kempthorne. You, yourself, signed the purchase order from the Ministry of Defense on behalf of Blackwater. Candidate Thirty-Two is once again Blackwater property. He wouldn't exist at all if not for us."

"Well, then I'll buy him off you."

"I'm afraid the asset is not for sale."

I'd had a similar conversation with a rather unpleasant man who thought he owned John. It hadn't ended well for him. But Blackwater wasn't one man. It was a vast operation with multiple tentacles. Cut one off, and it grew back. Mr McGovern having an unfortunate accident wasn't going to solve this problem.

"The Kempthornes and Blackwater have enjoyed a prosperous relationship over the decades. I've rarely intervened in your operations, but my investment can very easily be severed."

"Mr Kempthorne, you were the one who drove this project through. The surviving candidates were all given the green light after your *personal* involvement. Prior to your input, the project had been shelved, along with the candidates themselves. Frankly, the purchase of the embryos to begin with skirted a few ethical issues, and we'd have rather not acknowledged the entire project."

"'Embryos'?" There had been mention of embryos on Kage's documents too. "At what point did Blackwater purchase the latent children?"

"Oh, we didn't purchase them. We—Blackwater that is—sponsored the candidates from conception. We essentially *made* them."

"Wait..." My mind worked, only now putting some rather nasty pieces together. "You weren't sold them as infants?"

"No, Blackwater loaned them out—the children— and paid their host families to support them as they matured. As you can imagine, raising children isn't easy. And now that we're seeing results—results you wanted, I might add—you want to remove our most valuable asset, the most promising candidate for controlling latency?"

I'd made a mistake, all those years ago. But before me, my parents had made a bigger mistake. John Domenici wasn't a Domenici at all. If that was the information he'd discovered, and he'd believed I'd known, then it was a surprise he hadn't outright killed me when he'd thrown me against the bar.

I rubbed my neck, the bruises now faded but the memory fierce.

The candidates had just been numbers in a spread-sheet. I'd needed a powerful latent. One I could control. Blackwater had them available. One who'd shown remarkable self-restraint and promise. A military man with a troubled past. Regrettably, at the time, I hadn't thought any deeper than that. He'd been a tool, and for that, I was sorry.

But John was so much more than a number, so much more to me than the idea that he'd make a reality. And even if he no longer wanted to be with me, I could do this for him. I had to. Because it was right. I wasn't leaving this conference room until Blackwater relinquished all rights to John.

"Mr McGovern, I restarted the project on a whim, and it's really not of interest anymore. Let's shelve it and move on, shall we?"

McGovern's smile was the pitying kind. "That's not your call to make. While we appreciate your investment, you have no authority over Blackwater's research."

I sighed and removed my phone from my jacket's inside pocket. "I think you'll find you're wrong." Ignoring the rampant blast of text message notifications landing on-screen, I opened my photos folder and showed Mister McGovern the name of the man who now owned a controlling percentage of shares in Blackwater.

Sean McGovern's smile fled, leaving disdain behind. "When did this happen?"

"Last night. Twenty seconds before trading closed. Kempthorne Enterprises owns Blackwater, and if you refuse to cut John from the project then I will personally shut you down. Deny my request and you'll leave this room unemployed."

"How dare you." His cheeks flushed. "This is absurd. I wasn't told—We do important work here. You can't just waltz in and buy us!"

"Important work manipulating latents with Ink and god knows what other heinous experiments on human beings, born of test tubes or not. Work my parents began and I am a single word away from ending." I knew what it was like to be brought up an experiment, a tool, one tick-box away from failure, and the fact Blackwater existed at all undermined everything I was trying to do.

McGovern shot to his feet. "If you close Blackwater down you will lose millions, perhaps billions, in compensation for reneged contracts."

"Military contracts. Yes, I am aware."

"Why? That candidate is everything you wanted!"

"Yes, he is." I stood and re-buttoned my jacket. "Make it happen, Mr McGovern, or Blackwater is finished." I thrust out my hand to shake on the agreement.

He looked at my hand, my face. A little twitch tugged at his mouth, and then his pretend smile was back. He grabbed my hand and squeezed as if he meant to take it off. "I see the apple does not fall far from the tree. Very well. You'll get your wish. Candidate Thirty-Two will be struck from the project."

"And nobody from Blackwater is to touch him. Understood?" He nodded. "A pleasure doing business with you." I headed for the exit, satisfied it was done. They'd surrender him. And the moment I was certain John was safe, I'd shut them down.

"Mister Kempthorne, the fact you are a latent and you continued to invest in what we do here has me questioning your real motives."

"A question nobody but John has the right to know the answer to."

I'd been fighting fires since the world had realized bad boy billionaire gay latent Alexander Kempthorne had not, in fact, perished when his private jet had gone down in the middle of the Atlantic Ocean. The Met police had questioned me on my whereabouts during the window of time when Jordan had been killed. Unfortunately, John was my alibi, and he'd understandably gone to ground. I hadn't been arrested, but I'd been warned not to take any *vacations*. The IRL had made it clear I was on their naughty list, but at least they were unlikely to hog-tie me and throw me on a plane back to the States, whereas the American LOA would. They'd have to get in line.

Kage could have been anywhere... but he was the least of my concerns.

Where was John?

Even if I knew, how could I go to him? I couldn't.

In a rental car, I pulled up outside Ravenscourt. The house was cold, dark, and horribly empty, and I lasted fifteen minutes before locking it up and leaving. I couldn't face Kensington, not without Jordan, and Cecil Court was closed. Running on autopilot, I checked in at the Savoy and planned to drown my sorrows in the hotel's dramatic gold and black Beaufort Bar.

At around 11pm, while I stared at my whiskey, mind meandering around the subject of John, Kage Mitchell walked in, looking untouchable in black trousers and a black turtleneck, with his hair slicked back and eyes sparkling. He sat in the chair opposite, leaned back, and smiled.

A few beats passed. If I did anything violent, I'd be arrested and locked up, the key thrown away. It would almost be worth it.

"I didn't think they let murderers in here," I said.

"They let you in."

I imagined reaching across the table and lighting his bones up with trick, but that would be too quick a death. "How did you find me?"

He laughed. "Cecil Court has been seized, you hate your own company, so Ravenscourt is out, and Kensington? It's just not the same without your butler. But the Savoy? Could you be any more predictable?"

I clenched the whiskey glass tighter. "When you lay dying on Cecil Court's kitchen floor, I hesitated, just for a moment. I should have listened to my instincts."

"Like you did your friend at the academy, who you let die?"

"Well informed, aren't you?" I swirled the whiskey in its glass.

"Don't pretend you saved me out of the goodness of your heart when we both know you don't have a heart."

True enough.

"You only saved me to impress Dom."

If he was going to bring John into this, then it wouldn't hurt to remind him how he'd screwed that up. "He cared for you. Even when you turned on us, he wanted to believe you were one of us... He fought for you." I set the glass down on the side table and leaned forward. "You could have had John. In the beginning, he was all yours and I wouldn't have stood in the way."

A muscle in his cheek jumped. He leaned forward. "He killed my brother."

"What happened to your brother was tragic, but that wasn't on John. Easy to blame everyone else for your own mistakes, isn't it?"

"Like you do?" he snarled. "Dom knows who you really are. The spider in his web, all the threads leading back to you."

I'd used the same analogy for Montgomery and missed it every time I looked in the mirror. Or perhaps, instead of a spider, my life was a murder wall, the red threads I'd cast out all pointing back to me.

"There's only one thing I don't understand." Kage smirked. "What was your endgame, huh? Or do you just like to fuck with people's lives?"

I didn't have to tell Kage anything. But as I couldn't reach across and light him up, I'd make him hurt another way. "John Domenici is mine to fuck with how I wish, and the fact that pisses you off is really just a happy accident."

He laughed again, masking most but not all of his flinch. The words had hurt. He knew he'd lost John.

"You just can't get your head around why John chose me, when you could have given him everything he's ever wanted."

The laugher vanished, leaving his eyes stone-cold again. "You're a vicious, self-centered, murdering sociopath, so no, I don't understand why he keeps going back to you—but this time, Kempthorne, he's not coming back. He knows what you are. He knows you've controlled him from the beginning. He knows he's your experiment. He knows everything."

"Not everything." I picked up my drink and took a gulp, suddenly needing it.

Kage's satisfied laugh crawled beneath my skin. "You're never seeing him again."

I flicked my gaze up to find his smile as bright as always, so full of satisfaction. He thought he'd won. "If you threaten or hurt John in any way, I will burn all of London and everyone in it, just to get to you. Do not underestimate what I am capable of."

"I'm relying on it." He pushed to his feet. "The world is going to see you both for the monsters you are."

I lunged, grabbed him by the back of the neck, and yanked his face close to mine. To anyone nearby, it appeared as though we shared a secret, something inti-mate. Kage's eyes widened. He tried to pull free. I tight-ened my grip, stopping short of choking. "You will regret the day you made an enemy of me. Run. Run now. I will not warn you again. You crossed the line when you killed

Jordan. He was *family*. Now there is *no fucking line, Mr Mitchell.*"

He tore himself free, stumbled and almost tripped over a table, and righted his jacket, hastily smoothing his hair down and glancing around to make sure we hadn't been observed.

I reclined back in the chair and finished my whiskey in a single gulp, then saluted him with the empty glass.

Hate blazed in his glare. He stormed from the bar, slamming the door behind him.

Kage Mitchell was a dead man walking.

## 12

D<sup>om</sup>

"So, let me get this straight..." Gina, seated with me and Cas at the little kitchen table in their flat, held up her hand and bent one finger down. "Kage has gone psycho and wants Kempthorne and you dead." Another finger went down. "You're like some powered-up latent who can tap into the source of all latent power." Another finger bent. "Blackthorn—"

"Blackwater."

"Blackwater is some super-secret shit that paid the Domenicis to raise you?"

"Yeah."

The last finger went down. "And Kempthorne knew this whole time?"

"Yeah, that covers most of it."

She flopped her head back and blinked at the kitchen ceiling. "This is a disaster."

"It's something." I'd showered while Gina helpfully cleaned my clothes—it was that or burn them—then wolfed down some cereal and dressed in the freshly dried t-shirt and trousers. Only then, feeling halfway to human again, I'd told her and Cas everything.

"It's about to get worse," Cas drawled. She'd been browsing her phone for any clues as to where Kempthorne might be and showed us the screen.

"*Kempthorne Enterprises in hostile takeover of military research company, Blackwater*," Gina read aloud. "He's doubling down on this?"

Cas shrugged. "It fits his whole evil villain agenda thing he's got going on."

I slumped in my chair, folded my arms on the table, and buried my face in them. "Yeah, but he's not like that."

"Dom," Gina sighed. Her little hand rested on my bicep. "When do we start thinking that maybe he is?"

"Never?" I couldn't. Even now, after everything he'd done and kept secret, I couldn't hate him. I'd been pissed off, and I still was, but the rage had faded behind what was beginning to feel a lot like despair. I lifted my head. "You don't get him. Nobody does. His whole life he's thought himself the villain, right? But there's always a reason behind all his sneaky shit. I have to talk to him. He'll tell me what's going on."

"He's literally lied to you since you met," Cas said. "You think you can trust whatever excuse he comes up with next?"

"I dunno. I can tell when he's holding back. Maybe."

"He killed Renick," Cas continued, shrugging when Gina and me stared. "I'm just sayin'... His parents experimented on latents, apparently so does he. The apple don't fall far from the tree. Maybe he enjoys it all a bit too much?"

"No, he wouldn't... His mum..." I wasn't going to tell her the abuse Alex had been subjected to, but there was no way he'd do the same to others. Would he? Ruthless, focused, relentless. He'd use anyone and anything to get what he wanted. Did that include me?

"Ease off, Cas." Gina tried to soften the blow, but maybe Cas was right. I had a blind spot when it came to Kage, but when it came to Kempthorne, I couldn't see around him. He'd become my life, my everything. I'd follow him anywhere, into anything. Had he tricked me this whole time, turned me into his latent pet? But why? What was the point? So he could fuck me? That didn't make any sense.

I chewed on my thumbnail. I couldn't believe he was bad, even if it looked that way from every angle.

"I'm gonna take a walk." I needed to move, to think. I scooped up my jacket and threw it on, over my Nessie shirt.

"Be careful. We don't know who's watching..." Gina called.

Soho was a great place to get lost, especially at night. Old London, full of nooks and crannies, overhanging houses and gnarled alleyways, among countless quirky bars and shops. The rain had passed so the bar patrons were spilling out onto the streets. Music thumped, taxis trundled by, splashing through puddles. This was London. This was my home. And far beneath my feet, the source throbbed.

It had always been there. I'd always heard it—London's heartbeat—I just hadn't been able to tune in like I could now.

If I wasn't a Domenici, if I'd been created in a lab somewhere, what was I? Was I even human? I was me, right? Just because I'd learned some shit, it didn't change who I was today. Christ, my heart hurt, right behind the ribs, as though it had grown thorns to protect itself.

My phone rang. "Hey, G..."

"Dom, so I think I've found him. There's this conspiracy thread on Reddit that I used to keep an eye on while you guys were in hiding. A bunch of people never believed he'd died. Anyway, they've switched to trying to track Kempthorne down. I mean, there's some insane stuff on there, like he's a vampire." She chuckled. "Can you imagine? I mean, actually yeah, it kinda tracks—"

"G, he's not a vampire. I'd have noticed. Focus?"

"Oh yeah, right. They reckon he's in London. Which makes sense, I guess. He'd come back, right? There's nothing in Scotland for him—"

"Where in London?"

"It's kinda obvious, when you think about it. He's not gonna go home. There's nothing there for him either, so—"

"G, seriously. Where the fuck is he?"

"He's at the Savoy."

"The big-arse hotel all the celebs stay at?"

"Yeah."

"How the fuck am I gonna get in there in a Nessie T-shirt and boots? They'll call the cops before I've left the cab."

"Come back to the flat. Cas has an idea."

lexander

The Gentleman's Lounge at the Savoy served drinks on velvet napkins. I'd never thought much of it, but when my whiskey arrived, sliding across the bar on the little patch of velvet, I could hear John asking me what the point was. I'd have struggled to answer him. Like most things in my life, he called it all into question, and I loved him for it.

The lounge was quiet. Kage hadn't been back since the threat the night before. A few people chatted together in a seating area, while a handful of others sat at the bar, like me. I dug my phone from my pocket and frowned at its blank screen. The bloody thing hadn't stopped vibrating in days. I'd neglected to charge it, for my own sanity. The whole world wanted pieces of me, and I was done, just for tonight.

I stared at my drink, my dead phone next to it, and fought to keep all the bad choices from my head. I hadn't ever wanted to do anything wrong. My past decisions had always been for the right reasons. Or so I'd thought. Now I wasn't sure. I wasn't sure about a lot of things. If I didn't have John, then I'd have to adjust my world again, go back to the way things were before. Somehow. Cecil Court, Kempthorne & Co... It was all gone.

Someone leaned against the bar to my left a little too close for comfort. Hopefully, they'd order and leave.

The well-dressed guy raised a hand, and perhaps there was something in that gesture, or his stance, that triggered recognition. My heart almost lodged itself in my throat. His hair had been swept back and styled under control, but I knew how stubborn those locks were, and how they liked to curl. My fingers itched to reach out and tease them free but the rest of me was far more intrigued by everything. The suit was an exquisite fit. He'd hitched one foot up on the stool's footrest. The trousers hugged the curve of his backside and his firm thigh.

"What is your most expensive drink?" he asked the barman, attempting to hide his East End accent by putting on what he'd call a posh voice.

The barman arched an eyebrow. "Crystallo Vodka, Sir."

I waited to see if he'd ask how much. Instead, he turned to me, raked his gaze over me, then turned back to the barman. "He's paying."

I fought a smile and nodded at the barman. John kept

his gaze away, tracking the barman's movements as he prepared the drink. The vodka arrived in a slim, frosted glass. The barman left and John eyed the drink as though it might come alive and assault him. "So, what is it?" he asked. "Filtered through crushed diamonds or some shit?"

"Hopefully not the latter. Taste it and find out."

He picked up the glass, chinked it with my whiskey glass, and downed the vodka in one gulp.

"It's also fifteen thousand pounds a glass."

John choked, spluttered, and wheezed. The barman hurried over, but I waved him away with a laugh.

"Fuck." John exhaled. His eyes glistened and some of his smoothed hair had escaped to brush his jaw. "You could have warned me." He coughed against the back of his hand, but he was grinning, and that was all I cared for. If he was smiling, then we were all right. The relief made me giddy. He was here, he hadn't left. Or he had, but he'd come back, and that was... *everything*. I swallowed a sip of my own drink, clearing a swell of emotion.

John raised his hand. "Yeah, I'll..." He cleared his throat, forgetting too smooth out his accent, and tried again. "I'd like another, please."

The barman again glanced at me. "Leave the bottle," I said.

"Of course, Mr Kempthorne."

"I'm not gonna ask what the whole bottle costs." John snickered.

"It's probably best you don't." I finished my whiskey. John refilled my glass with vodka. His smirk had gained a sly quality. Mischief danced in his eyes, although that could have been the potent vodka. Anger simmered there too. I wasn't off the hook yet.

"You look good," I told him.

He preened. Then pointed at the shiny Oxford shoes. "I fell up the hotel steps. Why are all the floors polished? It's a bloody death trap."

I laughed, and he chuckled along with me. His being here was impossible. I did not deserve him. Perhaps he was back to tell me it was over.

More of the vodka went down for both of us. We didn't speak; there didn't seem to be a need to. He was thinking though, his mind working out his angle of attack. Whatever method he chose, I'd already surrendered.

"So... Here's what we're going to do." His rough hands bracketed his glass and when he next spoke, he kept his voice low. "There's one of those swish men's rooms here, right?"

"One would presume."

Glancing around, he spotted the door to the toilets and nodded. "I'm going to go in there and after a few minutes, you're gonna follow. Once inside..." His eyes flicked up and locked on mine. "You owe me a bathroom fuck. I'm either goin' to fuck you, or you're gonna fuck me. I haven't decided yet, because in case you hadn't noticed, I'm still fuckin' pissed at you. Either way, we're doin' it."

Lust ran through my veins, cool and sharp, like the diamond-filtered vodka, burning me up while at the same time shivering down my spine. "All right." I ached to have my hands on him, to open him up and fuck him deep, but with the look he was giving me, it seemed as though I might be the one under his hands. My chest tightened, heart racing.

John downed his final vodka, caught my eye one last time, pushed from the bar, and sauntered across the lounge to the men's room. There had better be a lock on that door. We were going to need it.

The next two minutes were some of the longest in my life. I settled the bar bill, tipping the barman handsomely should he suspect anything, then crossed the lounge, my heart a drumbeat in my chest.

The men's room didn't have a lock, but it did have furniture that could be propped against it.

John leaned against the far wall, arms crossed, expression smug, his arousal upsetting the fine cut of his suit trousers. I grabbed one of the chairs, wedged it behind the door, crossed the room in three strides, thrust a hand into John's hair, and kissed him hard. He moaned into me, tongue thrusting in, all traces of anger gone. I'd missed this, missed him so much it hurt to have him back. I'd been so afraid I'd lost him that the world had lost all meaning, and now he was here, in my arms again.

He ran both hands up my chest, locked my shirt in his fists, and in a blur of movement and muscle, he'd bent my arm behind my back and pinned me face-first against the fine velvet-embossed wallpaper. I'd been thrown worse places.

John's breath scorched my ear. "Don't even think about escaping."

"Frankly, escaping is the last thing on my mind."

"Just tell me one thing." His free hand, the one not

holding my arm bent against my back, slithered over my hip and dipped. He made short work of my trouser fly, then wrapped his fingers around my erection, stealing an involuntary moan from the back of my throat. "Are we a lie?" he asked.

If I said yes, I got the impression I might not be leaving the bathroom intact. Luckily, *that* would have been a lie. "We are real." My reward was him sliding his fingers down my shaft. I rested my forehead against the soft wallpaper and closed my eyes. I needed this, him, now.

"You knew Kage was out there, you knew about Blackwater, did you ask me to marry you to distract me?"

"No..." He squeezed my cock, the sharp side of pain. A shudder went through me, not entirely uncomfortable. "Yes... Some."

"We're telling the truth, Alex. And if you want us to continue to be a thing, you need to start being straight with me. Tell me, did you somehow maneuver me into Wordsworth for that showdown with Montgomery?"

"John, no, never. Wordsworth was all Montgomery—"

"Are you fucking with my life?"

I opened my mouth to reply, but his hand jerked me off, and for a few seconds, his hand was all I cared to think about. Then he stopped, leaving me adrift and gasping, desperate with need.

"Answer the question, Alex," he growled against my cheek.

"Can you be more specific?"

He pulled on my arm, spun me around with surprising strength, and slammed me back against the wall, this time facing him. Perhaps I was supposed to be afraid, but being manhandled by John had the opposite effect. I'd rarely been more aroused.

Fury burned in his glare. "Answer the bloody question."

There was no easy way to answer this one. A lie, he'd know. But the truth sounded so much worse.

"Alex," he growled, and that part of him the military had honed began to spark behind his eyes. He'd always had it. His passion, his fight, his drive, fueled by the need to do good.

"I love you," I blurted. He knew it, but it was worth repeating, especially as he might need reminding soon.

Some of the icy fury melted, but not all. "Answer the fucking question, Kempthorne."

I swallowed. "Yes."

"Yes, you're fucking with my life." He stepped back, staggered a little. "How?"

"It's... a lot for a bathroom discussion."

He pointed. "You stay there, with your dick out, Kempthorne, and tell me, because if we go back to your room or anywhere else, then you'll do what you do, distract me all over again, and I'll fall for it, because I can't stop falling for you. So spill. Now."

Dropping my head back, I blinked at the lights. "You were one of many Blackwater candidates with extraordinary tricks. I'd been looking for someone like you for a long time, someone special."

"Me? Or my trick?"

"Your trick. The fact you can touch the source,

commune with it. I've always known you were capable. It was imperative for everything I had planned."

"And what do you have planned?" The smiles from earlier, the mischief in his eyes, it was all gone now. I suspected we weren't going to be finishing our bathroom fuck after this.

"A way to cure latency," I said.

"What?"

"You and I, John. Together, I believe we can unravel latent tricks, we can cure them."

He frowned, and as the seconds passed, his frown darkened. Then he pulled the chair from the door and left. Again.

I tucked myself away, attempted to tidy my shirt and hair, and dashed after him. "John, wait."

He walked bloody fast. I chased him from the bar, into the hotel foyer, surrounded by glittering hotel opulence and sparkling guests, caught his arm, and pulled him around. He yanked from my grip, hands curling into fists.

"Alex, stop."

"Please... don't leave again." I knew how it sounded and didn't care. "We can work it out."

"You don't get it. I trusted you." He spread his arms and backed away. "Everyone I trust turns out to be a dick, so I'm done... I'm done with all of it."

"John, wait." My heart raced for a very different reason now. If he walked away, I'd never see him again. He'd vanish. He knew how. I'd had a taste of my old life, without him in it. I couldn't go back to that. I wouldn't survive it. I needed him. "Please, I know I've ruined everything. I wish I wasn't like this, but I don't know how to be anyone else. I've ruined everything—I know that, John—but I didn't do it to hurt you. That was never my intention."

We'd drawn an audience, including the concierge, who was on the desk phone, probably calling security. I had seconds to stop the love of my life from leaving me, and I had nothing to negotiate with. No leverage. There was only me, Alexander Kempthorne, the man who didn't exist, the boy who was made, everyone's favorite villain. I didn't know how to be who John wanted, or needed, or deserved, but I wanted to be that man for him. I'd do anything for him. Whatever he wanted...

...including walking away.

## 14

# D<sup>om</sup>

Alex stood in the middle of the Savoy entrance lobby, hair a mess, shirt untucked, and his face so wrought with agony that I almost went to him, just to make it stop hurting inside. The whole foyer full of guests had stopped to admire our drama. They all knew who he was, but not me, especially in my toff disguise. I was just some guy who Alex Kempthorne owned in every way.

The truth hadn't made anything better. The pain had just gotten more acute.

It hadn't hurt inside when we'd sat at the bar and I'd polished off half a bottle of vodka that cost more to buy than a house. It hadn't hurt when he'd kissed me in the men's room. It didn't hurt when I was with him and the world, and our past, and all that shit left us alone. When it was just me and him, it was perfect.

But there were lies, and then there was him manipulating me for years.

Alex swallowed. He glimpsed all the people staring, only now seeing them. He straightened and swept his hair back. "You're right," he croaked. "I'm sorry." And with those two words settling in the quiet foyer, he turned and jogged up the sweeping staircase.

He meant it. He'd meant all of it. He'd just laid his heart bare and because I was pissed, I kept batting it away, but I didn't want to go. I wanted him. It was always him. Lies, an' all. I just didn't know how to handle the mountain of crap he'd dumped on me.

"Shit..." I started after him, taking the stairs two steps at a time. On the above gallery landing, the elevator doors rumbled closed. I sprinted into the stairwell and up to the next floor, but the elevator continued to count up. On the fourth floor, I shoved through the fire doors and caught sight of him walking down the plush corridor underneath sparkling chandeliers.

"Alex?"

He stopped.

I started forward, breathing way too hard. "I'm sorry too, okay? Everything is fucked, and nothing makes any sense... except you."

His head turned, but he still didn't look over his shoulder, or at me.

"I didn't leave you. I just *left*." I didn't even know what I was saying, not really. The words stuck in my throat. I kept on walking, quicker now, in case he got any idea about disappearing behind one of the hotel's giant doors and locking me out. "Kage dumped a load of shit on me and I should have known it was all twisted up, but I can't see straight with you because you keep hiding important stuff from me."

"I know, it's not your fault. Just go, John. I can't be who you want."

"What?"

He started walking again.

"No, wait…"

He sped up. And just like I'd feared, he waved a card at one of the gold-gilded doors and vanished inside, slamming it closed behind him.

"Hey." I thumped the door. "You're a prick, you know that?" Bracing both forearms on the door, I bowed my head. "I know you can hear me. So listen, Kempthorne. My answer is yes. You hear me? It's yes. And you had better open this bloody door in the next five seconds or I'm gonna burn it down and get us both banned from here for life. I mean… that's not a problem for me, but I figure you like it here, so—"

The door jolted open just enough for me to see his intense eyes. "Yes to what?" he asked.

"What do you think?"

"I… don't know?"

"I think you do."

His eyebrows lifted and his eyes widened. He definitely knew.

"Wait." The door slammed in my face.

"Excuse me, sir." I blinked at a big guy dressed in all grey and couldn't figure out if he was security or the butler, or where he'd come from. "The management has kindly requested that you and Mister Kempthorne discuss your misunderstandings elsewhere."

"What?" Was he speaking English? Was he kicking us out? "You can tell the management to shove my misunderstandings up their arses. These rooms are insanely expensive, the vodka is overpriced, and I'm having an important conversation with my boyfriend—"

The door opened. Alex dropped to a knee and presented me with a ring nestled in a velvet box. My first instinct, like before, was to leg it. But all of this had kicked off right around the time I'd screwed this up once already, so maybe that hadn't been the best reaction.

"Hm..." I pretended to consider it.

"Really?" he growled, his blue eyes alight. "John?"

"Maybe you should say the words, so we're clear." My fucking heart was going to leap out of my chest.

"John Domenici, will you marry me?"

"Fuck, yeah."

Alex blinked.

I glanced at my new grey-clad friend. "You witnessed this, right, so it's real—"

Alex grabbed my arm, hauled me inside, slammed the door, and plastered me to the wall with a kiss so bloody hot there was no ending it there. I grabbed his face in my hands, thrust my tongue with his, and drove him backward, in the general direction of the bed. He fought with my jacket, managed to pull it down my arms, where it got stuck. I shoved him away, flung the jacket off, and fixed him under my glare a few feet away, his face wrecked, his whole rich git persona crumbling, revealing

the *real* person. The kinda messed up, vulnerable, maybe a bit psychotic, superintelligent, flawed, but amazing man who was all mine.

"I'm sorry," he said. And I believed him.

"Get on the bed."

Alex backed to the bed and climbed onto its edge, on his knees. I approached, wanting nothing more than to devour every inch of him, but we'd get to that. I stopped in front of him, face-to-face, and looked over all the tight lines around his mouth and eyes, the frown creasing his forehead under his messy fringe. He knew he'd fucked up. I'd already forgiven him, but he didn't need to know that. Not yet.

Stroking his jaw, I teased my mouth over his, waiting for him to lunge. When he did, I pulled back, keeping just out of reach. He groaned. "You're about to torture me, aren't you?"

"I'm thinking about it."

"Anything," he breathed. A man like him, groveling? Just when I'd thought he couldn't get any hotter, he proved me wrong. He reached for my face, skimmed his fingers over my cheek, his face so wrought I wasn't sure how much of his agony I could take.

"I'm sorry I pinned you to the bar," I said.

"I deserved it."

"No. It was wrong. I don't... I don't do that shit. Not anymore."

"Sorry I lied about... everything."

"Yeah, I know." His lips brushed mine, a tease. He nudged my mouth open, gently asking, seeking permission.

"Can you ever forgive me?"

I dropped my hand and clutched his dick, making him groan some more. "Let's fuck around and find out." Shoving him back, he sprawled on the bed, legs bent awkwardly. I spread his knees, crawled between them, and pinned Alex under me. "Your hands." He brought his hands together. I grabbed both and locked them down, holding his wrists trapped, and hovered my face an inch from his. His eyes told a thousand different stories, but anyone who looked deeper knew the truth. All those lies were armor. And they'd all crumbled away, leaving the man bare.

"If you want me to stop," I whispered over his lips, "tell me it's raining." Before he could answer, I cocked my head and skimmed my tongue down his smooth jaw, then sucked at his neck and pinched his skin between my teeth. He arched under me, his wrists still pinned, and moaned my name. Summoning a tingle of trick to my lips, I kissed his shoulder, leaving a golden trail he absorbed. His breathing quickened, his body coming alive, his trick singing.

He was all mine.

---

The gold band, engraved with tiny Celtic markings, glinted on my finger. I rubbed it with my thumb, twirling it in the light. Seeing it there was going to take some getting used to. Was I even supposed to have a ring already? How did this all work? Should I get Alex one? What kind of ring would be good enough?

Gina was going to lose her shit.

While Alex snored lightly, I extracted myself from under his long limbs, showered, and brewed some coffee—the hotel had real coffee makers, not instant coffee. I figured they had to justify the cost somehow. And as I let Alex sleep, I flicked on the TV, keeping the volume low.

Protestors had set up camp outside IRL processing centers, waving their signs: *LUL, Lock Up Latents*. It didn't take a psychic to see where it was all going. Soon, the UK would be like the USA, maybe worse. There was no shortage of people who wanted all latents behind bars just for being latents. I'd been there. I'd prefer to die rather than be locked up again.

But what if Alex was right? What if we could *cure* latents?

*"Kempthorne-owned Blackwater research on hold. Ethics called into question. IRL to investigate."* The ticker across the bottom of the screen read. Huh. Kempthorne buys a major stake in Blackwater and then it gets shut down? That couldn't be a coincidence.

I turned on my phone and received six messages from Gina demanding to know if I'd found Alex. I sent a reply that I had, and then dug around the news sites for more on the Blackwater story. Blackwater was being accused of artificially enhancing latents. *Is Alexander Kempthorne building a latent army?* Was one of many theories bouncing around the Internet.

"Maybe he bloody should," I muttered.

"He should what?" Alex said, voice gravelly and sleep addled. He'd thrown on a fluffy white dressing gown that made him look like the devil in angel wings, and as he bent down to read over my shoulder, I planted a kiss on his neck. "Morning," he growled, probably hungover, definitely sex sore. We'd raided the minibar after the wall-to-wall sex, and if he was feeling anything like me, everything ached in the best way. As he straightened, he caught sight of the ring, smirked as though he'd won the lottery, and sauntered into the bathroom to shower.

I did some more Googling, avoiding conspiracy black holes, then found this gem: *Did John Domenici create latents?* The article was from a US newspaper and discussed an event at a small airport six months ago. It hadn't been picked up by the UK press. If they did see it, and partnered it with Kempthorne's evil plans for world domination, we were screwed.

Alex reappeared, dressed and back to his usual alert self.

"Tell me about this plan of yours to cure latents."

He poured himself some coffee. "I'm an absorber. I drain trick from latents, but if I take too much, it renders me unconscious. I have a limit. You, on the other hand, do not. You can summon as much trick as it'll give you."

"Yeah but, I've almost spiraled a few times." And none of those experiences were something I wanted to relive.

"Not when I'm with you."

Huh. That was true. He'd always caught me before I'd lost control. "So... you absorb and I... what?"

"Feed excess trick back to the source."

"But I've never done that." Was it even possible?

"You've pulled from the source, you have a connection. You and I together are able to push and pull trick between us. It stands to reason, if I drain them and feed you the excess, you can funnel that trick to the source."

He made it sound so simple. "Has anything like that ever been done?"

"Not to my knowledge. But if you can draw from the source, then you can also push it back."

"And this was your big idea? Your plan for me?"

He breathed in and fixed me in his sights, dark eyes sharp with intent. "I thought you had potential, yes. But you should know, I had no idea you weren't a Domenici. I was only told you were a viable candidate for what I needed, nothing more. My involvement only goes back a few years. Whatever transpired before that was all Blackwater."

That tracked. He'd gotten involved when he'd bought me from the military. "If I'm number thirty-two, then there are other candidates out there?"

"It's possible, yes. Likely even."

"Blackwater had fifty embryos." I'd seen that much on Kage's documents.

Alex rubbed his forehead. "Kage told you this?"

I moved to the breakfast bar and leaned closer. "Hey?"

"I'm sorry, John. I should have told you from the very beginning, but initially I wasn't sure you were even viable, and then, well, I... feared the more you knew, the more you'd pull away. I thought I'd lose you."

He almost had. "We'll get through it, like we always do."

He didn't look convinced, but I didn't doubt us. We'd survived everything else. What the hell else could go wrong?

"Not all of the embryos survived into adulthood," he added. "Blackwater let that slip when I spoke with them recently."

"You bought Blackwater out?"

"Yes. It was the only way to intervene in their control of you."

So he'd been moving the pieces again, shifting things around behind the scenes, as he did so well. "And did you stop them?"

"Yes. I threatened to shut Blackwater down."

"Nice."

"The gears are in motion to close Blackwater anyway. I wanted you safe before that happened."

"So you're not planning a secret army of enhanced latents to take over the world like the Internet says?"

"No." He smiled, but his smile faded, his mind working.

I chuckled. "No... Don't go there. If those candidates are anything like me, they're better off not knowing they were created in a lab and their lives are all fake bullshit." Alex winced. I waved his silent apology away. "It's done. I'm dealing. If we can really cure latents, it might even be worth it."

"It's a theory. We won't know until we try. And until recently, you weren't capable."

That was what the little trick-testing visits to the stone circle had been about. And I'd thought he'd just been curious about my burgeoning trick. But it was all good. I knew now. Knew it all.

I circled the counter and pulled my man into my arms. He put his coffee down and came easily, the pair of

us slotting so well together it had to be right. "Will you promise me, no more surprises?"

"No more surprises." His genuine smile grew, softening his eyes. "You have my word."

Yeah, okay. We could do this. We were going to be all right. "You think I'm ready to save latents?" It sounded like the kind of thing someone with my power should do, but I still wasn't convinced I was the right guy to do it. Maybe the two of us were, though.

With his thumb on my chin, he tipped my head up. "There's only one way to know."

"Find someone who doesn't wanna be a latent anymore and make their dreams come true?"

"It would certainly be a start. Do you have anyone in mind?"

"No, but I know someone who will."

## 15

Alexander

We were about to return to Hackney, Business-controlled territory, but this time we wouldn't be in my Aston and I wasn't bound and gagged by Charles Renick's associates. This time, John rode in the passenger seat of my rented Ford while I drove. We'd talked. He knew it all now, everything, and against all the odds, he was still by my side, reinforcing the fact I did not deserve him, but I was going to bloody well try.

The ring on his hand caught my eye more often than I cared to admit. We had a great many external forces converging against us, yet it all paled in comparison to the fact he'd said *yes*. And I hadn't needed to maneuver him into it. He'd made his choice. He'd had ample opportunity to leave. It hadn't even been my idea, not the second time. He'd said yes... to be with me.

Trepidation and excitement swung me wildly from terrified to thrilled.

We were *engaged*.

"...right and then a left, back there," he said, then twisted in his eat. "We missed it. What's going on with you?"

"I fully admit to being distracted." I pulled the car over and waited for a gap in the traffic to turn around and head back while John half-smirked in the corner of my vision. "Do you have any preference for a wedding? A registry office, church, clifftop hotel in Devon?"

"You're kidding, right?" He laughed. "I didn't even know we could, you know... get hitched."

"Gay marriage is a right we do still have. Although, it's not something I've dwelled on in the past." We were hopeless. Perhaps Gina would be the best person to ask for advice.

"So you don't actually have a plan for the Big Day?"

"To be fair, I didn't actually expect you to agree."

He laughed again. "What happens next?"

"I have no idea." And that was the truth.

We turned into the street he'd pointed out earlier and approached a few 80s-built concrete high-rises that should have been demolished years ago.

This was John's old neighborhood. His world, growing up. And as soon as we pulled into the cracked and overgrown closed-down hardware store parking lot, his mood rapidly darkened.

He stared out of the window at graffiti-painted walls

and trash-scattered pavements. "People always said I had his eyes, yah know?"

John's eyes were beautiful. Fine, with dark, long lashes. Typical Italian, and so like his father's, at least from what I'd seen in photographs of the man. The blue of John's irises, I'd assumed to be inherited from his mother. Given recent revelations, that was obviously not the case. He didn't share any DNA with the Domenicis. We'd likely never know who his donors had been.

"Do you want a fancy event?" he asked, switching back to our earlier topic.

"I really don't mind."

"My mum can't come..."

"A shame. I'd like to meet her."

He snorted. "Oh, she'd love that."

We fell quiet with just the sound of the car engine idling. Outside, the cityscape of cracked concrete, overflowing dumpsters, and rusted shopping carts left a lot to be desired. Someone had bent the CCTV cameras over, all were smashed, and nobody had bothered fixing them.

"It's not a beach view, is it," John said.

"It has a unique industrial charm."

"When I was a kid, I'd kick a ball around right over there, until I got beaten up by Nick the Prick and his gang. Dad took one look at me and told me I had to hit 'em back harder." He laughed at the memory, so it couldn't have been as bad as I imagined. "A week later, I got Nick alone and broke his nose, but I couldn't come back 'ere. His lads would've killed me."

What would this *Nick* think of him now? If I'd gotten to this Nick, he'd have had a lot more than a broken nose.

We waited some more, the quiet between us a comfortable one.

"Do you think we'll survive all this to even get to our wedding day?"

Cassie emerged from behind a collapsed chain-link fence and sauntered over to our car, hands in her ripped-jeans pockets.

"I think," I began, watching Cassie stride closer, "together, you and I can accomplish anything."

Perhaps if we succeeded in what we were about to do here, we might change the world for the better and buy ourselves a break. We could hope. Hope and I had a troubled past, but John's return had me softening to the idea.

"She's here," Cassie said, "but she's jumpy. You'd better talk to 'er."

I tailed behind John and Cassie, down a ramp, onto the ground floor of a disused multi-story parking lot. The young woman who waited in the shadows was probably no older than early twenties. She had her hands thrust into her jacket pockets and glanced around her as though expecting the police to leap out at her. The cold and echoing interior of the parking lot certainly wasn't the most relaxing of surroundings, but we had few alternatives where our test wouldn't be observed.

"I'm Dom, this is my partner Alex," John said to the girl. "Jodie, right?"

She nodded, the movements jittery.

"Is it true? You can cure me?" She looked at me, a little uncertain, but I let John reply. These were his people, his territory.

"We're going to try."

Jodie chewed on her lip. "And you don't wan' anything? I ain't got no money. But you know, there are other ways." Her gaze found me again, implying something I didn't catch.

"No, nothing, but listen. It might not work, okay? We're just going to go slow and see what happens. If you're not comfortable, just tap out, all right?"

Jodie glanced at Cassie.

"They're legit," Cassie said. "They won't hurt you."

"All right, so what I gotta do?"

John and I had discussed how this would work. Instead of connecting with the source and launching it outward—like he'd done at the American airport, *creating* latents—he needed to draw Jodie's trick through me, into him, and back through his link to the source. I absorbed and kick-started the reaction, he completed the circuit. In theory, it should work, but we'd never attempted anything like it.

If we succeeded, it could change *everything*. If we failed, well... we'd all end up with headaches and jittery tricks for a few days.

John glanced at me, smiled, and appeared relaxed for Jodie's sake, but concern tightened his face. "I've got you," I whispered. He nodded, trusting me in this, if little else. If the worst happened, and things got out of control, I'd absorb them both, swallowing any risk they'd spiral. I'd wake up feeling hungover, but we'd all recover.

We couldn't try this anywhere else, or with anyone else. If word got out John and I were tapping into the source, our fragile status as free latents would quickly change.

"All right," John said, standing next to me. "This'll do."

I smiled at Jodie and held out my hand, waiting for her to take it. "If we succeed," I said, "it's likely you'll no longer be a latent. You won't have a trick."

"I don't wan' it. Never did. I just want a life."

"You're sure?"

She took my hand and gripped it hard. "Yes."

John took my other hand. We knew trick could transfer through us. Trick naturally flowed between latents, but between John and I it was always easier. All he had to do was channel it downward back into the waiting source. There were no standing stones here to shore him up, no wide-open space to absorb a shock should things go wrong, just concrete pillars and me.

It would have to be enough.

## 16

D<sup>om</sup>

I hadn't been this nervous since Jamie Davis had sucked me off as a kid in the filthy block of flats' stairwell, not far from where we stood now. Coming back to this part of London town to cure latents seemed like a weird dream, but here I was, my hand in Alex's, siphoning off trick he'd absorbed from a woman we'd both just met, with Cassie on lookout.

The source was close here, humming with potential. I hadn't been able to hear it before. But I'd changed.

Alex's hand tingled. The trick he'd absorbed flowed into my hand, into my veins, wrapping all of us in shimmering golden light. The flow was smooth, calm, controlled, and with Alex's grip tightening, I mentally reached for the source.

It bubbled so close it seemed insane that not every latent could feel it. We stood above its flow, the four of us small compared to its brilliance.

I could do this. I just had to draw Jodie's trick through Alex, into me, and send it back where it came from.

It began to *move*. I couldn't tell if it was Alex's trick or Jodie's, or even mine, but it was flowing. Alex kept the flow restricted, kept it smooth, and maybe... just fucking maybe, this was going to work.

The source yanked. My grip on it slipped. Trick jerked downward, diving way too fast. Alex's breathing quickened. The light we threw out shrunk closer, tightening, *crushing*. It was taking too much. What if it took my trick? What if it took Alex's? That wasn't the deal. I had to slow it down, get it back under control. I pulled, trying to ease the current—and the bloody thing snapped, reversing in a blink, suddenly flooding *upward*.

I had hold of it, just like I had in Scotland, just like I had in America, and now... I wanted *more*.

All of it.

Why not?

Why shouldn't I take it?

A small voice somewhere far away reminded me this was the same psychic shock artifacts were infused with, and those voices sounded a lot like the ones telling me to take it all and burn the world. Like the knife, like the pen, like all the artifacts that had tried to tempt me to the dark side. I knew this was bad, knew if I gave up, the trick would take me, swallow me, and I'd spiral out of control. But so what? I'd take half of fucking Hackney with me, revenge on a world that had kicked me like a can down a street.

"John!"

Hands gripped my shoulders. Alex was right there, but so far away too. A river of gold flowed between us.

He looked into my eyes.

If he absorbed whatever I was doing, it would kill him. This wasn't just trick, it was the source, rushing through me. It had almost killed him before, on Montgomery's desk in Wordsworth. I couldn't let him take it. It would burn him up. I shoved, pushing him away. He vanished, drowned in the rushing river of power. Or I was the one in the river. I couldn't tell, couldn't see anything beyond the pouring golden waves. I wasn't bloody having him sacrifice himself for me again. Not this time. Was this spiraling? I'd have already gone up like a firework by now. No, this was something else. Golden light spilled upward, no longer under any kind of control—at least, not mine. Down, up, all around, it flowed, washing through my veins in waves, filling my lungs, my heart, my head.

I tried to grab at it, but my fingers sailed through, leaving swirls in the light.

Alex's hand plunged through the light, caught my arm, and yanked, hauling me out of the golden river and back into my solid, shivering body. Disorientated, I staggered and fell against Alex.

"Run, go!"

I ran, or mostly stumbled and tripped. Alex pulled me along behind him, over cracks splitting the ground from under our feet. Golden trick bubbled up, poured outward, and wisped into the air, lashing at us as we dashed past. Nearby pillars crumbled, trick leaking out of them, swallowing the rubble. It was everywhere, growing, climbing.

"Are you seeing this?"

"Yes!" Alex hissed, hauling me along.

We sprinted from the collapsing building, toward the waiting Ford.

Cas was there, running... Where was Jodie? "Wait, the girl!"

I stumbled. The ground slid away. The car, if I could just make it to the bloody car! Alex's hand vanished, and I dropped like a fucking stone. A rumble, like thunder, startled me. On my hands and knees, the car so damn close but too far away, I glanced behind me. The entire multistory parking lot glowed, lit by jagged veins of source ripping through its structure. And those veins were coming for me. They snaked across the ground, cracking the earth, snapping and darting like living things.

Until they got to Alex.

He spread his legs, hands at his sides, a pillar against a flood. But as the source split and tried to flow around him, he lit up his trick. Sparks flew, the two massive opposing forces clashing.

"Don't! No!" This was Wordsworth all over again. He couldn't contain that much power. It would tear through him, turn him to dust.

I spread my hands on the ground and plunged my trick down, reaching for the source, and when a connection struck, I thrust every damn piece of will into it—*Back the fuck off my man!*

It must have worked, because the source spluttered, its snapping tendrils recoiled, and Alex had hold of me again, manhandling my numb body into the back of the car, seconds before I passed out into silence.

The car rumbled down the single-track driveway to where Ravenscourt loomed in the dark, quiet and cold and more unwelcoming than I'd ever seen it. Usually, to my latent senses, it groaned and breathed as though alive. But not this time, or maybe I was too battered to feel it.

Gina met us at the front door. She snapped at Cas, blanked Alex, then fussed around me. The fact I hadn't stopped shivering for twenty minutes wasn't helping my argument that I was fine.

She sat me on the big sofa in the comfy lounge and wrapped a blanket around my shoulders.

Cas looked on, arms crossed, chewing on her bottom lip, while Alex stood by the fireplace, his back to me, all moody and dramatic. The whole Save the Latent experiment could have gone better. But we were all still here, so it could have gone worse too.

Gina reappeared with a mug of hot chocolate.

"I'm fine, okay? But thanks." I wasn't ever saying no to hot chocolate. I cradled the mug in my hands, hunched in the blanket, and breathed, finally less shivery and more like myself. "Jodie? Did she get out?"

"She's fine. Scared, but fine." Cas said. "She legged it out of there the second shit started to go wrong."

"It shouldn't have happened," Alex said, turning to

face us. His expression was all business, which meant he was masking everything going on inside his head.

"I think I fucked it up," I sighed. "It was working, but then I panicked and it's like..." I struggled to even find the words. "Like a hundred artifacts in my hands all at once."

"No, it wasn't you." Alex settled into one of the wing-back chairs by the cold fireplace. "The source tried to take you."

"Yeah, I kinda, maybe, let it?"

He lifted his gaze. "We'll work on it. Next time, we'll slow down—"

"You almost killed him!" Gina shrieked. "There won't be a next time, Kempthorne. Whatever experiment that was, it's over. You're done."

He weathered her onslaught with a blink. "That's John's call."

All eyes turned to me. I wanted to tell him we could try again, but we'd only narrowly escaped. "We just tore a hole in Hackney and almost killed a woman. I'm not doing it again anytime soon. I'm not ready."

He leaned forward. "We can't give up after just one set back."

Gina snorted. "You don't give a shit about Dom. You just care about your investment."

The entire house and everyone in it held their breath.

"Gina, be very careful," Alex warned.

"Guys, c'mon, I'm fine..." Arguing wasn't helping. "He's fine. We're all still here. It just needs some fine-tuning—"

"If he cared for you, Dom, he wouldn't ask you to do that again."

"Don't second-guess my feelings, Gina," Alex snarled in a voice I'd rarely heard from him.

"Someone needs to because everyone is collateral damage to your plans. It's always been that way. I don't like Kage, he's a dick, but he was right about that. If Robin were here, she'd kick your arse." Cas tried to hold Gina back, but she was having none of it and shook off her hand. "No. He needs to hear it because there's nobody left to tell him. All of this, everything, Robin, Jordan, Kage, it's all your fault. And I'm not losing Dom for some stupid experiment." She pointed at Alex. "Your parents screwed you up, but that doesn't mean you get to do the same to Dom."

Power fizzled unseen against the back of my neck and lifted the fine hairs on my arm. Oh shit. Gina couldn't feel it, but Cas did. She urged Gina to back off, reasoning with her to leave the room and take a breath.

"Alex?"

His dark gaze flicked to me, trick sparked inside his irises. "She's right," he said.

No, she wasn't. It just looked like that from the outside. "Guys, can you give us the room?"

"Dom." Gina sighed, all the fight deflating out of her.

"I've got this, it's okay..." I gave her what I hoped to be a reassuring smile and watched Cas escort her from the room.

"She's scared," I said, once the door was closed.

Alex dragged a hand down his face and stared at the cold fireplace. "So am I."

I forgot, sometimes, that he wasn't anywhere near as

invulnerable as he let everyone believe, including me. "We all just need to stop and breathe for a second."

"We aren't getting out of this, John." Finally, he faced me, his eyes glassy and tired. "We tried walking away and it didn't work. All we have left is somehow making *this* work, making it so we're indispensable. I began, years ago, wanting to save latents. That was why I had Kempthorne Enterprises reinvest in the Blackwater projects. Now I just want to save us—save you."

"We'll figure it out."

"How?"

I shrugged and sipped my hot chocolate. "I dunno, but we will."

He shifted from the chair to the sofa at my side, angled toward me with his arm over the back of the cushions. "If we don't prove we're worth keeping alive, they'll come, and they'll separate us. They will run their tests, and when they're satisfied they've drained every last drop of knowledge, they'll kill us."

"Who are 'they'?"

"The IRL, the military, the Department of Defense, a private outfit. Any number of organizations."

"Pick your poison," I mumbled.

"If we don't cure latents, if we don't prove we're good, then it's just a matter of time. You asked if we'll see our wedding day? No, we won't. Not if we don't change things."

Add Kage to the mix, and we were screwed. I'd known what he was saying was true, I just hadn't wanted to think about it.

I set my drink aside and leaned into him, welcoming

the solid weight of his arm coming down over my shoulders. There would be a way out, we just couldn't see it yet. I *had* to believe that, because if I didn't, then what was the point in fighting? "Even when the odds are against us, we always come out swinging." My dad had told me that. He'd been wrong in a lot of things, but not that.

"A sentiment I agree with." Alex's fingers stroked my arm. I leaned into him. "I will never stop fighting for us."

"Er, fellas." Cas poked her head around the door. "There's a load of cars coming down the driveway and they don't look friendly."

I threw off the blanket. Alex leaped to his feet. Considering everything he'd just said, there was no way we were hanging around to chat with whoever was bringing in the muscle.

In the hallway, Gina handed Alex his phone and coat. "I'll stall them."

Alex ushered me down the hall. "Out the back, John. Go."

We hurried out Ravenscourt's back door and plunged into the waist-high grass of the acres of fields behind the house. The sound of car doors slamming punctured the night.

"Keep going." Alex's eyes flashed in the dark.

Dogs barked and whined.

"Christ..." We couldn't outrun dogs. Once they got our scents, they'd track us for miles.

Alex veered right. "The river, this way."

A river. Right. That might help throw the dogs off, but all I saw ahead of us was a whole lot of gloomy trees, a long sprint away.

The dogs fell silent. Not good. Quiet dogs were *tracking*. I glanced over my shoulder. Flashlight beams swept the grass near the house. At least eight agents, or whoever they were, fanned out. IRL, LOA, didn't matter. They were coming for us.

Alex's long legs had taken him several meters in front of me. He could run like the wind. I was built for stamina... The ground tilted. Alex stumbled. My boot slid, and I almost sprawled on my arse behind him. His hand shot out, caught my shoulder, and then we were scrabbling and skidding down a steep slope, leaving an obvious trail in the grass that a sight-impaired Pomeranian could track.

I heard water but still didn't see a river. Just a thick wall of trees. At least if we got among those trees, the brush might slow the dogs. Alex glanced behind, checking on me. I swear, even in the mirky greyness, I thought I saw a smile. Was he enjoying this? He smirked, then nearly tripped when his foot disappeared up to his ankle in sodden mud. I staggered into the reeds behind him. Mud slurped around my boots. Alex heaved himself forward.

A blur to my left drew my gaze. "Look out!" The dog sprang for Alex. I sent a trick-infused card toward it, blasting it in the side. It yelped, sprawled in the mud, but was back on its feet too bloody fast and lunging for Alex a second time.

Alex pulled on his right leg—stuck in the mud. Behind us, shouts rang out. My trick had probably lit up our location like a beacon. I flung a second glowing card toward the dog, blasting the mud between it and Alex,

scaring it back with a yelp. It began to bark. I didn't want to kill it. I didn't kill animals, or people, if I could help it… but…

I grabbed Alex's thigh and heaved with him. The mud gave, we both fell elbow-deep into the gloopy, foul-smelling muck, but we were free. Alex crawled through the rushes. The dog continued to bark. I had to shut it up. I tried to grab a fresh card from the deck. My mud-coated fingers slipped, and the card fluttered into the brackish water, sizzling out.

I didn't even see the second dog, just Alex's trick flare, turning the world brilliant white for a blink, and I heard the *thump* of the dog thrown backward. I assumed it was a dog, not a person. He flung another whip-like lash of light and the barking dog fell silent.

Alex caught my arm again, half dragging me out of the worst of the mud and into a sprint between the trees. "You killed the dogs?"

He didn't slow, just kept on running, dashing around trees and sprinting over gnarled roots. "I don't care if it's dogs after you, people, or the bloody queen." He crouched, dropping behind a bush. I knelt beside him, breathing hard. His eyes flashed again, his smile back, but laced with that razor-sharp line warning the world not to mess with him. "If it comes down to you or them, I'm saving you every time."

"This is probably the wrong time, but your ruthless streak is hot as fuck."

"I'm glad you approve."

He parted the brush, and there, down a short drop, was the river. "You first," he said. "It gets deep halfway across. If we get separated, I'll meet you at the old red phone box south of here, on the roadside. Go."

I grabbed his face, slammed a kiss on his lips, and wanted to say more but didn't have the words.

Forehead to mine, he smiled. "I love you."

Oh Christ. "Love you more." I tore from his grip and plunged into the cold river. Water tried to grab hold and drag me downstream. My boots slid over slimy rocks. Pushing against the current, I glanced back. The bank was empty.

"Alex?"

Flashlights stroked over nearby trees. Where was he? C'mon... I scanned the bank, searching... And there, farther down, running along the river's edge. The prick, he was leading them *away*.

My boot slipped, the river caught me, I dropped. Water rushed up my nose, down my throat. I scrabbled, turning over, tried to grab the rocks, something, clawed at a branch, and pulled up, breaching the surface with a gasp. The flashlights were farther now, but still there. More dogs barked. I panted, saw the bank was close, waded over, and crawled out. The agents and their dogs were all on the other side... The same side as Alex.

I stayed low and crept from the river, boots and clothes sloshing in the cold grass.

*Alex had better bloody be at that phone box.*

## 17

**A**lexander

Had there ever been a better sight than seeing John sitting on the ground, propped against a red phone box at the side of the road? He had one leg pulled to his chest, the other stretched out. His disheveled appearance only added to the view.

I trudged up the road. The moment he spotted me, he shot to his feet, his grin worth more than any possession, but it soon faded. "You prick," he growled, starting forward, his face turning thunderous. "You deliberately led them away."

"Yes."

"I'm going out of my mind waiting here, and I've got no fuckin' idea if you're all right—" He flung his arms around me, squeezing. His sigh warmed my neck. "Don't pull that shit again. We stay together. We *always* stay together."

I folded him close, breathing him in, absorbing his shivering, his strength, everything he gave. His anger was worth it. I'd always save John first.

"Come on, let's get off the road."

We trekked for several miles until finding a Premier Inn on the outskirts of a town. Thankfully, they didn't ask questions. John and I checked in under our fake names and retreated to the room to clean up and regroup. We stripped, showered, washed our clothes in the bath and hung them all over the room to dry. John, wearing just his damp Nessie T-shirt and a towel around his waist, rummaged through the small selection of tea and instant coffee, making himself at home.

I had a towel around my waist, grabbed my drying shirt, then flicked on the TV and wished I hadn't. "Oh dear."

"Now what?"

John sauntered over, saw the news, and his face dropped. "Oh Christ. Was that us?"

A disused multistory parking lot in Hackney had collapsed into a sinkhole and appeared to be leaking what the journalists were calling *unknown radiation*. All latents everywhere knew what the golden light shimmering out of the rubble was. Trick. Or more precisely, the fuel behind their tricks. The source.

But that wasn't the worst of it.

The video clip of John and I fleeing the scene was clear enough for us to be instantly recognizable.

John groaned, flopped onto the bed, and covered his face with his forearm. "Can't we just catch one break?"

I eyed the angle of the video. It had to have been filmed from the abandoned B&M store. I'd been sure we weren't being watched. But I'd been distracted, and clearly wrong.

The net had closed another notch on our freedom.

John grumbled about our bad luck. With his arm over his eyes, he didn't see me watching him, didn't see my face as I worried how to make it through this with our lives intact.

Our time together was running out.

"We could go back to Scotland?" I suggested. As plans went, it was weak. But I was running thin on ideas.

He removed his hand from his eyes and arched an eyebrow. "Because that went so well last time."

There were other countries, countries with more lax views on latents. Some with not so great views on gay marriage. But nowhere would shield us for long. Persecuted at every turn.

The TV news reporter prattled on about new laws being rushed through parliament that would mean all latents would have to be tracked and issued curfews. I jabbed at the remote, turning the TV off, then flung the remote at the wall. It shattered, spectacularly.

"Better?" John frowned.

"Not in the least."

"You know what, if we were as bad as they say, we could start a few fucking riots, build a latent army, set fire to shit. Burn it all down. Be latent fucking kings." He flopped back again, arm over his eyes. After a few seconds, he peeked out. "That's actually not a bad idea. There is one place we can go. One place they'll never find us."

I knelt next to him, then lay on my side, head on my hand, and stroked up his Nessie T-shirt, relishing the firm warmth of his chest. His solid strength grounded me, made the world stop spinning. His heart thumped under my palm.

When the source had tried to swallow him in Hackney, and I'd blocked it, I'd felt its fury. It had matched my own. Nothing and nobody was taking John from me, not even the source of all latent power.

He said something, but I'd been too lost in admiring him. "Hm?"

"The Business."

"What about it?"

"Nobody will snitch, not on me, and as you're mine —" He wiggled his ring finger. "—they won't dare."

"You want us to join an organized crime gang?"

He shrugged. "Renick's gone. There were a few other lieutenants, but none with the balls to lead. It's probably fractured now. We just need someplace to lay low. The Domenici name has gotta be good for something?"

The last time I'd crossed paths with the Domenici Business, I'd been gagged and tied to a chair, and not in the entertaining way. "They are unlikely to accept someone like me." Gay latent billionaire. For all my survival skills, I didn't know John's world and would likely get a knife in the back.

"You're kiddin' right?" He snorted, grabbed my hand on his chest, and slid it lower, planting it confidently over

the hard ridge under his towel. "You do that controlling *Alexander Kempthorne* thing you do, and nobody will dare cross you. Shit, they've just seen on the news what we're capable of." He shifted his hips, driving himself against my hand, and his eyes widened. "I know for a fact there's an opening for the King of Hearts."

If his arousal was any indication, it appeared as though he *really* liked the idea.

"We let it slip you killed Renick," he went on. "And you'll do the same to anyone who fancies trying their hand at stopping us."

I cupped him, massaging enough to make him squirm and his eyes sparkle. The idea had its appeal. The threads of a plan wove together. I smiled and hooked my knee over his firm thigh. "What exactly is this Alexander Kempthorne thing you believe I do?"

He tried to fight a smile, only succeeding when my grip tightened and his groan overrode the smirk. "The face you make where you're about to crush anyone and anything in your way."

I straddled him and pinned him between my thighs, my own towel slipping free. He waggled his eyebrows, so I nipped his lip, freeing his moan. "I suppose the world already thinks me a villain, so let's show them one."

John came alive, back arching, body writhing. He clung to my back, pulling me down, needing me— needing us—in a way that amazed and surprised me every time. I ran my hand up his chest, assessing the quickest route to having him slick for me.

He pushed up and I swooped in, taking a nipple between my teeth. John's hand clutched my head, fingers locking in. I needed this, needed him, needed our bodies and tricks blurred together, becoming one. I tore from the kiss to get a look at his face and fell into his eyes. I'd done terrible things, lied to him over and over, and he still loved me. That was the true miracle in all of this.

"You remember that time in the Premier Inn you promised you were going to fuck me hard?"

I did recall that, although I hadn't said those exact words. "You'd just escaped Wordsworth. You believed you owed me. That hadn't been the right time."

"Now you *owe* me, Kempthorne." His mouth teased mine, dancing around a kiss. "You're going to fuck me so hard, everyone in the rooms around us will know exactly how it's done."

I needed no more encouragement than that, and scooping my arms under his, I jerked him up, onto his arse, only to flip him over. He grunted a small sound of protest. I dug my fingers into his backside, spreading him. His hand flew out, grabbed at his clothes drying over the chair beside the bed, and in seconds he had the small bottle of gel in his hand. I pushed down between his shoulder blades, made quick work of the gel over his hole and over my straining length, then thrust inside him so suddenly, and so deep, he choked, then growled and clutched the sheets. "Yes, fuck me. Do it."

Rough and mindless, I pounded him into the mattress, chasing the high that came from fucking John.

"Ugh, shit," he spluttered, and tried to get a hand between him and the sheets. "Fuck, yes, ream me you bastard."

I grabbed his hips, pulled us both down and onto our

sides, and reached around him, grasping his hard erection. John was mine, arched against me, head thrown back, my mouth on his neck, hand on his cock, my dick buried deep. I held him so bloody close, making him a part of me, and pumped, relishing his moans, twitches, and gasps until he spilled hot cum over my fingers. The thrill of it tipped me far over the edge, freefalling into ecstasy, climax riding me until we both came down, hot, slick, and breathless.

We lay together a while, breathing hard, our skin ablaze with shimmering trick. If I'd had my way, I'd have never let him go.

He turned his head, catching me in the corner of his eye. "Guess we'd better hit the shower again, huh?"

## 18

D<sup>om</sup>

The multistory parking lot shimmered and glowed, its pillars lit up with trick like a Christmas tree. As Alex and me had destroyed it a day earlier, this had to be a dream, right? But it didn't feel like a dream. Grit crunched under my boots. The air smelled of spilled diesel and muddy water. I looked for Alex, for Gina, anyone, but all the buildings looming nearby were silent.

I'd been with Alex. He'd railed me hard... I was here. Whatever this was, it was happening.

Follow the light, isn't that what they say? The dream didn't seem to be ending anytime soon, so what else was there to do? I ventured toward the parking lot and its rippling trick. Maybe this was one of those waking hallucinations—

The dream switched, like a buffering video glitching a few frames, dumping me in a vast cathedral-like chamber with enormous arches sprawled overhead, and at its center, twitching and sparking, hung a huge, shimmering liquid ball of... trick? I shielded my eyes, but its glare still burned. This wasn't right.

Metal bars enclosed the large pulsing orb, encasing it, *trapping* it. Ladders and elevated walkways encased those bars, creating a scaffold. Thick braids of wires fed to banks of machines, like veins feeding the orb, or taking something away.

My feet carried me closer, close enough to reach through the bars and touch it. But if I did that, it would swallow me. It was hungry. So viciously hungry, like an artifact was hungry, it demanded and crooned and sang, *wanting*.

I'd been here before.

When I'd lain in a Wordsworth cell, losing my mind, my dreams had brought me here. The Thames was nearby, so close its chill and the smell of thick mud laced the air. This place was in the heart of London. The source... flowed from here. From this exact spot. But the source was a river. A flowing stream. This was something else.

I hovered my hand outside the bars. My trick leaped, surged, and snapped into the orb—connecting—I gasped, jolting awake in the plush surroundings of my dad's old office. "What? How?" Pain stabbed at my skull. "Fuck."

"John?"

Alex was here. I blinked at him, waiting for my

thoughts to catch up with reality. Right... Hackney. The Snooker Room. We'd come back to the Business, where it all started for me, and we'd come back to *own* it. Christ, whatever that dream or vision had been, I couldn't deal with it, not now.

"Are you all right? What happened?" His hand landed on my shoulder, absorbing, soothing, calming.

"Thanks," I sighed. "I'm fine. It's nothing." I hadn't been asleep. Between one blink and the next, my mind had been somewhere else. Someplace the source took me. But the images were fading like shadows at dawn. A church... no, but definitely underground, with dripping water and some kind of immensely powerful beating heart of trick.

"John?" Alex leaned in, his cheek next to mine. "Are we good?"

The office door swung open and a big guy stormed in. Big, as though he could bend me backwards over his knee and snap me in half. "What the fuck, Domenici?! What are you doin' 'ere?"

I raised my hand, igniting the trick, freezing gorilla guy in his tracks. "Who are you?"

Cas had given me the rundown on who was left in the Business, and who to avoid. She'd been among them, used as a latent to traffic stolen goods, maybe used for other things too, although she hadn't outright said it. Hopefully this guy wasn't one she'd warned me to avoid.

He sneered at us both. "Name's Trevor."

Trevor Beets. High up on the food chain, one of the tough nuts I'd need to crack if Alex and me were going to pull this off. "Here's how it's going to be, Trevor. The Business is on its knees. If something ain't done, it collapses. We're here to change that. In exchange, you keep quiet about who we are. Everyone's happy."

Trevor snorted. "Bollocks to that. Fuck off back to Knightsbridge or wherever you call home now, faggot."

Okay, this was going to take some Domenici finesse. I dropped a card from my sleeve, charged it, and flung it at Trevor. He reeled, blinded, and while he stomped about, trying to regain his balance, I vaulted over the desk, got him by the throat, shoved him backwards against the desk, and pressed a second card to his chest, over his heart, igniting the trick through my hands—just enough to make his shirt smoke and give him second thoughts. "I killed the king," I told him. "The guy behind you, he killed Renick. So ask yourself, do you really wanna die for something you don't even fuckin' believe in."

"I believed in it," Trevor grunted, but fear showed in the whites of his eyes. "You want this, Domenici? What for? Huh? Why you back now?"

"Maybe I'm sentimental. Maybe I got nowhere else to be. Does it matter? I am back, and you're all gonna fall in line."

He peered down his nose, probably weighing up whether he could turn me into mincemeat before I turned him into a human firework. He was bigger than me, more muscle, but he couldn't fight the trick. With a huff, he nodded. "All right. I ain't got no beef with you. So long as you get shit done. Can't say much for the rest."

If we had Trevor on board, there was a chance the others would fall in line.

I nodded, so did he, and we had an understanding. If

he stepped out of line, he'd take a dip in the Thames. Good, this was progress.

I let him up and took my eyes off him to glance at Alex.

Alex's trick danced, lashing across the desk in a dazzling whip. Something metallic pinged and skipped to the floor. A dagger. And it had been meant for me.

Alex's trick looped around Trevor's neck, choking the man. "Try that again," Alex warned, his tone scalpel thin. "And we'll see how quickly it takes for your eyes to boil from your skull."

Trevor gagged and bucked, clawing at the burning threads of light choking him. I wasn't about to get in the middle, but if Alex killed Trevor, it would make this a lot harder. Alex crossed the floor, his trick still coiled around Trevor's neck, and picked up the dagger. He slammed it tip-first into the desktop, leaving it thrumming in the wood.

He looked Trevor in his bulging eyes. "Do we have an understanding?"

When Trevor nodded this time, he meant it. Alex's trick uncoiled and Trevor stumbled back, wheezing hard. After a few seconds, he readjusted his shirt and collar.

I leaned against the desk, arms crossed, all casual-like, as though I hadn't narrowly missed a dagger to the back. Alex, the suave bastard, straightened his cuffs beside me. Christ, he was hot when he got his murder on.

"You wanna see your dad's place?" Trevor grunted.

"Yeah," I replied, sounding like I knew what he was talking about, when I had no fucking clue my dad even had a *place*.

"I'll get the car." Trevor sniffed and slunk from the office, his ego taken down several pegs.

"That was the hottest fuckin' thing anyone has ever done for me," I said.

"I'm always happy to threaten bloody murder for you, John."

"We just might pull this off."

Alex's smile twitched. "We just might."

What followed was a whirlwind tour of my dad's life—a life I'd washed my hands of the second I'd left him dead in a ditch. Trevor drove us to a UStore, where a lock-up housed stacks of boxes full of documents that the Met's Organized Crime detectives would sell their firstborns to get their hands on. But the real treat came in the form of a palatial apartment in Shoreditch with a stunning view of Tower Bridge and the jagged Shard high-rise.

Alex stayed quiet through much of our tour, absorbing the spoils of a long-dead crime lord, or maybe he was just giving me space to process the fact my dad had been fucking loaded, and nobody had cared to tell me, because I was the gay latent son who had turned his back on this life and didn't deserve to know.

Trevor loitered by the apartment door while I drifted through the vast space, pulling sheets off the furniture, revealing what were probably designer leather sofas underneath. "This place was my dad's?" I asked. I hadn't known about the Shoreditch apartment. Neither had Mum. He'd have come here to do *business* with people on the wrong side of the law, fuck women, pay them to fuck him, fuck people over. Everything was so bloody perfect it made my guts churn.

"It's legit," Trevor grumbled, still not happy about being downgraded to tour guide for the night. "He was careful to keep some things in the right books. When he... died, it got locked up, like the rest of that shit you saw. We only needed the Snooker Room to run the Business."

The apartment had been here the entire time, collecting dust?

There had been times, right after I'd left the military, when I'd had nothing but the clothes on my back, until Alex had bought me. And this fucking apartment had been sitting here all along?

Alex clicked his fingers, said something to Trevor to make him leave, and the door clicked closed. He found me at the big windows, hands in pockets, staring out at London.

"Are you all right?" His hand eased around my hip, and just like that, half the weight I'd been carrying lifted from my back.

"Yeah. Why wouldn't I be?"

But he knew me better than that. He also knew not to push. He glanced behind us at the glossy apartment. "It's a lot to process."

"Not really." I sighed. "He never wanted me to have any of this. They all had instructions to make sure I didn't get it. He was a bastard with multiple lives. He lied worse than you—no offense. This place... it's not a surprise."

Alex smiled. "The fact you're here now means you won."

I turned my back on the view, breathed in, and tried to switch my perspective to a positive. Alex was right. My dad would turn in his grave knowing I was standing in his apartment with my fiancé right beside me. "Those documents we saw at the lock-up, you can bet there's shit in there about trafficking latents. IDs, shipping manifests. There's no way Renick masterminded all that. That was my dad."

"What are you thinking?"

I knew what had to be done. I'd known all along. "I'm going to dismantle everything from the top down, starting with the trafficking. That shit stops now."

"It won't be easy." Alex drew me against his side. "They'll fight you, once they realize what you're doing."

"We'll be careful. The drugs, guns, whatever else the Business trades, it's over," I said, thinking aloud. This felt right. Nothing had felt right since Kempthorne & Co had collapsed. But this? Bringing down the Business, saving latents? I could do this. We could even spin it to our advantage. "If we go to the Met, they might even offer us a deal, keep us protected from the LOA and IRL, give us some room to breathe."

"Hm, high-risk. It will take some intricate negotiations."

"That's what I got you for, right?"

"Indeed." He tilted my chin up and kissed me on the forehead, and there was no way I was letting him get away with being that cute.

I grabbed him by the arse and yanked him tight

against me. "But first, we're gonna fuck on every one of these posh sofas and surfaces." Guilt tried to wriggle in, some part of me from years ago too scared of my dad to risk his wrath. "Is that fucked up?"

"Perhaps, but I'm not the best judge of morals, and you certainly won't hear me complaining when I bend you over that table."

## 19

John

The next few weeks passed in a blur of intel gathering and damage control, with a few broken limbs and black eyes for anyone who disagreed with the Business's new management. Alex took to threatening people as well as I should have expected. He played the polite, sophisticated gentleman so well that I sometimes forgot he was more than capable of cold-blooded murder. So far, we hadn't yet needed to reach for the murder option, but everyone knew it was on the table.

Kage was ominously absent. And my waking-dreams... Yeah, that shit wasn't going away. Neither was the hole in the ground in Hackney. Or the cries for latents to be locked up. Some peaceful protests had turned violent, resulting in more latents being shipped off to institutions like Wordsworth.

I couldn't fix that, but I could stop East End latents from getting chewed up by the Business.

The Shoreditch apartment had begun to look like Ravenscourt's dining room, complete with a murder-wall for Alex to obsess over. But instead of Montgomery as its centerpiece, we were bringing down the Business. Alex and Gina had ensured the Met were on board, so long as we produced the goods, including proceedable legal evidence on multiple lieutenants.

All we had to do now was buy time.

We had our breathing room; it should have been all good. So why then did I wake almost every night drenched in a cold sweat? Why, when I closed my eyes, did I see the underground arches and the pulsing orb. Alex had stopped asking me if I was okay. We both knew I wasn't. And if I didn't figure it out soon, the dreams might not let me go.

"John, I've found something—"Alex was seated at the couch, documents sprawled over the coffee table in front of him. He leaped to his feet and joined me at the break-fast bar, where I'd been waiting for painkillers to kick in and numb a raging headache last night's dream had left me with.

He'd been examining every slip of paper from my dad's storage unit. Receipts, statements, trying to connect the dots so we had leverage with the Met, but this was the first time he'd looked so grim.

Adoption papers.

Candidate Thirty-Two.

I pushed them back across the bar. "I don't need to know."

"It's not so much what they are, but the return address." He tapped the sheet of paper. "John, this is important," he urged, carefully, like handling broken glass. "When you told me about your dreams, about the arches... It could have been any number of underground reservoirs or chambers in London. The whole city is strewn with caverns and voids, but this..." He pointed out the address. "*St Katharine Docks*, that's a Blackwater address."

"Okay..." I still wasn't seeing the connection, but my head was also pounding so hard that thinking was secondary to breathing.

"St Katharine Docks is mostly offices now, bars, and some nice apartments in a vast warehouse overlooking a marina. The whole area was originally overhauled in the early 70s, and more recently redeveloped again. The warehouse housed Blackwater's offices until ten years ago. And your dream... Those arches. Beneath that warehouse, there are Victorian vaults with arches just like the ones you're describing."

"Yeah but... what does it mean? I don't get it." I rubbed my throbbing head.

"Perhaps nothing. It could be a coincidence. But this suggests a possible, granted slim, link between Blackwater and your dreams."

"You know, a sexy bastard once told me coincidences are also facts," I quoted him.

"Indeed."

"Send Gina. She's perfect for this. She loves poking

around." If there was any shady shit going on at St Katharine Docks, she'd find it. Maybe my dreams were just dreams. Maybe it was PTSD from Wordsworth, only now catching up with me. Who knew? But Gina would find out if there was anything suspicious happening in those offices now.

Alex called Gina, brought her up to speed, and sent her off on a mission to be careful but find out everything. When she asked to speak with me, Alex checked my face and told her I was in the bathroom. Ending the call, he sat next to me and laced his fingers with mine.

"I'll call her later," I said.

Gina was worried, but I had nothing to tell her that I hadn't already.

"I have a private doctor," Alex suggested.

"It won't do any good." This wasn't a physical thing. The bloody dreams had started when I'd touched the source in Hackney. Whatever was going on, it was a latent thing, and no normal doctor was going to cure me.

"You should rest..."

I hadn't been sleeping. As a light sleeper himself, every time I woke up, so did he.

"I think I'm gonna get some air." I unlaced my fingers from his and climbed off the stool.

"I'll come—"

"No, it's fine. I won't be long."

I left before he could argue and win, like he always did. Since Scotland, he didn't like to let me out of his sight for long, but I needed space. We'd survive five minutes apart.

Outside the apartment building, the late summer sun

baked the pavements and painted the sky blue. St Katharine Docks, opposite the Tower of London, was a thirty-minute walk from my dad's place. Too far to trek alone, considering Alex and me were Latents of Interest. Although, if I kept my head down—No, it wasn't worth the risk. I reached into my pocket, seeking the familiar feel of my cards, but the pocket was empty. In my urgency to get outside, I'd left them behind—

The vision, dream, whatever the fuck it was, hit me like a sledgehammer to the back of the head. The weightless sensation of falling scooped me off my feet, but I didn't hit the ground. And from one step to the next, I was back in the arched chambers, surrounded by cables and equipment, while the orb throbbed menacingly behind its bars.

But this time, I wasn't alone.

Shadows moved, sliding over brick walls, under arches, across the floor. Like spilled ink down a drain, except the drain here was the orb, drawing them to it, as though it beckoned me. It *wanted* me. It had almost had me in Hackney, before Alex had stopped it.

It glitched and sparked, beating like London's golden heart, and as the shadows slipped through its bars, the orb swelled, pulsing bigger, swallowing the bars inside itself.

It was *unstable.*

And with that thought, came the fear. It wasn't a single spiraling latent. It wasn't even the source. It was the beginning, the epicenter, the *origin.*

Jesus Christ... it was also a ticking bomb.

Bigger, it swelled, filling the underground cavern,

swallowing the arches and all the shadows, the machines, until finally, it swallowed me.

---

I came around to the sounds of a rumbling engine and car tires bouncing through potholes. The minutes swirled, stuck between waking and sleep, my mind and body too slow to catch up. My head pounded, pooling heat down my neck.

"Before you think about using your trick, you should know I have your mom."

Kage?

What.

The.

Fuck.

"You-fucking-piece-of-shit," was what I tried to say, but a rancid cloth filled my mouth, muffling the words. He understood the sentiment though, and chuckled, one hand on the wheel, cruising the car through some part of London I could only see partially through the windows.

Fuck him. He didn't have my mum. There was no way, she was too well-protected. I kicked at the opposite door. Once. Twice. Kage tossed me a furious snarl. I told him to fuck off through my gag and kicked again.

Then the car's speakerphone rang a number.

"'ello?" my mum's voice came over the speakers.

I froze.

"John, baby, is that you?" Her voice quivered.

My whole world narrowed to a single, sharp point. Kage had my mum.

Kage ended the call. "Do as I say, and she'll be fine."

He had my mum.

He had My. Fucking. Mum.

I couldn't lash out, despite wanting nothing more than to set the car on fire with Kage in it. I couldn't do a bloody thing until I knew she was safe. And Kage was counting on that.

"There you go. I know you can be reasonable, Dom," he said, so smug. "Stay calm, and we'll get through this together."

Shit, why had I trusted him before? Why had I let it get this far? If I'd just let Alex kill him, he wouldn't have my mum and I wouldn't have been tied up in the back of his car going who the fuck knew where.

Christ, Alex was going to lose his shit. "'ey," the gag muffled me again. "Ougig." That was meant to be 'you dick.'

"We can chat later. I'm looking forward to it, in fact. Just you and me."

"Ug-ogg."

He laughed. "What the hell was that back there? I wasn't expecting to have to scoop you up off the sidewalk. You're welcome for the save, by the way." He glanced over his shoulder. "You feeling okay?"

*Was I fucking feeling okay?!* I kicked the door and sent a string of swear words through the rag. As soon as I knew Mum was safe, I was going to punch his perfect smile down his throat. Not even my dad dared touch Mum once I'd gotten big enough to swing a right hook.

"This was inevitable," Kage continued, still cruising the car through more of London's traffic. I caught snippets of trees and sky, but not much else. "You and me, ending like this. Since we first met in that alleyway, remember? I almost shot you. I'm glad I didn't, just to have you before Kempthorne fucked you."

He was messed up.

"I should have shot you though, in that alleyway. Would have saved my brother, saved a lot of lives. You fooled me. I thought I knew you, I thought you were good. Maybe I just wanted to believe it so much that I missed all the signs." His thoughts must have drifted or he got bored of his own voice because he fell quiet for a few more miles. I writhed my hands behind me, trying to stretch the tape he'd used to bind my wrists. By now, Alex had to know something was wrong.

Alex could—*would* do anything. Would he spiral?

"I saw the ring." Kage huffed and drawled, "Congratulations." He pulled the car off the road and onto an uneven, bumpy track. "It'll never happen, but I admire your optimism. People like you don't get happy endings."

The car rolled to a halt. He cut the engine, climbed out, and made his way around to the rear passenger door. If I could rush him once I was out... Pin him, beat the shit out of him... He yanked open the door and shoved a gun in my face. "Get out. Slow and easy."

I shuffled forward, got my legs under me, and fell out of the car. Kage grabbed an arm, hauled me upright, and shoved me ahead of him. "Go."

We were in what appeared to be a gas works, or oil storage, surrounded by vast white silos that had to be full of gas or petrol. Not the best place to be carrying a firearm.

"Up the steps."

I could see where this was going. All the silos had metal steps. The one in front of us was likely about to become my home. What if it wasn't empty? What if he was going to drown me in petrol? Christ, was he that far gone?

"Dom, move."

The gun poked the back of my head. I trudged up the clanging steps, all the way to the top. The wind whipped my hair around. The storage site was huge. Acres of silos, with the wide mouth of the Thames estuary in the distance. Even if Alex knew I was missing, he'd never find me in time.

Kage bent and heaved up the solid steel hatch. It twanged over, ringing the silo like a bell.

"Get in."

I looked at the black hole and then his serious face. No fucking way.

"Get in, Dom."

My throat constricted. I tried to swallow without much success.

"Get in, or I'll be sending pieces of your mom to Kempthorne."

Inching closer to the open hatch, I peered inside the darkness. If there was a bottom, I couldn't see it. Petrol fumes burned my eyes and scorched my nose. What if it was full of petrol?

Kage shoved—I reeled, toppled, hit the edge, and dropped through the air, through darkness. It felt like forever—terror froze my lungs. I expected to hit petrol, to drown in the next few seconds. It wouldn't take long. The gag meant I'd swallow it, my bound hands would sink me to the bottom.

My hip slammed against metal, buckling my leg under me, and some part of me screamed in agony, bursting bright white across my vision. But I wasn't drowning.

Kage's blurred silhouette appeared in the hatch hole, backlit by bright sunshine. He smirked, and the lid slammed closed.

## 20

Alexander

John Domenici had vanished so many times that I'd developed something of a sixth sense in detecting trouble, and right then, I knew he was in it. Trying his phone and receiving no answer was usually how these things began, and this time was no different.

He'd left his deck of cards behind on the kitchen counter. They sat there, their corners peeling and bent, their artifact throb a mild push and pull.

I knew, without any doubt, John was no longer in Shoreditch. And with that knowledge came a cascade of possible scenarios.

Someone in the Business had taken him, or the IRl, or his battery had died—unlikely, but possible. I'd need to eliminate every possibility and proceed assuming the worst-case scenario.

My phone rang, still in my hand.

John's name displayed on-screen.

Well, then. I was overreacting. "John—"

"Let me stop you there," Kage purred. "John can't come to the phone right now."

Murder was too good an end for Mister Mitchell. "What have you done with him?"

"So far, nothing."

An icy calm froze all thoughts, bar one. Save John. Kage had him, somehow. The fact Kage was using his phone was proof of that. They couldn't be far, not yet.

"Let me speak with him."

"Not possible, he's sleeping."

The line was echoing with a monotonous drone. A vehicle. They were traveling. Kage had rendered John unconscious, that was the only way to ensure he'd stay quiet in the background, or Kage had already dumped John's body somewhere—no, not enough time for that, in central London, in daylight. John was *with* Kage, probably inside a car. He'd hadn't left the apartment more than half an hour ago.

"Bring him back to me now and this doesn't have to escalate."

"Oh, it's escalating. You can bet on that. Wait for my instructions."

The call ended and I stared at the phone, hearing Kage's words echo over and over in my mind.

My heart thumped, pushing trick-infused blood through burning veins.

I should have spent more time trying to track Kage down, should have gone with John, should have killed Kage months ago, should have left Kage to die, should have done a hundred things. But none of that helped John now.

Wait for my instructions.

No, I wasn't waiting.

Kage had John. And I was getting him back.

## 21

D<sup>om</sup>

I'd managed to work my tied hands under my arse and picked at the tape with my teeth enough to pull them apart. With my hands free, I pulled the gag out and used the crook of my arm and sleeve to filter the stifling petrol fumes from every breath.

Petrol sloshed around my boots. My eyes burned, streaming with tears. I squeezed them closed. There was nothing to see anyway, just a tantalizing glimpse of light squeezing through the hatch too high to reach.

I'd been in some tight spots, pinned down by hostile fire, surrounded by LOA dicks, almost spiraled on a London dock, but being stuck in a petrol silo was right up there at the top of the I'm-Fucked list.

The petrol was deliberate. One tiny spark from my

trick and boom, I'd be confetti. Kage was a clever bastard. Christ, I knew how to pick 'em. He'd had me in his sights from day one. He'd flashed a smile, sold me a gay sob story, and like an idiot, I'd been suckered right in.

Now I was locked in a petrol silo. Idiot of the Year, that was me.

Alex would come. He'd try my phone. Kage had it. Had Kage connected with him? Alex would burn him to ash—but not yet. He'd make sure I was safe first. He'd be working on that. Even with limited resources, he'd find a way. He always did.

He'd come for me. He'd have come for me in Wordsworth if I'd given him a few more days. He'd come for me when Greyson had kidnapped me in America. He'd bought me from the military, tried to keep me safe. He'd come for me here too.

I rubbed my thumb against my finger. Where was my ring? It wasn't on my finger.

Had I dropped it? I knelt in petrol, sloshed through it, stirring up more fumes. The ring... It had to be here. I needed it.

I couldn't see, my eyes burned.

Gasping into my sleeve, I slumped against the inside the silo.

He'd come... Until then, I couldn't do a fucking thing but sit and breathe through my sleeve, trying not to pass out, and think about Alex, about Gina, about my life, about whether we were going to survive, about the origin and its dreams, and what the fuck I was supposed to do about it. Why had it chosen me? John Domenici, an East

End council estate latent, Candidate Thirty-Two, now dumped in a silo, probably about to die.

"C'mon, Alex."

He'd said I always saved myself, but I really needed him to drag me out of this hole. My head lolled, the ache splitting my skull apart. *Stay awake...* What if I closed my eyes and never saw Alex again?

---

## 22

A lexander

The Rouge café, a short walk from Cecil Court, had been a favorite haunt of the Kempthorne & Co team. They sold amazing pastries, made great coffee, and today, Kage Mitchell was sitting in the sunlit window, sipping his cappuccino while eyeing my approach over the rim of his sunglasses.

The trick itched to be free. I could have blasted him through the window, killing him before he drew breath to beg for his life. He had it coming, but not before I retrieved John.

I sat at his table, folded my arms, and stared at the man who stood between John and I. I'd wager there wasn't a more dangerous place to be in all of London. The second I no longer needed him—that precise moment—I'd destroy his mind, body, and soul.

"D'yah want a coffee while we chat?" he asked.

A smile crawled onto my lips.

He lowered his cup to its saucer, sank a hand into the pocket of his coat, which was draped over his chair, and placed two items on the table between us.

A ring. And a scratched old-style British pound coin.

The ring was John's—proof Kage had him. The coin was mine; I'd thought it lost in America. An artifact with the psychic burn of my sister's death flash-burned into it. A death I'd thought I'd been responsible for. Technically, I had killed her. Regardless of the truth. But the coin had lost its burn, turning it into a worthless old coin. He'd neutralized it.

Kage said nothing. After a few minutes had passed, he smiled and sipped his cappuccino. "No threats, Kempthorne?"

"The time for threats has long passed. Where is John?"

"We'll get to that." He pressed a finger on the coin and pushed it toward me. "I had an authenticator read it. I assume you know what they found? You can take it. It probably has sentimental value?"

"What do you want?"

"What do I want?" He chuckled. "Interesting question. If you'd asked me that months ago, I'd have said I just wanted Dom. And we might have had something, him and me, but you were there, and it was always you. Alexander Kempthorne, the sun Dom orbits around."

"This isn't just about jealousy."

Kage leaned in. "It's about you getting away with everything, over and over again. You're a danger to everyone around you. It's about John getting caught in your orbit, and how you've turned him into something *wrong*. You knew what he was, you've always known. You shaped him without his knowing. You've fucked him every way and he doesn't see it. He's a tool to you, like we all are. And now you create latents. You can open fissures in the source like the one in Hackney. Montgomery was a saint next to you. You need to be stopped."

I spread my hands, inviting him to do his worst. "Then arrest me, Agent Mitchell." He didn't move. Because he was no longer an agent. It seemed his superiors didn't agree with his assessment.

"Deny it," he sneered.

"I can't. You're right—about all of it. But you're so very wrong too. At the end of the day, wrong and right are just semantics. Tell me where John is and I'll kill you quickly, instead of the torture you'll shortly be experiencing."

He laughed and removed his phone from his pocket. He flicked it open and played a memo of my voice: *"John Domenici is mine to fuck with how I wish, and the fact that pisses you off is really just a happy accident."*

I blinked. "Is that supposed to concern me?"

He shrugged, scrolled some more on his phone, then showed me the screen.

*Kempthorne wanted by police for the murder of Charlotte Kempthorne. Do not approach. Considered highly dangerous—*

He took the phone back. "Someone sent the authenticator's report to the cops and the press. Looks like you're back on their Most Wanted list." He grinned, so pleased with himself. "How many times can you slip the noose, Kempthorne? They're coming for you and if they lock you up, you'll never see John or freedom again."

"You seem to be confused... I don't care what happens to me. I never have. But you should. Because if I'm stopped from finding John, whoever stands in my way will die. It will be their blood on your hands. *Tell me where he is.*"

Kage smirked, in that charming way he did, and rose to his feet. He tossed a few five-pound notes onto the table, his contribution for the coffee, I assumed, and a signal our meeting was over. If he thought he was leaving, he was wrong.

I caught his forearm and trickled some trick through my hand, warming him up. "Sit down, Mr Mitchell. We're not finished."

Kage grasped my shoulder. "You've got bigger problems." He nodded toward the window.

A woman with a professional-looking camera stood outside the window, taking photographs through the glass. Behind her, someone else was on their phone, glancing my way.

Instincts had me freeing Kage's arm. He patted my shoulder and whispered, "They will hunt you down and rip you to pieces. Everyone wants a piece of you."

The laughter in his voice crawled under my skin and set my fury ablaze. I grabbed his hand, twisted, and slammed him face-first against the tabletop. The table skidded. His half-finished cappuccino shattered across the floor. Kage bucked. I pinned harder and drove his face against the shiny surface, a vicious lick of glee snapping at my smile. Someone screamed. Shouts bounced around the little café. I leaned over Kage in a position I imagined John had fucked him in a few times before too. "If John were here, he'd tell you I'm all out of fucks to give."

Kage writhed under me. Teeth gritted, he panted through his nose and glared as though he could burn me up with his stare alone. "Let me up. If I don't get back to John in time, he'll die."

I slammed a hand onto the table, grabbing John's ring next to Kage's face.

The photographer was still there, snapping away. I'd give them something to print in their wretched newspapers.

"Everything you do," Kage panted, "proves I'm right."

I lifted off his back and wrapped my hand around his neck instead. "I never said you were wrong." I shoved him forward, letting him go just enough to give myself room, and then kicked him in the lower back. He flew head-first through the window. The entire pane of safety glass shattered, raining pieces over Kage, the pavement, the people taking photos. He landed on his side among startled pedestrians, most of whom had their phones out. I stepped through the broken window, ignored the shouts for someone to stop me, grabbed Kage with my left hand, and punched his cheek. Skin split. Blood burst.

More shouts and screams went up, but they were far away, as inconsequential as buzzing flies. Kage gasped, and I landed a second punch.

A hapless bystander began squaring up, about to try

to do something exceedingly stupid like get in my way. I thrust out a hand, trick ablaze, and caught the would-be hero's gaze. A single shake of my head was enough for him to think twice.

Kage coughed and spat blood near my shoe. He smirked and wiped his bloody mouth on his sleeve. "You're really famous now."

The crowd had their phones out, filming everything. Fuel to my fire. I grabbed Kage's neck and spilled trick in, almost choking him. "Tell me where he is."

He gaped, mouth opening and then closing. His fingers clawed at mine. The satisfaction from finishing him here in broad daylight would almost be worth losing everything for. Almost. I eased off, and he gulped air.

"Hey, latent prick! Get the fuck off 'im!"

"Yeah! Get off him!"

There were more now, the crowd growing. They jostled, moving closer, getting braver as their numbers swelled.

"Lock up latents!"

"That's Kempthorne!"

"Kempthorne! He's mad!"

"Stop him!"

I surged more trick to life, lighting myself up in its halo, and the crowd lurched backward, but not for long. What had begun as a few bystanders was becoming a mob. And Kage knew it. He smiled from the ground at my feet, playing the victim. "They're coming for you," he smirked. "They're *all* coming for you." Blood ran between his teeth and down his cheek. Blood shone on my knuckles. John would have stopped me by now, he'd have stopped me from getting this far.

I stepped back.

"Oi, Kempthorne!"

A glass bottle flew from the crowd, missing me by an inch. Someone shoved my shoulder. Hands caught my arm, pulling me around. Snarling faces, swinging fists. Their hatred burned, just like trick.

"Lock up latents!"

They were everywhere, pushing in, hands clawing. Distantly, sirens wailed. The authorities wouldn't arrive in time to stop this. A punch landed in my ribs. "Oi, Kempthorne!"

I'd lost sight of Kage, lost sight of everything. Faces full of hate filled my vision, and fists hurled. Some landed, some went wide. I twisted, shoved, but there were too many, too close, pushing, pulling. Couldn't move, couldn't breathe. Fear, like the kind I'd known when strapped to an examination table, raced through my veins. No air. Chest crushing tight. *Too much!* Trick exploded outward, flooding the street in light, leaving silence in its wake.

My sawing breaths heaved out of me.

People lay on the pavement, in the road. Motionless.

I staggered.

*So many people.*

I'd had no choice.

Nearby alarms sounded. Windows had blown out; glass glittered among the fallen.

The nearest victim shifted, coming around, and

groaned. Not dead. I hadn't killed him. Others were moving too. I hadn't killed them, but I could have.

I stepped around the moaning bodies, picking my way between them.

"I'm sorry," I muttered. "I had no choice..."

I hadn't meant to hurt them. Just like I hadn't meant to hurt my sister, like I hadn't meant to hurt John. I didn't want to hurt anyone, but it always ended the same way. Was Kage right? Could I have stopped this? Did I want carnage?

I fell into a run, dashed down a narrow side street, jumped some steps, and slumped against the rear wall of a Chinese takeaway, hidden by stinking rubbish bins and an abandoned trolley. The sirens were back, getting closer, *coming for me.* They should. I'd almost killed those people. Wanted to.

My phone rang, jolting me out of the mental spiral.

"Hey... you okay?" Gina asked.

"I er..." I rubbed my face and checked both entrances to the side street. "Yes. I'm... okay."

"—tailing Kage," she added. "Kempthorne? You there? Listen, I saw what happened... It wasn't your fault, okay? They would have killed you."

"Just stay on him." I ended the call, dropped my head back against the wall, and *breathed.*

Gina was wrong.

I'd wanted to kill them all. Kill everyone. Exactly as Kage had planned.

D<sup>om</sup>

A rope ladder dangled from the hatch. The thing had just appeared as though I'd dreamed it up, or maybe I was so far out of it, it had been there all along. I grabbed that sucker and hauled myself up every rung, wheezing like a fifty-a-day smoker. When I reached the top, I crawled out, collapsed on my back on the top of the silo, and blinked at a billion stars. Had there always been that many stars in the sky? My head spun, my guts heaved, and every inch of my skin itched like dried paper trying to turn to dust.

"Breathe," Kage said.

*Breathe?* I raised my middle finger. It was all I could muster.

I'd been so close to passing out and drowning in an

inch of fucking petrol that he didn't get to tell me to breathe. He didn't get to tell me anything. As soon as my head stopped trying to pound its way out through my ears, I was going to beat the shit out of him. Although, the shadows on his face suggested someone had gotten there before me. Whoever they were, they should have bloody well finished him off. Although, if they had, I might never be found.

"Your mom is fine."

He just had to remind me he had her.

"Just so long as you do everything I say."

I hated him, hated my fucking life, hated—

The vision struck like it always did, rolling over me and dragging me under. The origin, the shadows, all mangled together in a pulsing orb of dark and light, and the bars, gone now—I gasped back into the now and covered my eyes with my petrol-soaked hand. "Fuck." My voice was wrecked, throat scorched by fumes. I panted some more, breathing through the pain. "Kage... why?"

"Sit up."

No, fuck him, I was going to lie on my back and stare at the stars. I could die like that, it'd be okay...

"Dom... C'mon, sit up."

He gripped my hand and helped haul me upright, then handed me a bottle of water. I drank half of it in seconds, stopping only to breathe, then choked on air and water.

Kage crouched close. His face conveyed something like concern, as if maybe he'd gone too far.

"Listen," I wheezed, "whatever this shit is between us, there's something else happening. There's this... thing...

It's unstable. It's trick, but, it's like... the beginning, the origin. It's under London. There's a... chamber... with arches and shit. It's there. Okay? That's where the source comes from. And it's unstable—I said that, but you have to listen—" It sounded insane. But somebody had to know. "I think, it's like... it's going to blow. Or something bad is going to happen, and whatever you're doing, whatever fucking vendetta you've got going on, can it just wait? Can we just shelve it or something until this thing is out of my head, and then we can go back to trying to kill each other?"

He sighed. "You're hallucinating."

"Maybe..." I spluttered a laugh. "Maybe I'm fuckin' losing it? You left me in a silo of petrol you fuckin' twat!!"

"Finish the water."

I stared at the bottle of water in my hand, then at Kage. In the dark, under the stars, I couldn't make out all the intricacies of his features, just some bruises, his dramatic silhouette and how the starlight caught in his eyes.

Wait... that sharp glistening wasn't starlight.

"Oh fuck." It was trick.

He turned his head away.

"Shit, man, I'm sorry. I didn't know..." But he hadn't always had it. That shine was definitely new. It hadn't been there before America... It had to be me, didn't it? I'd done that to him. It was my fault. Christ, no wonder he was messed up. I couldn't have fucked him over any worse if I'd tried. "Since when?" I croaked.

"Since you *murdered* Greyson."

The helicopter crash, when I'd wrapped Alex in my

arms and sent out a blast of trick to protect us. Kage had gotten caught in that blast. But it hadn't killed him. It had *turned* him. I wet my lips, tasting petrol, then uncapped the bottle and finished off the water. "I er... I didn't mean to do that to you."

"Fuck you, Dom."

"Yeah, okay." I'd killed his brother, gotten him fired, and turned him into a latent. I'd fucked him, literally and figuratively. Saying sorry wasn't going to cut it. "I know you don't wanna hear it but Alex and me—we were trying to find a cure. That's what that crazy hole in the Hackney carpark is all about. It went wrong, but... it should work, in theory. I guess I could try again on you?"

"You're so full of shit, Dom."

"No, it's true. We were trying to help a latent, trying to absorb her trick and send it back to the source, but—"

"Just stop."

"I could try with you? Maybe it's easier with someone who's not... you know... meant to be a latent—"

"You'll say anything to save your ass."

"We're not fuckin' bad people, Kage. We're trying to do the right thing here. For fuck's sake!"

"Get back in the tank."

"Fuck off, no way." I tried to scoot backward, but with my head full of fumes, my balance was shot and the messages to run never made it any further than a few twitches. Kage hauled me up by the arms. "Don't..." I begged. "It'll kill me. I can't breathe. Kage, don't... Christ, please... I never meant to hurt you. Ever."

"But you did." He pulled a gun and pressed it to my

forehead. "Now get in the tank or your mom gets a bullet between the eyes."

"Please don't. Just leave her out of all this? Please, Kage... You said we had something once? You cared, I know you did. I can't go back in there."

He hesitated, just for a second.

"Please?" I whispered, never too ashamed to beg.

"I almost forgot." With his free hand, he dug into his coat pocket and pulled out his phone.

*"John Domenici is mine to fuck with how I wish, and the fact that pisses you off is really just a happy accident."*

Alex's voice. A message?

"Wait, what?"

Kage's aim dropped. The gun boomed. Pain burst across my shoulder. I staggered, my boot went out from under me, and I dropped, but from blind luck, I caught the edge of the hatch with my right hand and clung on, dangling in the gloom inside the silo. I couldn't go back into the dark. I'd die down there.

Kage loomed. His boot lifted. The treads got bigger. "—don't!"

Horrible, vicious agony flooded my fingers—I couldn't hold on, and when he lifted off, I fell.

A lexander

The King of Hearts.

I flicked the black-and-red playing card between my fingers. Not from John's deck—that sat safely in my pocket. This card had been among the papers in the Domenici desk I was now sitting behind.

Backed into a corner, enemies at every turn, there was only one way out.

The world and Kage wanted a war, I'd give them one.

Cassie opened the Snooker Room's office door, approached the Domenici desk, and tucked her thumbs into her cut-up-jeans pockets. "The latents are here."

"All of them?"

She'd gained a ring piercing that glinted as she

arched her eyebrow. "As many as would come. You're sure about this, boss?"

Was I sure? I teased the card back and forth. Just a playing card, not one of John's artifacts but it reminded me of him, of his life. A life that should have turned him into a villain. Instead, he'd become the opposite. A good guy. Kage had him, had hurt him, otherwise John would be here, by my side. I'd meant what I'd told Kage, I'd burn the world to save him. Of that, I was as sure as I'd been of anything in my life. "It's time."

Cassie led the way into the Snooker Room's main lounge area. The pool and snooker tables had been pushed aside to make way for at least a hundred latents. Most were dressed casually, a few wore suits. They came from all walks of life, but all were connected in some way to the Business. Some met my gaze with challenges in theirs, but most skipped their glances away, conditioned to quiver in fear by a world that hated them.

They worked for the Business, and the Business gave them a measure of protection. That was how it was painted, but they were slaves, each one of them, used because they were latents—threatened, bullied, black-mailed, trafficked.

That was all about to change.

"Many of you probably believe you know me." I walked among them, carefully examining each person, how they held my gaze, or didn't, whether they carried a weapon, what they intended to do, why they were here. They weren't hired criminals. Some had done questionable things for the Business, but most had been abused in some way, probably their whole lives.

"You think you know me, the same as the world believes it knows every single latent here. *We're wrong, we were never meant to exist, we're broken.* They don't see people, they see hate, and fear. They turned us into their enemy the moment we were born." At the front of the crowd, I climbed a few wooden steps to a scuffed stage. "For decades, we've let them wave their flags, tag our ankles, beat us, manipulate us, segregate us, and make us believe we should be punished for who we are."

All the faces were tipped toward me. Initial murmurs had died down.

I raised my right hand and spilled trick between my fingers. It coiled and writhed, alive at my touch. "If we continue to kneel, we will never be free."

A few whispers started up.

"Every single one of you has the power to make change happen, to make them see us for who we really are, not the monsters they've made us into."

"How?" The man who had called out was no older than John, with sandy-blond hair, haunted eyes, and a scar through his lip. It didn't matter who he was or the life he'd come from. All that mattered was how he was here, and what he did next. "What can we do?" he challenged.

I spread my fingers, showing the crowd my blazing hand. "On every poster, every IRL message board, every underpass, every road sign, burn your mark, leaving a handprint. Tell every latent. Being silent is no longer an option."

"Is that it?" He snorted. "They'll lock us up."

"Probably, but they lock us up for breathing. Wouldn't you rather be behind bars for a reason?"

He huffed but didn't argue. "Is this an order?"

"It's a choice," I said. "The Business no longer owns you. If anyone challenges that, send them to me."

More murmurs circulated.

"But this isn't about the Business, it's about freedom. Allow me to be clear, nobody is coming to save us. We must save ourselves. And that begins now. We *are* latents. We're stronger than them. They will see our handprints on every street corner, bus shelter, advertisement board. They will see *us*. And they will know, London is ours too."

Silence.

The kind waiting to be shattered. My heart thumped and the voices in my head told me that even if I just reached one or two, it would be enough. True change began slowly, in little gestures, in increments. It would take something larger to spark a chain reaction, but anything had to be better than the spiral of hate we were all trapped in.

Someone at the back clapped. Another joined them. Another raised their hand, their trick aglow. Another hand went up. Then a third. Until everyone had their hands alight and raised in unity, filling the room with blazing trick.

John would have loved it.

I nodded. "Begin."

I left the stage and instead of an angry mob ready to tear me apart, the faces surrounding me were full of fight and determination. Hate had no place here. The sentiment was true, but my motives were not. In truth, we were unlikely to win this fight. But that wasn't my objective. I needed to win them over.

"G's back," Cassie said, falling into step beside me as I headed back to the office. "An' she has news."

"Good."

"It's gonna be okay, boss man."

Was it? I'd lost any faith I'd had long ago and the panic tightening my chest cinched tighter with every passing hour John was missing. Squeezing his ring in my fist, I opened the office door and found Gina waiting with a map of London spread across the Domenici desk.

"I followed Kage from the café," she said, her tone all business-like. "He bounced around the tube stations, but eventually caught the overground line heading east. I wasn't sure where to go from there. But he has a canal boat, right? So, I figure he knows his way around the canals. I came back to town, took your car—thanks for that—and cruised around some of the marinas, then found a canal dock, or whatever you call them, here." She prodded the map. "Positioned right next to the overground line. Maybe I got lucky, I dunno, but I spotted him getting behind the wheel of an old blue Volvo. I tried to tail him but lost him in traffic." She ran her finger along one of the major roads leading out of London. "He headed east, not touching the motorways. I think Dom's around here." She circled a large chunk of south Essex, between London and Southend-On-Sea. It narrowed down the search area, but nothing like enough.

Kage Mitchell was intelligent, motivated, and focused. He knew how to keep John subdued, how to keep him from using his trick to escape. But how? He'd need leverage. Something John cared about more than his own life. "Cas." I looked up. "Distribute Kage Mitchell's photo to everyone on the Business's payroll and tell them I'm offering a million pounds to anyone who brings him to me *alive*."

"Sweet." She got to work texting her contacts, then dialed someone and took herself across the room to work her angles.

"Kempthorne?" Gina's soft query tugged my attention back to her. "You okay?"

"Kage can't hide in my city for long. Gina, get me everything you can find on John's mother. Ideally, her address."

"Isn't she in witness protection? How am I—"

"You're resourceful, you have Met connections. Use them. I can't approach them. The police will arrest me if we cross paths."

"What? I thought you were buddies with the coppers now you're snitching on the Business?"

"Mr Mitchell has revealed certain facts regarding my past that they were not previously aware of. Facts that implicate me in my sister's death." She knew the details. John had told her.

"Kage is just the gift that keeps on giving, huh," she grumbled.

There had to be other ways to find John, more leads I hadn't thought of, but when I tried to pluck ideas out of the air, they turned to smoke and vanished. I scoured the map of London and the locations Gina had pointed out.

"We'll find him," Gina said, dragging me back from my own thoughts. "He'll be fine. He's like a bad penny, you can't get rid of him. He's John Domenici. Nothing touches him."

But it did. He smiled and shrugged off the worst life could throw at him, but he felt everything. I set his ring down on the desk, over Shoreditch, on the map. "I asked him to marry me."

Gina fell quiet, then blurted, "Oh fuck—"

A nervous laugh fell from me. "That's what he said." But my laughter soon faded. If something happened to him, if I didn't find him in time—My trick churned just thinking it. "He said yes."

"Congratulations!" Gina circled around the desk, stopping short of hugging me, although she bounced on her feet. I spread my hands and she flew in, flinging her arms around me. "I love you, you know that right? I know I've said things, but... we're family."

I closed my arms around her and sighed. "I know."

She sniffed, pried herself from my arms, and attempted to hide how she dabbed her tears.

Cassie offered me her knuckles, which I'd learned to bump from John. "Fuck, yeah. If you guys can make it work, anyone can."

She laughed and shook her head.

"We need to find him," I told them.

"Hell yeah we do." Cassie eyed the map. "The Business has eyes everywhere. We'll find him."

John's disappearance felt different this time. All the times we'd been torn apart, we'd always found each other, but this time... There was more at work here, more than Kage's vengeance. Something else simmered below the surface, something too huge to grasp, too abstract to pin down. The latents, the Business, us. All of it spiraled around and around, caught in motion while being pulled irrevocably downward.

John's headaches, his dreams... It was all connected in a way I couldn't see, the answers elusive. On the street map, the iconic Tower Bridge caught my eye, and next to it, St Katharine Docks. "Gina, did you find anything at St Katharine Docks?"

"Oh shit, yeah. There were a lot of rich folks with posh boats and this." She showed me her phone. On-screen, the image showed a huge, uninspiring red-brick wall interrupted by several enormous ventilation ducts.

"And that is?"

"Industrial ventilation. You don't need those exhaust outlets just for offices. There's some serious air-moving shit behind there, but there's nothing nearby that warrants that kinda ventilation."

"The Tube?" Cassie asked.

"No, water table is too high there."

"How do you know so much about ventilation?" I asked her.

She shrugged. "Stuff like this is all over London. Fake house frontages covering up exhaust vents from all the underground tunnels and old streets."

"All over London?"

"Yeah, how do you not know this?"

"I do, I just..." I studied the London map again and recalled the maps we'd marked up in the past, high-lighting the weak spots in the source. "Wordsworth was located right over a fissure in the source," I thought aloud. "We know, where the source has breached the surface, latents spiral. What if those were just... tremors? Precursors to whatever John is seeing. He said there are brick arches in his dreams, like those at the St Katharine Docks."

Cas leaned in. "If what happened at Wordsworth was the teaser, what the fuck is the main event?"

Someone, somewhere knew more about this. St Katharine Docks, John's dreams... Montgomery was gone, my parents had been dead for years. Who was left?

"Blackwater."

## 25

D<sup>om</sup>

Boots clanged on the outside steps. The hatch creaked open and light spilled in. "Dom," Kage said. "Grab the ladder."

I didn't move. I wasn't sure I *could* move. My left arm tingled, mostly dead, apart from the occasional teeth-clenching spasm of pain from where Kage's bullet had winged me. My head throbbed, my throat was laced with glass, and every breath burned holes in my nose. I'd tried to breathe against the crook of my arm, and maybe it was working, I *was* still conscious, so there was that, but I was a few minutes from oblivion.

"Dom? Hey?"

If he wanted me out of the silo, he'd have to come down and get me.

"Your mom makes nice cake," he said, reminding me what was at stake.

She hadn't made the cake; she didn't bake. She'd bought it from the bloody cake sale. Maybe she'd told the nice American who had turned up on her doorstep that she'd made it, probably right before he'd threatened her.

"Shit," Kage muttered, then started down the rope ladder.

I peered through my almost-closed lashes while lying on my side, body sore, head heavy. *C'mon, you bastard... Just a little bit closer.* This was it. My one chance to get out of here. If I blew it now, I'd be dying real soon. And I wasn't ready to die. I had a bloody wedding to get to.

Kage set down in the silo, boots splashing in old petrol. He raised his right arm, covering his mouth and nose with his sleeve, and reached toward me.

*Now!*

I caught his hand—his eyes widened—and yanked, hauling him off his feet. He toppled forward, knee diving into the petrol, and I'd have liked nothing more than to pummel his face into the back of his skull, but I still had my wits and running now was my best chance of escape.

The swinging rope ladder blurred, but I managed to grab it and began to climb. It swung wildly, my head thumped, my eyes streamed. Thrusting my boots at the ladder's rungs was hit and miss, mostly misses.

Kage grabbed the ladder under me. With his weight on it, it stopped swinging, but it also meant he was right on my tail.

I clambered toward the light, scurried out of the

hatch, tried to slam the hatch closed, but Kage's arm flew up, catching it. I whirled, threw myself down the metal stairs. Somehow staying upright, I bolted toward a parked Volvo. Maybe, if I got lucky, he'd left the keys in it. I slammed into the passenger door, grabbed for the handle —locked. *Fuck.*

A shot rang out. The passenger window exploded. I recoiled, dancing back.

"Stay there!" Kage yelled.

I bolted. Rough ground tried to trip me up. My right boot landed in a pothole and my ankle buckled. I dropped, somehow saved myself from falling, but Kage hit my side, tackling me to the ground. My shoulder and cheek hit dirt. Kage's weight pushed from everywhere, hands scrabbling, gun coming for my head. A voice from my past told me I'd already lost, that I was too weak to fight him. That voice sounded a lot like my dad's. And I'd killed him, proving that bastard wrong.

I landed a right hook across Kage's face—throwing him off—rolled onto my front, and belly crawled. Fingers grabbed my ankle. I kicked him off. He grabbed again and yanked, dragging me backward across the gravel. My shirt rode up, stones grated my ribs. The gun aimed down. I twisted and batted it away. When he tried to swing it down again, I caught his wrist, shoving his aim over my head. And then he was right in front of my face, his eyes ablaze with trick, mouth twisted into a snarl. This close, there was only one thing I could do that would distract him. I thrust my tongue between his lips, mouthed his snarl, and snogged him like I had when we'd fucked—and for a second, he froze. That second was all I needed.

I snatched his gun and pressed the muzzle to the side of his head. We both froze, him straddling my hips, me breathing like a dying dog.

"Do it," he sneered.

Yeah, I should. Just pull the trigger and boom, no more Kage. He'd almost killed Alex. He'd killed Jordan. Alex wouldn't have hesitated. So why the fuck was I?

Kage snorted. "Prove you're the killer, English."

My arm burned, the gun wobbled in my trembling hand, but the shot would still blow half his brain out. It wasn't as though I hadn't killed anyone before. And he deserved it. Even Gina would have pulled the trigger by now.

Kage grabbed my Nessie shirt in both his fists. "Do it, John!"

Maybe it was the petrol fumes, or maybe I *was* losing my mind. Because I tossed the gun. It skidded against another nearby silo.

The shock on his face stalled all his fury. He blinked. I could have killed him, should have, but I hadn't. That didn't fit with the idea that I was all bad. And if that didn't, then maybe he had me all wrong?

His hand smothered over my face, smelling of petrol and dirt and that fancy aftershave he always wore. His fingers gripped my cheeks. He lifted my head and slammed it down—

—the boiling orb of golden-threaded shadows throbbed behind its bars in the underground vaulted space. Shadows poured over red-brick walls and under the arches. I moved toward the light, each step easier. My hands were shadows. I looked through them, through me. I was a shadow. And the source was calling me home.

## 26

A lexander

It had been years since I'd seen my sister, not as a shadow trapped in the study, but as a real, solid person. Although, the undulating highlands with their vibrant purple heathers and the clockface of standing stones weren't real. They couldn't be. So that meant the young blonde woman sitting on one of those stones, her face turned away, also wasn't real, even if she appeared to be.

A dream then. I rarely had them. But with John, I'd been sleeping more, dreaming more. And this one was new.

I walked the well-trodden path toward the stones, toward the girl sitting on one of the stones, her back to me.

"Why am I here?" My voice quivered, pitched a little

too high to be a man's. I might have been a boy again, but my mind was mine, and as wary as always.

"Always suspicious," Charlotte said, keeping her face turned away. "You get that from Mother." Charlotte had always been tall and slim, with a beaming smile. I'd loved her the way little brothers always idolize their older siblings, even when we argued. I had more happy memories of my time with her than at any other time in my life. But her being here now, something about it wasn't right. Apart from the obvious fact she'd been dead for well over a decade. Why wasn't she showing her face?

Whatever game this was, I didn't want to play. My past was always better left alone. "Is this about John?"

She continued to gaze away, over the moorland, toward the distance where grey clouds threatened rain. A chill settled over the moorland, as though the sun had been hidden by storm clouds. But there was no sun, just clouds above a vibrant landscape of purple heather.

And a stag. A huge specimen, muscular, in its prime, with vast antlers.

Charlotte saw it too. "John isn't with us," she said. "But he is close, Alex."

Did the stag have something to do with John? "Do you know where he is?"

"He needs you. We all do." The breeze teased her long hair.

"Yes, well... Specifics would be helpful."

"It was Mother, you know? It began with her."

Briefly, I closed my eyes. My mother and I... I'd loved her, more than anything, but a boy's love had never been enough. I was never enough. "What began with her?"

*"Everything."*

My phone rang. I jolted awake, seated at a desk in John's father's Shoreditch apartment, the dream already turning to dust among old memories. The clock read three fifteen in the afternoon. I'd been out for no more than a few minutes.

*John isn't with us.*

It hadn't felt like a dream.

*But he is close.* What did that mean? Close to her, to the dead?

Gina's name showed on my buzzing phone.

"Have you found him?" I answered breathlessly.

"I've found something. You at John's?"

"Yes—"

"Good, grab your keys and meet me downstairs."

I ended the call, grabbed my coat and keys, and met Gina outside. She nodded, her expression serious. Grey clouds hung low over nearby office and residential blocks. "You have a car nearby, right?" she asked.

"In the basement lot." She followed me to the underground parking garage and frowned as I blipped the key fob, unlocking the unremarkable Ford waiting in its bay. "The Aston was seized along with the rest of my assets," I explained.

"It's perfect for this."

We both climbed in. I started the engine and drove up the ramp, into traffic. "Where are we going?"

"You up for some trespassing?"

"It's on my list of crimes I'll be incarcerated for shortly, so what's one more strike?"

"Take a left. We're going to Coryton Oil Refinery."

"Sounds charming."

Gina worried her bottom lip between her teeth. "I think it's where Kage has Dom."

Well, that changed things, including my urgency. I slammed the Ford into gear and sped through the London traffic. "Why there?"

"Where's a better place to keep a latent from using their trick than around highly flammable liquid? It's right in our target area. And I just... It feels right. I'm not a latent, I don't do the voodoo stuff you guys do, but I know he's there."

That was more than enough evidence for me.

"And it's kinda weird, but Cas had a dream—"

"She's not the only one. Did it feature a stag?"

"Yeah, and she said there was a light and those moving shadows things. And the light called to her."

Perhaps John's visions had only been the beginning, and now more latents were seeing things? We were all connected by the source... connected to John.

A traffic light ahead blinked red. I dropped a gear, jerked the Ford from behind a line of cars, and raced through the red light, igniting a chorus of horns and narrowly missing clipping the front end of a London bus.

Gina's knuckles, where she gripped her seat, turned white. "I dunno, but maybe we can get there in one piece?"

I carved through more traffic, speeding up. *Nothing* could stop me getting to John. This was the best lead we'd had. He was there. I could *feel* it too.

We reached London's industrial outskirts in less than

ten minutes and sped past warehouses, factories, toward where a bank of storm clouds gathered.

"You think he's okay?" Gina asked.

We were minutes out from Coryton. We'd find him soon. He'd be safe again.

"Yes. He'll be fine." He was always fine. But I feared the worst. John always came out fighting, but every man, no matter his strength or determination, had limits. He wasn't immortal. And the people I cared for died, more often than I cared to dwell on. John had escaped death by the skin of his teeth too many times to count. Eventually, his luck would run out. *Not today.* I changed gear, planted the throttle, and demanded every rev the Ford had in it.

*John isn't with us, but he is close.* What did Charlotte mean?

Was he one of the shadows? A dead latent, animated by trick. A by-product of disturbing the source. No, I couldn't think that. He'd be fine. He was John. We'd been here before. He was *always fine.*

The landscape at the roadside changed, flattening out, scattered with rusted chain-link fence and cracked concrete. Ahead, the tops of huge white silos dominated the skyline. My trick simmered. John was close. All we had to do was find him.

The main gates had been chained closed and the old guard booths boarded up. I changed down a gear and raced the Ford forward.

"Oh sh—!"

The Ford plowed through the gates, smashing them open. But as the road ahead split, I slammed on the brakes, flung the car to a stop just off the track, and leaped out. Petrol fumes permeated the shifting breeze. The same breeze hissed though high grasses. Seagulls called. I closed my eyes. John was here... I just needed to focus.

"We're not driving in?"

"I don't want to alert anyone inside to our presence so they have a chance to hurt him before we can get to him."

Gina's shoes crunched on gravel. "Kempthorne. Tracks."

She pointed out a trail of disturbed gravel, where a car had passed by, leaving the gravel wet. That had to be the way. Quickly, we walked between the tracks. A rusted sign warned of corrosive chemicals and no naked flames. The smell of spilled oil laced the air, so heavy it tingled my tongue. The silos were vast metal drums, as big as houses. Fading light cast long, low shadows.

At the next fork, the tracks veered right.

"Maybe we should split up?" Gina whispered. "We're kinda exposed."

Silos flanked both sides of the track, creating a gulley we walked through. We *were* exposed. But I couldn't risk losing sight of Gina. "We stay together."

Trick sizzled under my skin, eager for freedom, to light the entire place ablaze and flush out Kage, but I couldn't risk hurting John.

As we walked, the tracks curved around a silo and an old Volvo came into view.

"That's Kage's car," Gina whispered. "He's here."

"Not another step, Kempthorne!"

The American-accented drawl came from our right, and there was Kage, between two towering silos, standing over John's motionless body. My mind glitched, screeching to a halt and skipping from thought to thought. John's face was cut up, bleeding. The Nessie T-shirt he insisted on wearing was scrunched. His knuckles bled. Skipped to Kage, and his clothes were all scuffed too, his long black coat filthy, his face bruised. John had done that. He'd put up a fight. But now he wasn't moving. Why wasn't he moving? Trick pooled into my hand—I'd burn Kage *slowly*, from the inside out, make him feel every cell burst.

"I wouldn't do that," he said, holding out his hand to stop our approach. "Dom is soaked in fuel. One spark and boom."

Panic fluttered around my heart. Fury tried to lurch me into action, but I couldn't move, not yet. Was John breathing?

"What have you done to him?" Gina asked, not brothering to hide the quiver in her voice.

"He tried to escape."

No. I didn't want to hear *excuses* or listen to his *reasons*. "Enough—" I started forward. Kage had nothing to hold over me, nothing to stop me with. He didn't even have his usual gun to wave around. He was just a man standing over my lover, about to spend his last few minutes on this earth.

"Kempthorne, stop." He took something from his pocket, some kind of trinket. The thing sparked and fizzled, and that same trick danced in his dark eyes. Kage had trick? "Come any closer and Dom burns."

But that meant... "You're a latent?"

"Newly turned, thanks to you two. You kept that secret

real well, Kempthorne. How you can make *more* like you. Do you know what it's like to wake up feeling there's something alien inside of you, some other power coursing through your veins, turning you *inhuman*. Can you begin to understand how that feels?!"

A few things realigned in my mind; Kage's motives, for one. "I imagine it's enough to drive a man quite insane."

He snarled, taking my words personally. "You'll pay. As we speak, the whole world is turning against you."

"Is that all you want? To tear me down? Congratulations, you've succeeded. Now let John go. We both know you're not going to kill him or you would have done so already." I took a step forward.

Kage's manic smile twitched. "He killed my little brother."

"Protecting me." Another step.

"He ruined my fucking life!"

"No. *You* did that." Closer. "I even gave you a second chance to make it right and you still failed. This isn't my doing or John's. Take responsibility for your own actions. I've warned you. I've given you chances to walk away." Close now, just a few strides away. I ached to look down at John, to see if he breathed, but I couldn't break eye contact with Kage. "It ends here."

His eyes widened. He wouldn't hurt John. Through all of this, he'd hurt me, but not John. He wanted me to suffer, me to die. Not John.

Kage opened his hand.

The artifact tumbled from his fingers.

Kage ran, but my world narrowed to that single

falling item. I was never going to reach it in time to knock its path from John. But I lunged anyway, moving too slowly, watching it tumble. Everything was *too bloody slow.*

The tiny artifact ignited a sudden rush of hungry flame. That liquid flame poured over John's body. Heat burst outward. Gina screamed.

John was *burning.*

I thrust my hands into the fire. Pain lashed up my arms. My skin sizzled, boiling. I reeled, fell. Fire. So much fire. His whole body was ablaze. *Think... think...* my jacket. I tore it off and tossed it over the flames, beating the heat down. My scorched hands sizzled with jagged agony. Some flames sprang back to life, feeding on petrol fumes. Desperate, mad with fear, I scooped dirt over John's legs, trying to suffocate the fire. It took too long. The smell... The horrible smell of burning flesh.

God...

His clothes were shredded, melted, black, or was that his skin? I couldn't tell. His face...

Gina moaned a horrible sound.

"Call an ambulance!" I snapped.

"Heal him!"

Yes... I... could do that. But my hands. Burned. Didn't matter. I pressed them to his chest, tried to focus, to summon the trick. Memories swam too close to the surface, memories of Robin bleeding out under my touch. Wasn't this inevitable? Everyone I loved died. John was already gone. Not breathing. No heartbeat.

"Alex! Save him! Hurry!"

*Save him.*

*Save John.*

I needed the source, I needed him, I needed focus—

Gina grabbed my shoulder. "What the fuck are you waiting for?!"

"I can't—" A sob choked me. I was useless, I couldn't do this. A failure. The same failure I'd always been. Not good enough. I couldn't even save the man I loved.

"What?!" Gina screamed.

My hands, my fingers all curled inward. I didn't feel them anymore. Didn't feel anything.

"Alex." She grabbed my shoulders, pulled me almost off my knees to look her in the eyes. "You have to save him now! Whatever it is you do, do it. You saved Kage! You can bloody save John."

"He's dead."

She gasped. Tears fell from her eyes. "No... No, he's not." She let go and sprawled over John, her fingers at his neck, his burned face. "No, he's not! He's not! There... There!" She grabbed my scorched hand and pulled me down. "It's there, his heart, you feel it? He's alive, Alex. You have to do this. Only you can do this. Just try?!"

"I can't Gina—I can't! It's John, I can't." I needed focus, calm, clarity, I needed control. But I was falling, and the world rushed by, and Gina cried and raged, and inside I was breaking into a million pieces. I saw John's accepting face when he'd realized I'd forced Trent Anderson into a cupboard, his smile every time I caught him watching me, his laugh at some bizarre social dilemma I'd stumbled into, the determination when he knew he was right, when he fought for others, when he'd surrendered himself to do the right thing. He'd healed me, he'd brought me back. I had to do this. I had to try. Even if it was hopeless, John always tried.

I placed my broken hands on him again, shoved the slippery fear and grief aside before they combined to drown me, and reached down, into that part of me where the power resided. It wasn't strong enough or bright enough, but I grabbed it and heaved. He wasn't dying here... Nothing was taking him from me.

Gina sobbed into a phone, calling for an ambulance. Kage was somewhere, nearby. But I blocked that thought out, blocked everything, and drilled down, seeking John's spark, his trick, his connection, the part of him that made him wonderful, and unique, and more worthy than me. I saw it then, a huge pulsing orb of shadow and trick, the vast, hungry thing he'd described from his dreams, swelling to encompass the bars holding it. *Consuming.* Shadows poured toward it, each one disappearing inside its blinding light. An origin. A beginning, where the source originated from. It wanted John, wanted him back. It wanted us all back.

*You can't have him.*

*He's mine.*

The vision or dream blurred, throwing me out and back into my own body. Trick poured from my fingers into John, filling his veins with golden light. More. I pushed it all, everything I had, and slowly the scorched, blackened marks on his face faded away, absorbed back into him.

It was working, he was going to be all right. My trick waned, my heart spluttered, its beat erratic. I knew what this was. It was an end. This was the price. He already had my heart. My life for his. I'd give it a hundred times over. He deserved to live. He was remarkable, better than me in every way. He'd save us all.

It was done.

I pulled my hands free and fell onto my arse.

Gina rushed in. "John? John? Can you hear me? Hold on. An ambulance is coming. You're going to be okay. You hear me? Hold on—just hold on."

My wrecked heart thumped out of rhythm, my trick fizzled and vanished. I wasn't sure if I could breathe, but that was all right. I'd saved him. I'd saved him, and that was a good thing. A good ending then... for me. I fought to keep my eyes open, fearing when they closed, oblivion waited for me on the other side, but weakness took hold, my eyes closed. If it was truly over, and I'd given my life for the man I loved, then I was ready.

## 27

Alexander

"I quit," Gina said, slamming a tattered bunch of flowers onto the end of John's hospital bed.

"Technically, you're no longer employed, but I appreciate the sentiment," I told her from the bedside chair which I'd spent the last three days camped in.

"You're bad for my health, both of you." She glanced at John, out cold, hooked up to monitors, and her anger softened. The doctors all agreed, there was nothing wrong with him. John was bruised and a little dehydrated but, otherwise, they couldn't explain the coma. He should be awake. He should have been chatting about the Business, about our next move, about how to find Kage, who'd vanished while I'd watched John burn. But he slept, alive, while his mind was somewhere else.

"Boss, you look like shit," Cassie said, just now entering the room with a tray of take-out coffees. "Go get cleaned up, we've got it from here."

"Thank you, but I'm fine." I hadn't left his side since I'd woken in a hospital bed, torn the ridiculous IV drips from my wrist, thrown on my clothes, cornered a nurse, and demanded to know where John Domenici was. They'd had him in a latent ward, his treatment the bare minimum. I'd almost spiraled then, but my trick had yet again abandoned me, all used up to save John, healing my hands in the process.

After several threats and a generous monetary donation, they'd moved John to his own room in the private hospital wing.

Cassie shrugged and handed me the coffee. "Nothing from our boy toy then?"

"No." Whatever Kage had put John through, his physical wounds were healed, but mentally, he wasn't in the room. I had a suspicion I knew where that part of him was—I'd seen it when I'd healed him. The red-brick archways, the violently writhing orb. It had hold of John. I wasn't giving him up without a fight. But how did one fight the source of all tricks?

"Thank you for the flowers," I told Gina.

"They're for John, not you." She snatched them back, marched to the basin to fill a jug with water, and tore off the flowers' paper wrap.

She was still prickly with me after I'd almost given up on John. I was angry with myself for that too. More than angry. I was a twitch away from drowning myself in a bottle of whiskey. If I hadn't drained my trick, I'd be spiraling. "Any further information on Blackwater?"

"Maybe. Blackwater is definitely connected with St Katharine Docks. Scratch the surface online and stuff from the 70s peeks through. Old redevelopment photos. Blackwater paid for the first rejuvenation of the area. Although, they were called some other name, but had the same correspondence address. Kinda weird for a military research company to invest in property? But there's nothing on-site to get a look at, Cas and me have tried. You need to speak with someone high up. I tried and they hung up on me, so—" She thumped the vase of flowers down onto John's bedside table and sighed at his restful face. "You do you and throw a load of cash at them or march in there and be all *Alexander Kempthorne.*"

I didn't feel very Alexander Kempthorne. "Kempthorne Enterprises is in the process of shutting down Blackwater. They won't be pleased to see me."

She shrugged. "So use that. Tell them you want to renegotiate or something, anything. You're usually the one with all the ideas. Do I have to do all the thinking around here?"

"We need to get in that warehouse building, see those underground vaults," I thought aloud.

"Can't. It's locked down tighter than a duck's arse," Cassie said. "We've been all over it. And I gotta say, I don't feel any weirdness around there. If there was some enormous glowing ball of trick underground, wouldn't latents feel it?"

"You'd think so."

Nothing felt right. Nothing added up. As though I was

a square peg trying to fit into a round hole. It was because John wasn't with me. Together, we'd have Kempthorne & Co'd the shit out of it, as he would have said. Perhaps this was what Kage had wanted. Not to ruin who I was, but to emotionally destroy me. He wasn't far off succeeding.

"Maybe you should get out of here for a bit?" Gina suggested. "Clear your head? You've been through a lot too, you know. What with all this and... Jordan."

Jordan. I still had his funeral to plan. If I went back to John's apartment, I wouldn't rest. I'd go over all the documents we'd uncovered, stare at the new murder wall, and wish I was by his bedside.

"Those things I said about you, you know... blaming you for, well, everything? I didn't mean it."

I waved her apology away and pushed from the chair, hiding my wobble. "It's fine, really. You're right. I'll go back to Shoreditch, freshen up. I'll be back at..." I glanced at my wristwatch, but it had died when I'd healed John. I didn't even know what day it was. "Later..."

John still slept. Every time I looked at him, I hoped to see some sign he was still with us. I bent and kissed him on the forehead. The heart monitor kept up its steady sweeping lines, no change. "Come back to me?" I whispered, stroking his ruffled hair. "Come back like you said you always would."

Gina said something about taking care of myself, but I'd already left and the door swung closed. I took a cab to Shoreditch. The driver chatted about the traffic, the weather, and I heard very little. I trudged up to John's apartment and found Trevor's enormous frame barring the door. "We gotta problem, Kempthorne," he drawled in his thick East End accent.

"Do I look as though I'm in any condition to help?"

"The fuzz are sniffing around. I thought you said you could keep 'em at bay?"

I had said that while planning the opposite. He stepped aside, allowing me to unlock the door and enter the cold apartment. Nothing had changed inside. Three days ago I'd left to rescue John, and I wasn't sure if I'd succeeded.

"Where's Domenici?" Trevor asked.

"Clearly, not here."

Whiskey. We had some, I just had to find it. I searched the kitchen cupboards, found the bottle and poured us each a glass.

"There's so much heat around you, me an' a few of us are beginnin' to wonder if you're worth the 'assle," Trevor said, picking up his drink. "The latents have all gotten the idea they're free now."

"They are. If anyone so much as touches a latent without their explicit permission, they face me, and I am not in the mood to be gentle. The latents are gone. The Business no longer owns them."

"Talk is, some people want you out."

Wonderful. A rebellion within the Business, John was out cold, and I didn't have my trick. Harvey Lloyd's life had been *so* much easier. "It's fine," I told him, taking a generous gulp of whiskey. "Everything is fine. I'll fix it all."

"That ain't gonna wash for much longer, Kempthorne.

And with no Dom 'ere, you're just another rich guy playin' with knives that'll cut 'im."

I leaned against the kitchen counter and pressed the cool glass to my hot face. "Be careful who you threaten, Trevor. It never ends well for my enemies."

"Like Renick?" Trevor asked while eyeing me, weighing his chances. He didn't know I was drained. If it came down to just muscle, he'd beat me to a pulp in seconds.

"Exactly like that," I said.

With a grunting laugh, he downed the whiskey in one gulp. "You got balls, I'll give yah that." He set the glass down, skimmed it toward me, and in the second I glanced away, his thick fingers caught me by the neck and he bent me backward over the countertop. "You ain't one of us. Fuck wiv us, and you'll be pushin' up daisies in some unfinished construction site."

He loosened his grip just enough for me to croak out, "Understood."

Huffing an unimpressed sound, he straightened and smirked. Happy he'd won. Behind me, unseen by Trevor, I'd grabbed a knife from the block. I revealed it now, and Trevor's smirk faded. We both knew I could have separated his ribs in seconds. He chuckled and nodded. "Yeah, I see why he likes you. Bit of advice, get Domenici back. Or the Business will come for you."

I let him go, watched the door close, listened to the elevator ping, and then there was silence.

The Met, the Business, LOA, Kage, Blackwater, IRL, Jordan's funeral arrangements, the public campaign of hate, but mostly... the fact John wasn't here. It weighed on me, body and soul, and the cracks had begun to show.

"Fuck!" I launched the glass of whiskey at the door. It shattered, raining whiskey. My limp trick sparked to life but soon fizzled to nothing. Bracing my arms against the counter, I leaned forward, bowed my head, and tried to rein the spiraling sense of panic under control.

I'd never been very good at being alone.

The new murder wall mocked me. Its lines leading around the Business, around the Domenici's, and to Blackwater. But ultimately, nowhere. I didn't care about any of it. I didn't even care about a latent cure, that distant dream I'd been chasing. Without John, it couldn't happen. Without John... I didn't know who I was anymore. Half of me had been torn out. And the rest was in tatters.

I lurched from the kitchen into the lounge and stared at the work we'd pinned to the wall together. Pictures, notes John had written in his chunky writing, pointing out connections. And there, among it all, there were my parents, there was Kempthorne Enterprises, and there I was, among them, the boy who was made, with his haunted eyes, his too-big school blazer. The screams still echoed in my head all these years later.

I'd have died for John, but I couldn't even do that properly.

Mother was right, I was nothing. A disappointment. A failed experiment.

I tore the photograph of my parents from the montage, ripped them to shreds, then snatched everything left on the wall about the Kempthornes, balled it all up into my hands, and summoned the dregs of my trick to turn it to ash. My trick sparked, surging, dancing, leaping free, teetering on the edge of losing control, on the edge of spiraling... I wanted it to *burn*. But it spluttered, died. I kicked the wretched coffee table away and dropped onto the sofa, surrounded by a mess of my own making. I couldn't do this. Not without John. I buried my face in my hands and cried. Out of everything, perhaps that was the most cathartic. To feel the tears, to accept them, letting them go. With nobody to watch, to comment, or judge, I cried until the tears were all dry.

Nothing had changed.

In my haste to destroy, several Blackwater documents had fallen to the floor, one an old article, with the smiling face of a man I recognized. Blackwater's Sean McGovern.

I picked up the article, noting the date: 1974. But that wasn't possible. McGovern hadn't been much older than me. He couldn't have appeared in an interview from the early 70s. His father, then? But the similarities were striking. Nobody was a carbon copy of their own parents.

A mistake... The publication date had to be wrong.

I moved to the table and opened the laptop we'd been using for research, found the corresponding file, and searched for the original online database. And there it was. The same photo. Definitely Sean McGovern, definitely from the 70s.

"Impossible?"

I had to speak to McGovern again. And I knew the perfect place.

After a few calls to Gina, she set up a lunch meeting

with McGovern. He'd been eager to discuss the future of any Kempthorne investments in Blackwater.

But first, I had to clean up so I at least appeared to have myself under some measure of control, despite coming undone inside. I stripped in the bathroom, decided to keep the three-day stubble on my chin, and stepped into the shower's blast of hot water.

John was going to be fine. I believed it, because the alternative was unthinkable.

The bathroom lights flickered. Just a few blinks, blackness, then brightness, all in a blink. It might even have been me... Three days without sleep was a lot. Exhausted, on the verge of a breakdown. It was a wonder I functioned at all.

I bowed my head under the hot water jets. I just had to hold myself together a few more days, until John regained consciousness. He'd be back soon. Together, we'd fix everything.

The lights went out, plunging the bathroom into darkness. But the shower still ran, and a sliver of light glowed under the closed door.

A chill crept up my naked back, scattering gooseflesh. Steam swelled in cooling air.

*"Is this your dream or mine?"* John's voice fluttered over my ear.

lexander

John wasn't here, not really. I was dreaming while awake. It had to be that.

*"You in the shower tracks as my fantasy, but everything feels... off."*

A cool, insubstantial weight skimmed my thigh. I'd know his touch blindfolded, in the darkest of rooms.

*"Someone wrecked the front room."* His whispers skimmed my ear, scattering the most delicious goose bumps.

"That was me," I whispered, afraid to speak should the moment flee. The shower still poured hot water over me, the steam misted, and John's feather-light touch roamed, trailing over my hip then taking a detour downward, sliding over my rear.

*"Al-ex?"* His voice glitched, stuttering, the connection briefly lost. *"Wh... go... on? Wait..."* His touch vanished, then a distinct, *"Fuck,"* sounded, followed by, *"I'm a fuckin' ghost, aren't I?"*

My chest ached, my heart breaking, but even now, he still brought a smile to my lips. A glimpse of smoke, that was all I caught as I turned my head. If I focused too long, he'd vanish. "Technically, I believe you may be a shadow."

*"You're go... argue wi... now? I knew... bloo... fuckin... ghost..."*

The more angry he became, the more his voice stuttered, cutting out. Too much and he might leave. If he calmed, he'd stay. "Touch me."

*"What?"* His voice sounded clearer. I almost believed he was here.

"Touch me again, John."

The weight of his hand returned, riding my lower back and skimming my hip. Whether this was real or imagined, it felt torturously good, and my body responded as it always did with John.

*"Hm, can shadows fuck?"* his almost-here voice purred.

"I doubt anyone has tried." His hand stroked between my thighs, cutting upward. Strong fingers cushioned my scrotum, then stroked higher, along my length. But when I dropped my head and looked through the steam and water dripping from my lashes, I saw mist and something out of focus.

*"Why won't you look at me?"* he asked.

"I'm afraid."

*"Of me?"*

"No. That you aren't here, and I'm the one dreaming. That I'm losing my mind."

I lifted my head, washed water from my face, and turned. My vision had adjusted to the darkness, but the steam still rolled where it met cold air, and where it met the shadow, it flowed like mist, creating a vaguely John-shaped figure in the shower that water passed through. His face was indistinct and as I reached out, my fingers sailed through him. I couldn't touch him. It only worked when he touched me.

*"Am I spooky and shit?"* I heard his smile, despite not seeing it.

"No." My heart broke a little more with every word.

*"Does... mean I'm dead?"*

"No. You're safe." I ached to hold him, but if I tried, whatever part of him was here would disperse. "Your... body is safe. You're definitely alive, John. Gina is watching over you."

*"But you aren't?"* The question was so faint I almost didn't hear it.

"I'm going to find you, to get you back. I'm going to fix this."

*"Yeah, I know you will... always do..."* Fading even more.

The lights blazed back on and the shadow vanished, chased from my hands. "John?"

Water hissed. I turned off the shower. "John?"

The pain came back tenfold. I'd had him and let him go. Slumping against the tiles, I dropped my head back and breathed. John wasn't dead, but he was... lost. I had to get him back. Shadows, the source, the origin, Blackwater...

Kage had been right about one thing. I was in the center of it all. My family, my name. And it was time to burn it all down to get John back.

## 29

Alexander

The table I sat at in the little Greek restaurant in St Katharine Docks nestled under an awning, in the shade, with a view of the imposing red-brick Victorian warehouses across the marina waters. McGovern was late, but his absence allowed more time to soak in the ambiance of bobbing yachts, bubbling laughter from nearby customers, and the chatter of strolling tourists. Until my phone rang.

*Withheld Number* displayed on-screen. I silenced it, but moments later, it rang again. Whoever they were, they weren't giving up. A withheld number couldn't be blocked, and I needed my phone on should Gina call regarding John. Six missed calls from Withheld Number in the last ten minutes. Usually, I'd turn the phone off, but today I did not have that luxury.

It stopped ringing.

I reached for my coffee.

It rang again.

"Good lord, who is this?" I answered.

"Oh finally, 'e does answer 'is phone!" The woman's cockney accent was thick, handed down through the generations like an heirloom. But it didn't help me decipher who she was. "Why d'yah 'ave a phone if you don't answer it?"

"I'm sorry, do I know you—"

"Now, listen, Kempthorne, you an' me need to 'ave a talk."

"I think you have the wrong num—"

"No, no I don't, you sound exactly like you do on the telly."

Oh, good lord, was this a fan? How had they gotten my number? I'd have to change my phone immediately, update Gina—

"Alexander Kempthorne, are you listening?" she snapped.

I hardly had a choice in the matter. "Madam, I don't know where you found this number—"

"You will not take that tone with me, sonny. You might think you're all 'igh and mighty in that Kensington palace of yours, but we both know it don't make you 'appy. None of it does. Believe me, I know, I've been there."

I opened my mouth to tell her I was ending the call, when John's query regarding his mother's safety came back to me and, very suddenly, I knew who she was. She couldn't be anyone else. "Mrs Domenici? Are you all right?"

"What? That's what I said. Now tell me, is my boy in trouble? He came to me, worried about you, you'd had a fight, I know... happens to the best of us, luv. Then he saw you on the news and he went charging off, but that isn't what 'as me worried, like... There was this Yank. He came to the charity cake sale and was a bit too interested in me wares, if you know what I mean. And then there have been these silent calls, and I need to know... And it worried me, like... was that American using me against my John? Is my baby safe?"

It was a lot to absorb. Kage knew who she was. He'd clearly been getting to know her, as he did rather well. He could easily have threatened John with her safety. "John is as safe as he can be," I said quietly. "Mrs Domenici, you need to get yourself somewhere safe—"

"Is my baby hurt?"

I couldn't lie to her. She'd know a lie. Mothers often did. "He was, but he's going to be all right, I promise you. You have my word."

"I believe you. You'll look after 'im, won't you? He thinks he don't need no one, but it's all talk. You love 'im?"

"So much it terrifies me."

"Good."

"Mrs Domenici, please pack a bag and find some-where safe to hide away for a few days. The American you met, he wants to hurt John, hurt me. And he will find you."

"Sweetie, I was doing this while you was toddlin'

around in pull-ups. Don't you worry about me. Just focus on my John."

Sean McGovern arrived along the marina-side, saw me, and headed over. "I'm sorry, I really must go," I told John's mother. "We'll talk again. Soon."

"We'd better." And with that mildly intimidating threat, she ended the call.

"Mr Kempthorne." McGovern beamed, hand extended for me to shake. "I was rather surprised to receive your lunch invite after your withdrawal of funding." Sunglasses hid his eyes and the truth in them. He shook my hand, and we both sat at the table with the sunny St Katharine Dock's marina as our backdrop.

The warehouse of interest was within my view. Luxury yachts bobbed on the surface between our table and it. Cassie was right about there not being any latent triggers. I didn't feel any significant latent push or pull around the building. But Gina's enormous ventilation vents suggested something was beneath its proud red-brick exterior.

The server breezed in and took our orders for drinks and lunch. "I must say," McGovern began, removing his sunglasses to set them down on the table, "I'm surprised you're happy to be out in public like this, with things as they are." I hadn't paid much attention to his eyes before, too preoccupied with forcing Blackwater to back off John, but there was something sharp and ruthless in their glitter.

The things he referred to were likely the most recent revelations regarding my sister's death. "*Things* are under control. Between you and I, I'm working *with* the police, not against them. The press will print whatever they want, much of it baseless gossip. I'm afraid the only shocking aspect I'm truly guilty of is daring to be a latent *and* gay. The rest is fantasy, cooked up to sell clicks."

McGovern continue to smile, as did I. It was rather like looking in a mirror. John would have called McGovern traditionally handsome, with a smooth confidence to complement his appeal. He turned heads, as did I. We made quite the devilish pair.

"So let's discuss the real reason you asked me here," he said while we waited on our food. "Kempthorne Enterprises has pulled out of Blackwater. I'm hoping you'll reconsider?"

"Perhaps... but as you may have gathered, I am not my parents. I'm sure they saw results, but I have not. I hate to chase good money after bad."

"John's progress isn't result enough?"

"John is not part of this discussion."

"Because you are in a relationship with him."

Not a question. "Is that a problem?"

"No." Some part of his snakelike smile might almost be real. "But it does help me understand your motivations for reneging on our contracts. You'll probably be surprised to learn that I'm not an unreasonable man, Mr Kempthorne. And I do have a heart. Candidate Thirty-Two is off the table, we understand that. In order for you to continue your generous contributions to our work, what would you like in return? A sweetener?"

"A bribe?"

He laughed. "Goodness, nothing as crass as a bribe. Merely a... gift. Let me be clear, Blackwater has a long, prosperous relationship with the Kempthornes. We'd like to keep it that way."

"Ah yes, my parents. My mother invested in your start-up, isn't that right?"

"She did, yes."

"Do you remember her?"

"What?" He blinked.

"My mother, you met her?"

His stifled laugh was a lie. "No, regrettably. She was long before my time."

"Hm... Did you know that Ink, as the Americans call it, is responsible for an estimated three thousand military deaths in the field, the majority being latents, and that doesn't include deaths from private use, which must surely be in the tens of thousands?"

"Mr Kempthorne, I'm not sure of your point or what you're trying to suggest, but Ink has saved tens of thousands of lives in the proper execution in the military arena. Illegal sales are not something we control. Perhaps I can have my people give you a tour of our facility? Put your mind at ease regarding our methods. All latents volunteer for our programs."

"They 'volunteer'? Hm." Coerced to volunteer, perhaps. Did he believe the lies, or was he very good at telling them? I leaned forward, rested an elbow on the table, and pointed across the water at the prominent warehouse. "What of that building behind you? What do you keep within its vaults?"

He followed the trajectory of my finger, admired the warehouse for a few moments, and without a reaction, found my gaze again. "That building, like Candidate Thirty-Two, is not up for discussion."

"Half a truth is often more dangerous than the whole. With the knowledge I have, I might begin to assume certain things, and while I am regrettably without some of the resources I'm accustomed to, it wouldn't take much more than a few phone calls to have the building inspected. For safety reasons, you understand?"

He fell quiet with his smile twitching, trying to mask his concern. "I'm impressed, Mr Kempthorne. Although, perhaps, I shouldn't really be surprised, you are your mother's son, after all." It was his turn to lean forward. "You're like her. The same tenacity. The same determination. You'd drag us all to hell and back, to get what you want."

I took the photo of McGovern in the 70s from my jacket pocket and placed it on the table.

He looked at it and then at me, unsurprised.

"It seems we both have our secrets," I said.

"What do you want, Alex?"

That was a good question. "Answers." I wanted John back, I wanted all of this to be over, and all signs pointed to Blackwater making that happen, but I also had to tread carefully. If they knew John was vulnerable, I'd lose him and any chance of saving him.

McGovern studied me again, turning over thoughts I couldn't begin to guess at, and sat back in his chair. "You want to see what's inside that building? Let's finish up here. I'll get the bill."

"Now?"

"Why wait?" He waved over the waiter, canceled our food order, and settled the drinks bill.

Why the sudden change of heart? Was it just my suggestion I knew more, or was there something else at play here?

After leaving the restaurant, we strode along the dockside promenade, basking in rare sunshine. Even the proud Victorian warehouse offered dramatic industrial chic, with no hint of anything insidious hidden beneath. We walked by the building, and its vents, then turned left, leaving the docks, as though heading toward the bustle of Tower Bridge, but McGovern entered a convenience store instead. Was this some wild goose chase? My frown was met with his soft smile, and not for the first time I wished John were here to relay whatever subtle social clues I was missing.

McGovern strode through the store, ignoring the shelves of goods, and keyed in a code at a back door. Once inside what appeared to be a normal storage room, he pushed a wheeled shelf away from the wall, revealing a larger steel door that did not fit among its mundane surroundings. A code went into the pad beside this door too. The locking mechanism thunked multiple times, the sound like hammers falling. Interesting.

McGovern heaved the door open and we entered a sleek, steel-lined corridor. At the far end, he opened a safety deposit box and held out his hand. "Your phone?"

"A friend of mine is ill. I'd prefer to keep my phone on me."

"Given the nature of what we're about to see, if you insist on keeping your phone, this is as far as we go."

From everything I'd seen and knew up until this point, it was clear Blackwater had a facility here, in the heart of central London. A facility hiding in plain sight. Why would a military research and development company need such a building in this location, a stone's throw from the Tower of London? How long had it been here? And whatever they kept stored inside, it could surely rouse John from his coma, if his dreams had been any indicator.

I took my phone from my pocket. "All right, allow me to text my associates—" No signal.

His smile hadn't changed, not on the outside, but something within the man peeked through, some other side to him. "We'll only be a little while. A quick tour, and you'll have your phone back again, Alex."

His familiar use of my first name set my hackles rising, but I handed over the phone and watched McGovern seal it away in the lockbox. John's status hadn't changed in days. It probably wouldn't change in the next hour either. But if it did, Gina was with him. "An hour," I agreed. "No more."

"All right." McGovern turned on his heel and approached the next door. He held up his watch—the lock clanged and the red light turned green. No keycode this time, just that watch. The door opened into an elevator. We stepped inside, McGovern hit one of the blank buttons, and the elevator car lurched *down*.

St Katharine Docks and its lock-gated marina were situated right alongside the Thames. At a time when central London land was at a premium, the relentless and resourceful Victorians had constructed the vaults *beneath* the warehouse by sinking huge metal cylinders into the muddy earth and pumping out vast amounts of water, creating a dry zone, and from there, they'd built the vaults with the warehouse above. Five men had died in its making. We were about to head beneath the Thames water level.

"I sense, Alex, that you perhaps do not trust me?" McGovern said as the elevator whispered downward.

"Don't take it personally. I don't trust anyone."

He smoothed down his jacket, fingers tugging at the buttons in what almost appeared to be a nervous gesture. "No, I suppose not."

"The photograph from the 1970's? Is that man you?" It still didn't seem possible that this outwardly charming businessman could be around eighty years old. I needed the truth to know what I was walking into.

The elevator slowed. "We're about to find out," he said.

The doors opened.

lexander McGovern led the way along a tunnel with a grated floor. Unlike other facilities I'd been given tours of, such as Montgomery's labs and Wordsworth, this tunnel wasn't meant for visitors. Steel rods held the roof aloft. Water trickled beneath the grate, under our feet. Ventilation pumps whirred. At the halfway point, steel walls turned to brick and the temperature dropped, raising the fine hairs on my arms. We'd stepped from new to old, and my latent senses began to tingle. We were beneath the dock, under the moored luxury yachts.

Had John been here, what would he have made of it? Would he have felt the psychic resonance in the tunnel, like he had at Ravenscourt and Wordsworth? The absence of resonance left my latent senses numb, but as an authenticator, his affinity with the past had been impressive.

McGovern opened another door with his watch, and the tunnel delivered us to a far larger open space, interrupted by dramatic vaulted archways above. The vaults, just like in John's dream. Even lit by harsh floodlights, they were beautiful. A hidden cathedral of sorts, a monument to a time when London's heart had pumped to the sound of steam and coal-fed machines.

"It's impressive, no?" McGovern said.

"Remarkable."

McGovern and I splashed through puddles. Passing under huge conduits of cables fixed above us, we merged into a vast central chamber to the astonishing sight of an enormous pulsating orb of black and gold. Banks of unmanned monitoring equipment lined the entranceway.

The enormous pulsing orb though... it defied explanation. The first thought that came to mind was of a star, captured and placed inside a prison. Of course, that was impossible, not least because stars were a hundred thousand times larger than our Earth, but... nothing else compared.

I drifted closer, expecting heat, but the air was cool. If anything, the air grew colder with every step. My breath misted. And the orb, for all its pulsing and shimmering, was silent. My eyes told me I saw something extraordinary, but the rest of my senses ignored it existed, including the latent part of me. I'd feel more psychic resonance from a simple doorhandle.

There was no doubt in my mind, this was the light

John had seen. The same light that had tried to take him when we'd tapped into the source in Hackney. Whether it was the source, or the origin, or anything to do with latents, remained to be confirmed. But it *was* real.

I stood outside its bars, rendered tiny by the orb's towering height and width. How could such a thing remain hidden in central London, mere meters from thousands of tourists and businesses. What was it for? Why was it here?

Moving behind me, McGovern approached my shoulder. Speechless, I had no idea what to ask him first and turned toward him.

But the person behind me wasn't McGovern.

I froze, trapped suddenly by the past and the present. A ghost, a memory, an impossible vision of a woman who hadn't aged a day smiled. She'd haunted my nightmares for so long that seeing her here now couldn't be real. "M-mother?"

"My Alexander." Her smooth, cold hands cupped my face. Large dark eyes warmed. "It's so good to see you."

# D<sup>om</sup>

*Alexander, tears are for the weak.*

*Hush now. Do not fight it. It will all be over soon.*

Jolting awake, I gulped air and grabbed at the bedsheets. Panic spun the world around me. Not my panic... Alex's... "We have to—He can't—"

Wait, my head, my body. I was made of stone; nothing worked. I had to move, to get to Alex, to save him.

"Dom! Oh my God, Dom, sit back. Dom... wait, calm down."

The room. The here and the then. The things I'd seen in the cursed pen, memories from a past that wasn't mine. I'd been in the light, and then *she* was there. Alex's mum, the woman who had tortured him, tried to turn him into something he wasn't, used him like an artifact...

Where the hell was I now? White walls, blinking machines, and Gina... Right, a hospital?

I tore the IV from my arm.

"Dom, Jesus, would you sit still!" Gina reached for me.

I grabbed her hands. "He's in danger. Where's my mum?"

"So are you, you idiot. Just breathe a second, okay? You're mum's fine. At least, the Met say she is. They won't tell me much—"

"No..." I tried to push her away, but the air was thick, the room tilting. I had to get out of here. I flung the sheets off my legs. Why was I wearing a dress? Where were my clothes? I stared at my knees, poking out from under a thin gown with tiny blue flowers printed on it. "What the fuck is this?"

"Dom, you need to chill for a second. You're in hospital, okay? Things happened, you nearly died. You need to take it slow."

"Hospital? No, I'm not."

"You're literally in a gown with your arse hanging out."

"This isn't..." This wasn't a hospital room, it was a bloody hotel room. The flowers, the comfy chairs, the nice pictures on the walls. Where was the peeling paint, the old machines, the weird little paper bowl for throwing up in?

"Kempthorne's money," Gina explained. "You got an upgrade."

"You're getting' the five-star treatment, mate." Cas? Cas was here. By the door. With a tray of croissants. Okay. I could handle this. I just needed to shuffle my thoughts around a bit. I'd gone to see my mum, then Alex and me had been at the Snooker Room, then my dad's swanky apartment, something had happened... Kage... Kage had been there. Then it had been dark, so dark... Nope. My head wasn't having any of it. Whatever trauma had fucked me up, I'd locked it away. It didn't matter anyway, because that was the past, and Alex was in trouble now.

"Where's Alex?" I asked Cas, but she'd put the croissants down and was looking at Gina, not me.

"There are feds or men in black or whatever here. I saw them at the desk while I was gettin' snacks. They was makin' a big fuss at the nurses' station. We need to get Boytoy outta 'ere."

Gina grabbed me again and hauled me off the bed onto wobbly legs. Cold air licked down my back and bare arse.

"Clothes?" I grumbled.

Cas shook her head. "No time." She snatched the folded wheelchair from where it leaned against the wall and snapped it open. "Sit. We're goin' for a ride."

I sat because my legs were fucked and my head was still half checked-out. Gina got the door and Cas wheeled me out. "Easy now..." Cas whispered. "We all just gotta look not-sus."

She had bright pink hair, and she was clearly stealing a patient. None of us looked not-sus. The three of us couldn't have looked more sus if we'd been wearing orange overalls.

Cas wheeled me into an elevator, where we sat in awkward silence as the floors counted down. Blood dribbled from my wrist where I'd torn out the IV. Stupid move, that. Whatever drugs they'd been giving me, I was probably going to need more of them soon, when my body stopped floating and my head was back in the game. "I think I'm high."

"Awesome," Cas said. "I wish I was."

The elevator doors rumbled open. Gina took the lead, and Cas wheeled me out of the hospital foyer with surprising speed, bumping me down a pavement. The wind tried to scoot up my gown and tease my balls. "Can we maybe get me some clothes?"

Gina had the phone at her ear. She flashed me a fake thumbs-up. We were all doomed.

Cas wheeled me under the shade of a tree in a fancy little garden full of manicured shrubs and artfully placed rocks.

"Kempthorne's not answering." Gina growled.

*Alex... the dream!* "She's alive," I blurted. "Kempthorne's bitch of a mother, she's not dead. I saw her." They both frowned, then pouted, as though I'd hit my head or something. I hadn't, had I? I couldn't bloody remember. "Look, I know it sounds nuts, but G, c'mon, this is me, I know what I saw—or dreamt."

"You've been out cold in a hospital bed for almost four days. Nobody but me and Cas has been in. And you're high. You're maybe not thinking too clearly right now."

"No, Alex's mum didn't... She's not..." I rubbed at my forehead. How could I make them believe me? The dream, or vision, or fucking astral projection, whatever it was, I'd seen the origin, with Kempthorne standing so small in front of it. The origin had wanted him, like it wanted me and every single latent in London. It called, but nobody was listening, or nobody could hear it. It had called and now Alex was right there, in the worst place for him to be.

"There's a light... Cas, it's the source, the origin, the fucking beginning! It's there. Kempthorne is there, and his mum... His mum... she's alive and she... Oh no." My thoughts cascaded, everything falling together at once. "Christ, you know when you split a bean bag open and all the polystyrene balls fall out?" Now Gina just looked worried. "That's my head right now, okay? So just cut me some slack here, but it's all real."

They glanced between them.

Cas shrugged again. "He's wearin' a nightie in a wheelchair. I ain't gonna argue with 'im."

"Okay, so listen, we thought..." *Calmly. Breathe. Slowly.* The thoughts slotted together, the pieces falling into place. Whatever drugs I'd been fed, they were awesome, because I'd suddenly never had a clearer thought and knew I was right. "We thought the Kempthornes were the first people to study all the latent stuff, right? Everyone thought that. They wrote the books on it all, yeah?" I'd seen that book in Montgomery's office. The bloody thing had been an artifact. *The Origin of the Latent by Dr J. C. & Dr M. N. Kempthorne.* Even Montgomery bowed to them, to *her*. "Montgomery killed her in that plane crash, or thought he had," I said. "So how is she alive?"

"Dom, you're not making any sense. Flag a cab," Gina said to Cas.

Cas snorted. "Nobody is goin' to wanna take his half naked arse."

"Cas, just try!" Gina knelt beside my wheelchair. "Dom, look at me." She chewed on her bottom lip. "You need to slow down, okay? You've been through like... a shit-ton. I'm worried about you."

"Gina, I know, I get it. But... Alex and me, there's a connection, and wherever he is right now, he's in trouble. And I know it has something to do with his mother. I just know it. The origin thing, I've seen it, for real... it's trapped and I think it's because of Kempthorne's mum."

"All right, fine," she huffed. "So Kempthorne's rich white bitch mummy comes back from the dead now. Why?"

"I think... she started it. All of it. She wrote the book on the origin of latents because she created us—somehow. Maybe that light, in my visions, that's the origin, right? I should have read the fuckin' book I found. But, it's becoming unstable. Without it, maybe she's fucked. She needs a strong latent, someone like me, an authenticator like her, someone like... Alex. An absorber, to... maybe syphon off the unstable source. Oh shit, I bet that's it. Me and Alex, together we can syphon off trick, send it back. She wants that."

"If she started all this, latents, I mean... wouldn't she be like ninety years old or something?"

"Maybe, I dunno... Latents became a thing in the early 70s. She was around then."

"You're telling me there's a crazy pensioner with a giant orb thing under London who is controlling all latents?"

"No. Not controlling. I don't think. When I saw her—"

"In your dream?" She frowned.

I frowned back. "She didn't look old. And controlling us?" Did the source control us? No. We *drew* on it. Didn't we? "It's possible, I guess. I dunno. I'm not a science guy. I just know that she's not dead, and if she gets to Alex, he'll be fucked. He can't handle her again, he won't. I've been in his head. I've seen what she did to him. He won't fight her."

"Why am I believing this when you look and sound nuts?"

"Thanks."

"Okay, bitches. Let's bounce." Cas reappeared, grabbed my wheelchair handles, and wheeled me to the curb to meet a startled cabbie.

"It's a long story," I told him while clambering into the back of the cab.

"That's a sight I did not need to see," Gina said with a snort, commentating on the gaping back of my hospital gown.

"Like you don't love my arse," I smirked.

Cas slid into the other side of the rear seat beside me and shuffled up to leave room for Gina. "Kempthorne sure does."

I laughed.

"Oh my God," Gina groaned.

"Where to?" the cabbie asked.

"Shoreditch." I dropped my head back on the seat headrest and closed my eyes, letting the motion of the cab soothe my frayed nerves. I had to get back to the apartment, clean up, grab some clothes, and figure out where Alex was. "When was the last time you saw Alex?"

"In the hospital," Gina said. "He was wrecked. He'd

been by your bed twenty-four-seven. I sent him home. That was... not yesterday, the day before? I dunno, the days are all messed up."

"You haven't heard from him since then?"

"It's not been that long," Cas added. "He's probably catchin' up on some z's?"

"Yeah, but Dom has a feeling, and his feelings aren't wrong, usually," Gina explained so I didn't have to spout off the soulmate weird shit again.

It was more than a feeling. The vision that had woken me wasn't a dream or some fantasy. I'd *seen* Alex, I'd been there, in the vaults, as a shadow. I'd seen him standing in front of the origin like a man standing in front of the sun. I'd feared he'd been about to reach through the bars and touch it, and knew that would have been bad. But when I'd tried to warn him... that room, that place, the shadows and me had no voices there. And then, she'd arrived. Kempthorne's mum. Her trick a boiling blackness wrapped in shining chains, kinda like the origin.

Kempthorne's zombie mum was not good news.

"Dom?"

"Huh?"

"We're here."

I blinked through the window at the Shoreditch apartment building. Gina opened the door and frowned again. She reached out, but I batted her hand away. "I'm fine. I can walk."

Cas ahead and Gina behind, they hurried me along, into the lobby and then the elevator, thankfully alone, so nobody else had to view my arse.

"Still nothing," Gina said, after trying Alex's phone again. "I don't like it."

"The boss man has a knack for findin' trouble," Cas agreed.

He was with his mum. She'd get her claws in him, she'd break him all over again. My blood rushed, my heart pounded. "I just need to get cleaned up and we'll make a plan of action, right?"

"He could be at the Snooker Room," Cas suggested.

The elevator doors opened and I hurried to my apartment door. "Key?"

"Oh." Gina produced the spare key we'd given her. She slipped it into the lock.

"The Business ain't happy," Cas said over my shoulder. "The latents are getting uppity, after Kempthorne did 'is rallying speech. Normals don't like it when we get mouthy."

"What?"

"Oh yeah, he went all *Avengers* and shit. It was epic. Now 'alf the latents in London are leaving handprints all over. It's pretty sick."

I'd left him for a few days and he'd started a revolution? None of that mattered. The Business, the agencies after us, even Kage. If the unstable origin went boom, we'd all be dust. It could even be worse than that.

I shoved open the apartment door...

... and there was Alex, standing in the chaos of a trashed front room, packing a suitcase.

He looked up. His floppy hair fell over one eye. "John?"

"Er... hi. I thought—"

He crossed the space in three long strides, then stopped short of hugging me. "You're well? You're in a gown. You didn't ride the Tube like that? Why didn't you call? Do you need to sit down? Tea? Do you want a cup of tea? Some biscuits? I ate all the custard creams, but there are Jammie Dodgers." He turned on his heel and headed for the kitchen area, which was less trashed but still a mess of used cups and plates left out on the side.

He flicked on the kettle, grabbed some mugs, and began making tea.

Gina's frown matched my own and Cas did the one-shoulder shrug thing.

"I called," Gina said. "Multiple times."

"You did?" For a few seconds his eyes turned glassy and thin. He blinked, snapping himself out of it. "I must have lost my phone somewhere. Never mind, I'll buy another." The kettle bubbled away and Alex fussed through the kitchen, looking everywhere but at us.

"Hey." I turned to the girls. "Can you guys maybe give me a minute alone with him?"

"Yeah. Definitely." Cas grabbed Gina's shoulder. "Good luck with *that*."

"Wait, Dom, take it easy. You need—"

"He's got this." Cas pulled her toward the door. "C'mon, leave 'em to it."

They left and, still standing there in my stupid paper-thin hospital gown with one hell of a draft down my backside, I tried to figure out what the fuck was going on. The murder wall had been torn to pieces; the front room was ground zero. That was Alex; I recalled something about that from another dream. But the suitcase full of clothes? His off-the-scale weirdness?

"I'm so relieved you're better." He lifted his gaze, and the corners of his mouth pulled down. When he came out from behind the kitchen counter and approached me, I still didn't know what to say. He stopped close enough to touch, but hesitated, as though there was something between us, something holding him back.

The pain on his face etched all his worry lines deeper. He hadn't shaved. Maybe he was trying for bearded chic again? "Are you okay?" I asked.

"Me?" He laughed but it was one of those short, sharp, brittle laughs. "I saw you *burn*." That last word caught in his throat. His hand shook when he reached out. I let him touch my face, worried, freaked out, still kinda floaty and half detached from reality.

"I tried to stop the fire." His fingers skimmed my cheek, then he snatched his hand back. "You don't remember?"

"No, nothing since I was last here."

"It's good you don't remember."

I caught his wrist. "Hey, you're not okay."

He blinked, looked through me, and smiled. "Please, sit."

I did need to get off my legs before they dumped my arse on the floor. Alex led me to the sofa, then returned to the kitchen to grab the teas and brought them over.

He shoved scraps of torn paper off the coffee table, set the teas down, and sat next to me, his knee touching mine and his arm draped over the back cushion. "Okay, let's get married."

"Er... okay. But haven't we already had this conversation?"

"Friday."

"What?"

"One call and I can have it all booked. I've already checked, hoping you'd be awake."

"Hang on. Wait—"

"I'll have to grease a few palms to rush it through—these things usually take at least a month—but I assure you, we'll have our slot. I've been in contact with a lovely little registry office in Cornwall. Nice quaint place, right by the sea. Far away from London."

"Alex, Friday is like... I dunno..."

"Two days away, yes." He rushed on, "Do you remember when we stopped over in Prague after faking our deaths and you said you'd like to see the city one day?" He leaned forward, took my hand, and slipped my missing ring back on my finger. "We fly out from London City Airport Friday night."

Was that what the suitcase was about? But he'd been packing *before* I got back. What he been planning, to pinch me from the hospital and take me away while unconscious?

"Where is this coming from?"

He sighed through his nose. "I refuse to lose you again." It didn't sound like a promise, it sounded like a threat. "I am done with everything and everyone. It'll just be you and I."

"But, I mean..." This was *a lot*. And a thumping had begun in my head, and my wrist hurt where a bruise was forming, and something like raw panic squeezed my lungs. "What about the Business? The agencies after us? Kage… and the vaults! We can't just leave."

"I don't care about any of that."

"Alex, the vaults and what Blackwater is maybe keeping there matters."

"It's nothing. I checked." He picked up his tea. "I went to lunch with McGovern. He gave me a tour of the place. It's just old storage. Nothing insidious at all."

I wasn't buying it. "Alex… Okay, hear me out, but is all this because *she's* back?"

"Who's back?"

He knew. He had to know. But he was going to make me say it. "Your mother."

"My mother?" he laughed. "Preposterous. What drugs were they giving you?"

"Alex, c'mon, I saw you there, I saw her."

He peered into my eyes. "My mother died a long time ago, John."

Then what I'd seen had been some kind of drug-induced messed up dream? "But it was so real."

"You need to rest. If you don't want to get married on Friday, that's fine. Perhaps it is too soon—"

"I do, I said I did. I just… I need a minute."

"It's a lot. I'm sorry. I shouldn't have thrown it all at you the second you walked in. Something clearly happened at the hospital—but you're all right, and you're here, and that's all that matters."

"Well, yeah… Cas and Gina wheeled me out of there. Apparently the LOA or IRL were about to snatch me up." Maybe a honeymoon in Prague was the perfect solution right now? If what I'd been seeing wasn't real, and there really wasn't anything inside the St Katharine Docks vaults, then we could ditch England for a Prague fling.

Alex sipped his tea, half watching me while pretending he wasn't.

I smiled. "We're gonna get married on Friday."

His smile was brilliant. "Yes, we are."

lexander

We had to leave. Now.

The sounds of the shower had cut off ten minutes ago but John hadn't emerged. He was probably still dressing.

John was alive. I'd wanted that, more than anything. But he was in terrible danger.

*She* wanted him too. And like the Kempthornes were infamous for, she'd stop at nothing to get her hands on Candidate Thirty-Two. I couldn't allow that, even if it meant lying, if it meant running far, far away, like a coward. I'd lie and run and risk everything to keep John safe.

If I told him what I'd seen, if I told him what I knew, he'd charge back into the vaults and try to stop it all, and he would fail. We couldn't fight this, we couldn't fight her.

Doctor Jocelyn Kempthorne. The woman who had died and come back. My mother.

I approached the bedroom door, pushed it open, and spotted John on the bed, asleep on his side, snoring lightly. He'd gotten as far as throwing on a pair of old jeans, but his feet and chest were bare, his hair damp and towel ruffled. I crept inside and perched on the edge of the bed near his knee. His chest bore the scars of past wounds. Resilient, brave, thoughtful. John Domenici was the most amazing thing to have happened to me. He'd changed my life, changed me. My love for him was a force all of its own, so powerful there was no controlling it, no ignoring it. All I could do was sacrifice it to save him.

Careful, so as not to wake him, I snuck around the bed and lay behind him, gently tucking him close. He smelled of shampoo and trick, he smelled like the only real home I'd known.

Olivia Barnes, Thomas Montgomery, even Kage Mitchell... Those enemies I could handle. But my mother? She was a monster.

And she'd left me with no option.

We had to run.

"Oh hey, sorry. I fell asleep. How long was I out?"

I pulled the sleepy-eyed John into my arms. "Not long."

He smiled and sighed, melting against me. "You know, I still can't believe I get to do this."

"Do what?"

"Hold you." He tipped his chin up and brushed my mouth with his. "Fuck you whenever I want." His hand slid up my thigh and captured my hip.

"Hm, as much as I want to..." I eased his hand back down before we got distracted. "I wondered if you might like to take a trip to Cornwall now, spend some time there before the big day."

"You really don't wanna be in London, do you." His gaze turned suspicious but kept its mischievous humor. "Premier Inn?"

"Please, no."

His eyebrows rose. "I thought you liked it?"

"I was being polite."

He rolled his eyes and flopped onto his back, hands laced behind his head and glorious chest so close I couldn't resist stroking up it to encircle then flick a nipple.

He laughed, grinning. "Go on then, tell me you've booked some fancy place where I'm gonna feel like a complete tool."

"You choose."

Surprised, he thought it over. "Glamping?"

He had to be teasing. "Torture me, if you must."

His snort suggested he wouldn't put me through that hell. "There is somewhere. I saw it on a postcard once, in the Headmaster's office after I'd been called in for the millionth time for a bollocking."

"Good, book it." I sat up and pushed from the bed. "I'll pack. If we leave now, we can be there this evening."

"Er, okay?"

I grabbed all the necessary items of clothing from the

cupboard and threw them into the suitcase while he finished dressing.

"I think Kage has my phone," he called out from the bedroom.

Then we were both phoneless, which perhaps could work to our advantage. No phone, no outside contact. Just John and I. I'd left mine at the vaults in my haste to leave. "We'll buy some on the way," I called back.

John appeared in the doorway, buttoning up a shirt. "What about Gina? We have to tell her. Her and Cas have to come, right? Gina will kill me if she doesn't get invited."

Another risk, but if I said no, he'd fight me on it and ask questions. "We'll call her once we've arrived. They can meet us on Friday."

John's face turned serious. He headed over, his gaze intent. I zipped up the suitcase but the bloody thing got stuck. A few tugs and it jammed up further.

"Alex?"

"Yes?" Another tug.

"Are you sure everything is okay? Besides the normal shit, I mean? There's nothing you're not telling me?"

The zip finally gave. "Everything is perfect! Are you ready? Let's go."

He frowned at me, or the suitcase, I didn't linger on his expression long enough to know. "Do you have everything?" he asked.

"Probably. What we don't have, we can buy." I grabbed my coat and keys and wheeled the case to the door. "If we go now, we'll miss the rush hour traffic."

John hung back, quietly running his gaze over the

mess we were leaving behind. A pang of fear squeezed my heart. I couldn't stand to lose him, and especially not to her. We'd get married, we'd go far, far away, and whatever happened to the origin and London, that wasn't our problem to fix. Not anymore.

Someone else could save the bloody world.

## 33

**D**om

Alex was the only one on the long stretch of sandy beach, probably because the evening air was bloody freezing, chasing the locals indoors. As I approached, he had his back to me, his trousers rolled up, shoes placed neatly next to him, bare feet shoved into the sand. The sun had just set below the horizon, staining the sky red.

The picture was so perfect I didn't want to ruin it by getting in the way. But I'd told him to meet me here, so... I had a bottle of wine in one hand, a blanket under my arm and a packet of biscuits in the other hand.

Tomorrow, we were getting married. That was kinda a big deal.

Would I be John Kempthorne? Would he be Alexander Domenici? How did the name situation work?

Everything had happened so fast, the fact we were doing this hadn't yet sunk in.

I knew I wanted it and knew he was so fucking awesome. Lying through his teeth, but awesome. He didn't even look real, sitting there in silhouette, the whole ocean in front of him. Since my trial run as a shadow, and in the last few days since waking in the hospital, reality was still a bit wobbly. But this, this was real. He was real, and all mine.

I trudged down the beach, boots filling with sand. The blanket slipped from under my arm, and I almost dropped the wine trying to catch it; the result was a less than elegant arrival. "Hey."

Alex saw my offerings and did that thing where he frowned and smiled at the same time. "What's this?"

"If you squint real hard, it's champagne and truffles and definitely not prosecco and chocolate Digestive biscuits from Tesco." I handed him the wine, considered laying the blanket down, but it was so bloody cold that I scrapped that idea, sat next to him, and threw the blanket over our shoulders.

"Twist top," Alex said, unscrewing the cheap wine's cap.

"Only the best for our wedding eve." Shit, had I messed up? I couldn't afford a diamond ring or actual truffles and I'd known he'd been fine with this, but now I was here and tomorrow was a few hours away, my head was trying to sabotage all my thoughts. Not helped by the fact he was hiding a shit-ton from me. Again.

"It's perfect." With the top off the wine, he frowned at the bottle and our lack of glasses, then lifted the prosecco to his lips and drank it down like it was lemonade. "It's good."

I should have brought whiskey. "Biscuit?" I offered, unwrapping the packet.

"So romantic."

"I know, right." It kinda was though. The big sky, smudged shades of blues and purples, the ocean all vast and dramatic, and the beach with just us on it. It really was perfect. No way was I ruining it by asking him why he'd had us both hurtling toward tomorrow as though it was our last day alive. On the drive from London, I'd almost asked what the fuck was going on, but for all his lies and bollocks in the past, this was different. When Alex couldn't fight, he ran, and he was running so hard right now it scared me. I didn't want to know why. Not until after we were married. Because it felt as though whatever it was might be the end of us and I couldn't handle that.

We fell quiet, nibbling on the biscuits, drinking from the wine bottle, wrapped in a hotel blanket, like two hobos with nowhere else to be.

"I have a surprise for you tomorrow." He smirked, dark eyes all mischievous. He nudged my shoulder with his.

"I hate surprises," I mock grumbled, taking a swig of wine. "Tell me now and I promise I'll act surprised."

"You'll like this one."

Maybe tomorrow we'd get our happy ending. But I'd learned when it came to the good stuff, I needed to enjoy it when it was right in front of me, not dream about a tomorrow that might never come. I'd skimmed death too many times, using up my lives. How many could I have left?

"Oh, I have these." He dug into his trouser pocket and handed over my deck of cards.

"Hey, thanks." They were warm from being snug against his leg. I shuffled them, making them glow, and laughed as Alex's hungry eyes tracked the movement. I dropped them into my back pocket, breaking their spell over him. It felt good to have them back.

"By the way," Alex said. "Did I mention I spoke with your mother?"

"What? No. Oh Christ, what did she say?"

"Well, she called me, quite out of the blue, barely let me get a word in, and proceeded to threaten me in no uncertain terms."

I winced. "That sounds like her."

"I think we both agreed you're worth going to hell and back for. You're a lot like her."

The warm little glow around my heart spread through me, then I remembered where I'd actually come from and the warmth faded. I glugged more wine.

"Blood doesn't matter, John. My mother and I were blood, and well, you know exactly how that played out."

I didn't deserve to feel bad about my shit, when his mum had tortured him.

"Choice can often be a stronger bond than blood," he added. "Choice is given, not taken. Your mother loves you fiercely. And you have a family in Cecil Court, in Gina and Cas, and me. You're surrounded by people who love you."

"You got all that from one phone call, huh?"

"Some."

He'd brought her up, so here was my chance to pry answers out of him, to figure out why he was so afraid, but I still didn't want to know, not until after tomorrow. "What was she like? Your mother? Was there any good?"

He gazed at the soft lapping waves. The cold wind ruffled his hair. And his eyes turned cold too. "She was brilliant and impossible. I wanted to be deserving, to have her see me, but she never really did. The only time we truly connected was in the study, when she..." He wet his lips and bowed his head. "I didn't see it for what it was then. When you're in the middle of abuse, it's normalized. I had no perspective. She was my life. I'd have done anything for her. But I wasn't a son, I was a tool she'd tried to forge into an impossible shape, doomed to fail every time."

*The boy who was made.*

I took his hand and squeezed it. His dark eyes glistened in the fading light, full of emotion. "The same goes for you. You have a family too. Gina, Cas, me. We love you for who you are."

"Thank you, John." He swiped at the corner of his eye and laughed.

I couldn't ask him if she was back, if she was the reason he was running. The way he side-eyed me now, half smiling, he *knew* that I knew. What a fuckin' crazy pair we made. He hooked an arm around my waist, pulling me in close, and we huddled under the blanket, watching the waves and the final strokes of sunlight vanish beneath the horizon.

34

D<sup>om</sup>

Gina had picked two classy suits the colors of deep, dark blue and suave purple, with Alex's being a shade darker than mine for no other reason than because he looked as hot as sin in darker colors.

The moment had arrived. And I definitely wasn't losing my shit in the registry office waiting room.

I'd chewed my nails down to stubs and developed a knee-jump.

Alex had gone off somewhere for unknown reasons, leaving Cas and me to stew as the seconds ticked down.

A cute little sign on the door read: *John Domenici & Alexander Kempthorne. 10.00am,* with silver swirls and little bells.

"You look like you're about to leg it."

"I'm good."

"You don't have to do this, you know that, right?"

"What?"

Cas sauntered over and crouched in front of me. "He's got all the money and power, he's hot as the devil, but he's also a freakin' mess of a guy with control issues, murder tendencies, and he kinda likes to pull people's strings. He's probably a great fuck, but husband material? I dunno..."

"You think I'm the catch of the year?" I snorted. "Pink, I was literally made in a lab somewhere, brought up by a mob boss who hated me, spent half my life beating the shit out of people, and used as fuckin' frontline fodder by the military. Alex is... he's like a whole other world, one I'm not supposed to touch."

"Why marry him then?"

"Because we *work*. I dunno... We're both fucked up, but when we're together, it just works. He's like my other half or something, and it's not just our tricks. I trust him with my life, with everything. And if that wasn't enough, I love him, even the murder tendencies part."

"Good. That's how it should be, I guess. So why are you freakin' out?"

"Because good shit doesn't happen to me," I whispered, as though if anyone heard they'd kick me out. "I want it so much it hurts, and I'm scared something is going to screw it up. Like... *I'm* going to screw it up."

"Not even *you* can screw this up. All you gotta do is say some words, sign a book, an' it's done."

Yeah, she was right. I knew that. But bloody hell, I was *afraid*.

"C'mon, mate. You've literally faced psycho-latents, drugged-up assassins, and crazy shadows. You've got this."

Right. Yeah. I had this.

There was also all the other shit that Alex wasn't telling me, and once this was done, he *had* to tell me. Everything we'd been running from would crash back in. But that was later, everything had to be later. I was getting married. To Alex. That was the now. And hadn't I told myself last night to live in the moment, not tomorrow? "Fuck, yeah, I'm getting married."

"Yes, you fucking are!"

The door to the register's office creaked open and a petite older woman with red hair and kind eyes shuffled out. "John Domenici?" I shot to my feet, and she smiled, obviously used to twitchy customers. "Come in. I assume your partner is nearby?" She checked her watch.

Oh Christ. What if he didn't show?

"He'll be here," Cas assured us.

The registry office was in an old Georgian building with huge windows, high ceilings, and all the fancy wall paneling. Rows of chairs faced a large ornate desk flanked by huge arrangements of flowers. More purple and white. My heart squeezed.

"Where's Gina?" I whispered.

Cas shrugged. "With Kempthorne?"

Why was she asking me?! I dropped my arse into one of the waiting chairs while the nice lady fussed about the big desk. A huge book sat on a pedestal nearby. The damn thing was an artifact; not a dirty one, but enough to have my trick twitching. It wasn't often I met an artifact that had a psychic burn from good stuff happening. It made sense though. People came here to pledge themselves to someone else, to give their whole lives to someone they loved. That level of emotional resonance repeated day after day was going to leave a mark.

My deck of cards thrummed in my pocket, their resonance a little stronger, heavier.

"You're a latent?" the nice lady asked, seeing me staring at the book. She didn't sneer or recoil, so I figured I was good.

"Yeah."

"We thought about having the book despelled but..." She smiled fondly at the book. "I've been told it adds to the ceremony, for people such as yourself."

I nodded. "It does."

The door rattled and thank fuck Gina breezed in wearing a fabulous all-purple power suit and hat. She carried six white roses. "Buttonholes!" With a grin, she flung herself at me, wrapped me in a bear hug, and then shoved a rose into my lapel.

"Gina, you look amazing." I kissed her on the cheek. "Thanks for being here."

She beamed. "You're kiddin' right? No way am I missing you and Kempthorne getting hitched." She handed a rose to Cas and the pair of them fussed over their pins and flowers. Cas even blushed a little.

"Oh, John! Sweetheart!"

I shot to my feet. "Mum?!"

Oh Christ, Mum was here, all dressed up in her Sunday finest. *How?* My gaze skipped past her to Alex making a quiet entrance behind her. His soft, acknowledging smile hit me hard. He'd done this. He'd brought her here. For me. The surprise he'd mentioned? It was Mum.

She pulled me into a hug, then shoved me at arm's length. "Look at you! The last time you looked this good was that day you was in court, remember? That bastard judge sent you down—"

Oh my Christ. "Yeah, Mum. Thanks. Now everyone knows."

"Oh, pfft, if they worried about that they wouldn't be 'ere, would they. Come 'ere." She yanked me into her arms again and this time I melted there, then opened my eyes and found Alex, somehow equal parts humble and smug.

"Thank you," I mouthed.

He dipped his chin and joined me in front of the big desk. "Wild horses wouldn't keep her away."

"Bloody right," Mum said with a sniff.

"Isn't it a bit... risky?" I asked them both.

"What? No," she said. "I'm just a family friend. The only Domenici here is you."

"Now, are all your guests here?" the registrar asked.

"Yes," Alex said.

"And are you both ready?"

"I am," Alex said with perfect confidence.

"Yeah—yes." I straightened next to him, relaxing only when he took my hand and squeezed, making me look up. His smile said everything was going to be all right; it said nothing else mattered, just him and me. It said he loved me.

"Oh! Just a sec..." Gina took a little velvet box from

her pocket, removed a ring, and placed it next to its partner on a little velvet cushion. The last few days had been such a whirlwind that I hadn't even remembered rings, but she had. She gave me the double thumbs-up and returned to her seat.

This was it. The Moment. The registrar began speaking about love and all the good that came from two people who had found each other despite the trials and tribulations of life, or because of them.

Alex had asked me to marry him, I'd told him to fuck off, and here we were.

As the ceremony went on, Alex's hand tightened on mine. I knew the words were important, but they didn't feel as important as knowing, inside, how right this was. It would always be impossible, him and me, but maybe that was why we worked so well.

We turned to face each other. The registrar collected the rings and handed them over. She spoke the vows for Alex to repeat. He looked into my eyes. His shone with trick, and maybe that glassy sheen of over-emotion he always tried to hide. This guy… He really did love me, and wasn't that the most impossible thing of all?

The door opened.

A tall woman strode in. Her dark hair had been pinned up, and her blue eyes shone as cold as ice.

"Alexander, Candidate Thirty-Two," Alex's mother said. "I've been looking for you."

Alexander

It didn't matter how my mother had found us—perhaps John's trip to the local supermarket to purchase wine had been flagged on Blackwater's beta-tested latent facial recognition software. Or our names appearing on a marriage registry, might have triggered some alert. It only mattered that she was here.

"Alexander?" Her voice sliced through me like a blade to the chest. I had no choice but to respond. To obey.

"Yes, Mother."

Gina gasped, Cas frowned. I didn't dare look at John.

"Now, 'old on a second." John's mother stood. "Who are you?"

Jocelyn Kempthorne zeroed her sights on Janine Domenici. They should have been the same age, but my mother hadn't aged a day since she'd "died." She appeared to be in her mid-forties and wore a pair of slim black trousers and small flower-print blouse under a red jacket. She appeared to be a lot of things, one of them human. But I wasn't entirely sure she was that.

She sneered at Janine. "Who I am is of no concern of yours."

"Mum—" John put his hand out. He couldn't see my mother's aura, or how her trick bubbled and lashed, a heaving mesh of golden light woven with thick black threads. But as an authenticator, he'd been able to sense her tumultuous trick. And sense the danger we were all in.

John's mum, however, was not a latent, couldn't sense anything, and had no idea who Jocelyn Kempthorne was or why her being here defied the laws of nature—defied life and death itself.

Mother held out her hand. "Come, Alexander."

If I didn't go with her and take John with me, she'd hurt, perhaps kill, everyone here. I wasn't losing anyone else.

I started forward. John pulled on my hand. "I must," I told him.

He radiated strength and defiance. His eyes narrowed, his trick glittering. "Don't."

We didn't have a choice. "*We* must go or she will end everything you and I care dearly for."

His brow furrowed. He searched my eyes for the truth, or an escape. I had nothing to offer. He'd known she was alive. He'd asked me, and I'd lied to him. He'd feared this, just as I had.

"I'm sorry," I whispered, aching to touch his face. "I tried to keep you from her. Another few hours, and we'd have been on a plane, out of reach for a while. I wanted this. Us. Truly. But this is as far as we go."

"No, Alex—"

"John, it's really very simple. If we don't go with her, the origin will spiral. Millions of people will die."

"Did *she* tell you that? Huh? Because I don't know if you've noticed, but Kempthornes are really good at lying. She will tell you anything. We're not goin' with her—" He swung his glare toward my mother. "You don't own Alex. Go back to whatever fuckin' hole you crawled out of." From his pocket, he removed his deck of cards, lighting them up.

My mother laughed. It hurt to hear. The memories tumbled, each one jagged and sharp, broken glass in my mind. "Quaint, really," she said. "And absolutely wrong." She dropped her hands. Trick bloomed around her, twitching and dancing to her summons, but not free. Hers was tightly lashed by darkness, by *shadow*. She was both light and dark, life and death. And the result meant she was more powerful than anything we had faced before. "You both belong to me!"

She raised her right hand, bringing with it vast amounts of twisting trick. Her aim diverted from me, toward Gina. In the next breath, she'd incinerate Gina from the inside out. John's trick surged. I attempted to heave mine to life, but it would be too late.

Kage Mitchell stepped into the room behind Mother.

He raised his gun, pointed at the back of her head, and pulled the trigger. The gun boomed. Her face disintegrated. Blood splattered. Screams erupted, and I watched Jocelyn Kempthorne fall.

My heart stuttered. The boy I'd been screamed inside my mind.

Kage swung the gun in an arc, aiming at John, and the debilitating ice I'd been trapped in since my mother's arrival shattered.

I launched a blast of trick across the room, scorching Kage's arm. He recoiled, dropping the gun, but summoned his trick, lighting himself up like a human candle.

No. He'd had his chances. I stepped over my mother's motionless body, grabbed Kage by the neck, pinned him to the wall, and yanked on his trick, absorbing it right out of him. He writhed, kicked, tried to shove me off, and I leaned in, staring into his amber eyes. His trick spluttered, his fight draining away.

"I warned you. I gave you chances. Make no mistake, Mr Mitchell, you will die in the next few seconds. My only regret is that I cannot prolong your suffering." His eyes widened. He breathed hard through his clenched teeth and clawed at my grip. If he hadn't burned John, I might have let him live. "Everyone, out!"

I glanced over my shoulder. Nobody had moved. Even the registrar stood dumbstruck. "This is not over," I growled. "Gina, take Cas and Mrs Domenici, leave immediately. Don't go back to London. Go anywhere else but there."

"But—" Gina began.

The body behind me—the remains of my mother—*twitched*. Trick shimmered in the walls, bubbled up through the floor, and connected with my mother, like slow-motion lightning feeding into her. Or pulsing veins. A bullet to the head wouldn't kill her. I doubted anything could.

"If you want to live, go!" I barked.

"Let's go!" Cas grabbed Gina by the hand, who then grabbed Mrs Domenici's. "She's not dead! Let's go, people!"

"John?" Mrs Domenici reached for her son. "John, baby?" The love on her face was real.

John gripped her hand but maneuvered her toward Gina too. "Go, Mum. It's okay."

All three bolted for the door, with the registrar close behind them.

"I killed your bitch of a mother," Kage spluttered, still captured in my grip.

"Unfortunately, incorrect," I sighed. "You've merely inconvenienced her."

I sensed John to my right. If he witnessed me kill Kage, would he hate me for it? We didn't have much time. Mother would be conscious in minutes, and on her feet right after. We had a slim chance to make it to the airport and catch our plane to Prague, unmarried but alive. But we had to flee now. I didn't have time to finish Kage slowly, to make him understand how wrong he'd been, how his own choices had led him here. I wasn't his worst enemy; he was.

"Do it," John said.

Kage's eyes widened. Even after everything he'd done, he still believed John cared for him. Kage masked his fear with a cocky, smug smile. His smile was the only weapon he had left. I'd absorbed his trick. His gun was gone. He was just one broken man, clinging to the shreds of a life he'd already destroyed. A better man would walk away. I'd tried that path, and here we were.

"You burned John alive," I said.

His smile twitched and died. He finally understood, this was his end.

"No, this isn't... right..." He clawed at my grip, even as I drew the drags of trick into me.

"It didn't have to be like this," John said to Kage, or to me. Either way, he was right. *Did* John blame me? If I didn't kill Kage, Kage would try again and again to hurt us, to hurt John. And if I did kill John's ex-lover, right in front of him, he might never forgive me. He said he wanted it to happen, but there was a difference between wanting it and seeing it through.

"Alex." John swallowed—I heard the click in his throat. "Your mother... is er... she's... coming around..."

Her power was growing again. The touch of it crawled up my spine and crept into my bones. The chances of escape were diminishing by the second.

Of all the people I'd vowed to kill, Kage should have been the easiest.

But I wasn't hesitating for him, or for me. John...

"Do it!" Kage barked. "Prove you're everything the world thinks you are, prove you're nothing more than a monster—"

A gun boomed. Kage's head slammed against the wall, blood and more splashed, his body slumped, his head lolled. I let him go, and he dropped to my feet, dead and twitching.

Good Lord.

John lowered the smoking gun. His face was grim, his mouth pressed into a thin line. "I should have done that when he executed a latent right in front of me. He's wrong, about all of it. He was always wrong." John tucked the gun into his trouser belt and hurried toward the doorway. "Let's get the fuck out of here before Death Becomes Her wakes up."

Bright sunshine blazed outside. Gina's rental car was no longer in the parking lot. They'd escaped. Good. We ran to our uninspiring Ford.

"We got trouble," John said, making his cards glow.

I could feel it too, an approaching storm building, rising through the ground *beneath us.* My mother was drawing on vast amounts of trick. More than any latent could contain. But she wasn't just *any* latent.

After unlocking the car, I dropped behind the wheel, waited for John to get inside, and started the engine.

"How is she so powerful?" he asked.

And now it was time to start talking. To tell him everything I'd learned since she'd made herself known to me in the vaults. "She's the first."

"The first what?" Did he really have to ask? Then the penny dropped. "Oh shit."

"My working theory is that every latent began with her. All leads, all threads, go back to *her.* She *created* latents, although I think latents in general were perhaps a by-product of her research. The original murder wall in Ravenscourt, her work that I continued? It wasn't for research. She was trying to track the spread of latency." I pulled the car from the lot, half concentrating on the light traffic in the Cornish town and half on recalling what I'd pieced together. "Decades ago, she harnessed psychic energy, the origin, and opened the door to power over life and death itself. She got what she wanted."

John twisted in the passenger seat, watching through the rear window. "Which was?"

"Immortality. She's alive *and* dead. A shadow and a latent."

He snorted. "And you're just layin' this on me now?"

"I don't know any of this for certain, and if I'd told you before now, you'd never have come here. You'd have rushed into Blackwater. We can't. You can't. She's the first latent, she's the beginning. And unless we run, she'll kill us trying to control the spiraling origin."

"Then... if I'm the messiah...?"

"She's a god."

He fell quiet, still watching the back window. "You saw the origin, didn't you? It's in the vaults at the posh marina, just like I dreamed?"

"Yes. And yes. Exactly as you dreamed, actually. It's controlled somehow, harnessed there by my mother. She's nothing if not brilliant, but it's slipping free, spiraling. It's unstable. It's escaping its bonds, and when it does break free, my mother's life work vanishes and so does she. She's rather dissatisfied with that projected outlook. The deaths of millions of people are an unfortunate side effect."

"She thinks we can stabilize it?"

I stopped the car at a junction, indicator on, and waited for a gap in traffic flowing by. "You're an authenticator and powerful, exactly like her. You tap into the source directly. I suspect she believes you can control it enough to get it back under control."

"And you?"

"If it goes wrong, I'm the safety net."

"You'll absorb the overspill of power? You won't survive that."

"She doesn't care whether I live or die, she never has. She only cares for her own life and her power. A power she's been trying to contain since her apparent death."

"She didn't die in a plane crash then?" He snorted. "Like mother, like son."

"She was never on the plane I believed my parents died on. Even if she had been, she probably would have survived the crash." I wasn't certain of any of this, but the more I voiced my theories, the more it seemed to fit.

"Why now?"

"Montgomery is dead. He's the only one, besides me, who could have identified her had she resurfaced. She'd been hiding, growing, feeding, like a cancer at the heart of London." I laughed a little but the sound was dry. "Everyone we've fought, they've all tried to harness the trick or make themselves a god, and all this time, one already existed."

"Christ..." John exhaled. "She told you all this?"

"She came to me in the vaults and demanded I help. We had an understanding. She believed I'd take you to her. When I ran with you to Cornwall instead, she clearly came looking. We should have flown out of England two days ago instead of—"

"Getting married?" He took two rings from his pocket. "I figure they're ours anyway." He grabbed my hand, slipped the ring on my finger, and grinned. "I fuckin' do."

Still stationary at the junction, I let go of the wheel and did the same with him. "So do I."

"There, see." He grinned and his whole face lit up with joy. "We don't need a piece of paper to say we're married."

The car behind honked its horn.

"I'm sorry..." I said. "I know you hate secrets, and some part of you hates me for keeping them, but I can't lose you in a pointless battle for a world that doesn't deserve you. I will always save you first, and if that means running, then so be it."

"Yeah, I know. And I knew you were running. I don't hate you, Alex. I wish you'd talk to me, but we're good."

Another honk.

"Christ, mate!" John peered through the back window, and his smile fell. "Oh fuckin'bollocks. *Drive! Now! Go!*"

Mother. And close, if the fluctuating trick was an indication. I flung the car into gear and launched it into traffic on the main road, swerving around oncoming cars. A glance in the rearview mirror yielded nothing, but my senses burned, the building pressure scorching my nerves.

"Where is she?"

"Up..." he said.

"Up?"

"I don't think your mum is human anymore."

I saw her then, or snippets of her thrashing vast, enormous whip-like appendages of writhing black and gold. Each one was easily the size of a Tube train, and each one moved like a snake, carrying *her* warped, shadowy form forward.

John took a card from his deck and wound the window down. "How far is the airport?"

His deck of cards were unlikely to stop her, but he'd try. "Too far."

## 36

D<sup>om</sup>

Alex's mum was a combination of trick and shadows thrown together and stirred into a swarm of psychic energy. She propelled herself forward on lashing whip-like tendrils of woven trick and shadow. Each one slammed down onto a car, a tree, or a building, driving her forward. I'd never seen anything like it—not in the military, not on the battlefield. She was a nightmare brought to life. Maybe this was what happened to latents who didn't spiral, latents who just absorbed more and more power, latents who didn't die. The trick and the shadows turned them into monsters.

Alex sped the car through traffic, blasting through a junction and sliding around a corner so fast, I struggled to hold on while leaning out of the window.

My cards weren't going to do shit to stop the angry trick witch, but what else did we have? I charged a single card and flicked it skyward. It struck the monstrous form, splashed her in gold, and vanished, *absorbed* into her. She didn't even slow. Great.

"Uh... We're er... we're gonna need bigger guns." We were fucked. Unless we could get to a dual carriageway and outrun her, but this was the depths of Cornwall; the nearest road wide enough to race along was hours away.

And she was gaining on us.

*"Come now, Alexander..."* The voice rang inside my skull like a bell, both blinding and deafening. I clutched at my head, trying to squeeze her out, and was dimly aware of the car swerving, Alex lurching behind the wheel as the voice stabbed at him too.

Railings loomed, and beyond that, the wide expanse of ocean. We weren't slowing.

"Alex!" I dropped back inside the window and tried to grab for the wheel.

*"You cannot run! You are mine!"*

Her voice tore through my thoughts, shredding them. Alex had his hand on the wheel, but his head was thrown back, his eyes closed and teeth gritted.

We hurtled toward the railings, toward the sea—

"Brake!" I snatched the wheel. The car flicked sideways, struck the railings side-on, and rolled. I'd been in enough wrecks to know to keep my arms tucked close, so I didn't lose them out of the window, but when you're being flung around like washing in a dryer, holding on is all you can think about.

The airbags blasted, metal screeched, up became

down, and then the dizzying tumble stopped. My seat belt clung on, holding me upside down, cutting into my chest and shoulder. Sand and dust crunched between my teeth. Scuffs on my hands and arms dripped blood.

The car's engine had died. Metal ticked. Something groaned.

All we had to do was crawl between the narrow, crumpled window gaps. I could smell the salt in the air, hear the waves tumbling. The tide was out; we'd landed on sand, not waves.

Alex hung limp, trapped by his seat belt, arms and head flopped forward.

"Alex?" I reached for his shoulder and gave him a gentle shake. "Hey?"

He groaned, then snapped his eyes open. Raw panic bleached his face.

"It's okay, we're okay. Alex, hey, look at me."

He gulped, trying to breathe too fast, but as he looked over his panic faded, quickly reverting to his stony-faced stoicism. He jabbed at his belt and fell forward, then did the same with mine, freeing me. I fell against him, tangling with his limbs in the crunched space.

"The window, go," he said, firm hands already on me, urging me out. The airbag on his side obscured his window. My side was the only obvious escape route. With the opening half buried in sand, I wriggled through, arse briefly getting stuck. Once out, I turned and reached in for Alex. "C'mon—"

The car lurched, then *lifted*. My fingers skimmed Alex's reaching hand, and then he was gone, hauled high into the air inside the floating car. Sand rained. I scrabbled backward.

Jocelyn held the wrecked car aloft by a looped tentacle, way out of reach. Her trick sparked, dancing across the car's undercarriage. If any fuel had leaked, one spark would set the whole thing ablaze.

I reached for my cards, but the deck was gone, lost somewhere when the car had rolled.

"*John.*" Jocelyn's brittle voice sounded in and outside my head. She may have smiled, but her face was difficult to make out among the threads of light and dark. "*Come now, you must see the futility of your efforts to escape?*"

Oh yeah, I saw them, but that didn't mean I was about to give up. I got to my feet, so bloody small in front of her. "Lady, you're beginning to piss me off."

To my right, people gathered near the sea wall and the broken barrier we'd crashed through. A few meters farther on, a slipway led onto the beach, probably for emergency vehicles. If we'd have hit that, we wouldn't have rolled, and Alex wouldn't be stuck in a car suspended in the air by his homicidal mother.

The ocean flanked my left. Behind me, a mile of sand. I didn't have my cards, but I was meant to be some kind of all-powerful latent, right? I could handle this shit. I funneled trick into my fingers and reached down, teasing more from beneath the sand, but the beach hadn't seen much trauma over the years, and sands always shifted. The source was weak. Or maybe Alex's mum had already absorbed all the power?

"Put the car down."

"*Hm.*" She raised the car *higher*, tilting it onto its side. I still couldn't see Alex. Was he all right? If the witch killed him, I was going to go nuclear on her ass.

I raised a hand. "I feel like we got off on the wrong foot. Maybe we can talk about all this, huh?"

*"I trusted Alexander to bring you to me. He failed. Such a disappointment."*

Christ, and I'd thought my dad was a dick. Alex's mum was right up there on the list of worst parents ever. "I'm here now. So what do you want? Tone down the whole,"—I waved my hand—"storm-witch thing, and let's chat. Nobody needs to get hurt. Put the car down."

*"Hurt? Do you want to know hurt? A lifetime's worth of research deemed too dangerous, too costly, too unethical—They shut me down."*

"Hm, yeah, terrible... I can't imagine what they were thinking. Why don't you tell me all about it, after you put the fuckin' car down."

*"I killed them. One by one, and with each new death, my power grew."* She raised her free hand. *"Imagine it, John. Untapped energy, right under our feet. Imagine what it feels like to control it all. Religion speaks of gods, but religion didn't find one. Science did."*

The smell of petrol saturated the air. This had to end. Now.

"You're goin' full cliché bad guy on this huh?"

The storm witch suspended on lashing tentacles churned. *"You don't understand. None of you insignificant people understand."* The crowd had caught her eye, all of them filming. We were probably being livestreamed on social media. *"Every latent is my creation. You all belong to me!"*

"Hey, hey." I drew her attention back to me. The last thing anyone needed was a rampaging latent god on the news. "We can talk. You and me. I'm like you, right? An authenticator?"

"*There is no discussion. Candidate Thirty-Two is mine and you will obey. You must stabilize the origin.*"

I sighed; this was depressingly familiar. "Or maybe you shouldn't have fucked with nature and we wouldn't be in this mess to begin with?"

Her shadow trick-infused body stilled and her lashing tentacles writhed inward. When her gaze narrowed on me, my own trick simmered in my veins, fighting *my* control. Pissing off the crazy witch who held Alex thirty feet in the air was not my best idea.

"You know what? Okay. Yeah, sure. Put the car down, let's do this. You and me. We'll fix your science project, just like you want, but you gotta put the car down. Alex is in there. You know that right? There's petrol all over the place. You don't want to kill him or you would have years ago." I pointed at the wet patches on the sand beneath her. "I'll do whatever you want, just put the car down and let Alex go."

The intensity of her focus burned on me.

"*You believe I'm foolish enough to trust your word?*"

Trust issues. Typical Kempthorne. I raised both hands and snuffed out my trick. "What am I gonna do? You're the powerful one. I'm just a boy from east London."

She began to lower the car, and herself, toward the sand. If I could get her to switch from psycho-witch mode to Mrs Kempthorne mode, we might have a chance.

When the car had thumped down, Alex scrambled through the window. He slipped something into his pocket, but his quick shake of the head kept me from going to him. "Mother." He turned and lifted his gaze. "I never did get the chance to thank you for everything you've done for me."

Uh oh. What was he doing?

She planted her feet on the sand. *"My dear, it was all for your own good."*

"Of course." Alex's smile was razor sharp. To the untrained, it appeared to be friendly, but it came with a vicious barb. He started to make his way across the sand toward her. "And I'm sorry for deceiving you." He flicked a hand toward his head. "You know how I sometimes get. Such a disappointment. I'll try and do better."

She raised her hand. *"Yes, Alexander. Come with me now. You were made for this, after all."*

He took her shimmering trick-infused hand. "Hm." He half-chuckled. "Yes. I was, wasn't I?" From his pocket, he withdrew a playing card, one of mine, and slammed it against his mother's chest. Trick surged under my feet, lurching up at Alex's command. It blasted through him, into the card, *into* his mother. Light flared—light like only he could throw out—so bright and vast and devastating it bleached the world white.

I heard a scream hidden among the roar of power, or I thought I did.

What if he killed her? What happened to her power, what happened to the origin? I couldn't see Alex, or his mother, just whiteness, but then slowly shapes began to form, color bleeding back in.

Alex stumbled out of the glare and grabbed at me. "Go... We have to go."

"Is she dead?" I stumbled along with him, boots sinking in the sand.

He didn't answer, just pulled me away from the fading light.

"Alex, is she dead?"

He looked at me, trick burning in his eyes. "No."

No? He'd blasted her with enough trick to level a town. How could she not be dead? "How do we stop her?"

"We don't."

But we had to try. I dug my boots in. "Alex, she's weak now, right? You must have weakened her—"

He whirled, face stricken. "There is nothing we can do but run!"

"Forever?"

"Yes, if we must." He grabbed at his hair, distraught. "John, don't do this."

I understood why he wanted to run—why, in his mind, it was the only way out—but I couldn't walk away. It wouldn't end until we ended it.

"John, please don't? Please... Let someone else save the world."

It was a nice idea. But who? I could touch the source. I could control it. That meant there was nobody else out there who could control *her*. I had to do this; I was made for it. "Candidate Thirty-Two, right?"

His face was so pained I almost went to him. We'd get on that plane and run the fuck away and keep right on running, but it wouldn't last.

"I gotta do this."

He sighed, wretchedly defeated. "God, I know."

I flicked my fingers, sparking trick alive, and reached for the source. A glance over my shoulder revealed the afterglow of Alex's attack on his mother was melting, and within its heat haze, his mother's shadow moved. We didn't have long. I rushed Alex and caught his face in my glowing hands, knowing it wouldn't hurt him. It never had. "We go to her, you absorb her trick, just like we did in Hackney, and I'll funnel it back to the source. Okay? We can do this. You and me, right?"

"But it didn't work in Hackney."

"It will this time. "

"It nearly killed you."

"That was my fault. I almost spiraled. I won't this time. We can do this."

His hand gripped my arm, fingers digging in. "I can't lose you."

"And I can't do this without you."

"Why must you be the hero?"

"Someone's gotta try, right?" I pulled him into a quick kiss and pressed my forehead to his. "We can do this, I know we can."

He nodded—the trick in his eyes bright with determination but also fear. I dropped my hands, took his in mine, and pulled him toward his mother's lashing trick. Alex would absorb her, and I'd funnel all that power back down to the source. In theory, it made sense. But our first attempt was an almighty fuckup that had blown a hole in Hackney. I couldn't get it wrong again.

"*John Domenici.*" Jocelyn's voice crackled inside my head, its edges barbed. "*You think you can control me?*" A lashing whip of trick and shadow burst out of the shrinking light toward me. I had hold of Alex's hand, and with the other, I reached out—and connected.

Trick tore over me, into me—hers, my own. Alex's rushed in too. And all I had to do was wrestle all of it under control so Alex could drain his mother dry. She wasn't going to make this easy. But we could do it, we had to.

Alex's trick surged, lurching through me and into his mother, hooking in. He yanked, his power immense, and I opened a conduit to the source flowing all around us. Alex had to absorb, and all I had to do was open the door so all that unleashed power didn't kill us.

It worked...

The flow was strong, a pulsing, powerful beat of energy from Alex's mother, through him, into me, and eventually back where it belonged. It felt right, as though this was why I was here, the reason I'd been made the way I had.

A shattering scream erupted and Alex's mother tore away. A storm of light and trick and shadows lifted her into the air, dwarfing Alex and me. A whirlwind of sand blasted us backward. My trick spluttered, and Alex stumbled. "I can't... I can't let her do this," he said. When his gaze met mine, the determination was still there, but tinged with sadness, touched with goodbye.

He was about to spiral and take her with him.

"No—"

He bolted into the storm, yanking on the chaotic flow of trick all around us, and pulled it all into him, setting himself ablaze with brilliant-white trick. If he reached her, he'd bloody go off like an atomic bomb, destroying himself and her and probably half of the seaside town.

"Alex!"

Jocelyn Kempthorne rose higher and higher into the air. Trick sparked from her in forks of lightning. The sky turned purple and churned, and the ocean's waves heaved higher up the beach as she pulled more and more trick from the fabric of the world and channeled it into her.

Alex was almost on her, a shining star to her storm.

"Oi!"

Cassie? I saw her shock of pink hair near the broken railing, saw her raise an enormous book. "Want some trick, bitch?" Cas slammed her hand against the huge book's hardcover. "Get a load of this!" Light, like Alex's but funneled into a narrow beam, shot from the book, straight into Jocelyn's chest. She screamed. Trick boiled and then bubbled over. A blast wave knocked me off my feet, dumping me onto the sand.

I coughed, spat gritty sand to the side, and fought to stand again. By the time my head had stopped spinning, Alex's mum had vanished, leaving a huge crater in her place. Was she dead? Had we done it?

Alex lay sprawled on his back. He coughed and shoved himself up onto his elbows. I stumbled toward him, checking the beach, the waterfront, and the ocean itself for any sign of Jocelyn. Nothing. The sky was clearing too.

Alex grabbed my offered hand and let me pull him to his feet. "You all right?" I asked.

He coughed again, brushing sand off his tattered suit. "Nothing is broken. You?"

"Fine. Yeah. I think."

We peered into the crater. It was so deep, bedrock peeked from the bottom. "I guess if you dig deep enough, you still don't reach Australia, huh?"

"Woo!" Cas yelled. "Did you see that?" She waved the book. "The power of love, bitches!"

I frowned. "Did she steal the wedding registry book?"

"It appears so." Alex ruffled his hair, shaking sand free.

The book from the registry office that newlyweds signed had been powerful, I'd sensed that, but not dirty. The power Cas had just summoned, though, had been right up there with the kind that usually blew latents to bits. Cas was clearly fine, high-fiving Gina. Maybe because its burn had been a good one, it didn't affect latents in the same way as a dirty artifact.

Alex arched an eyebrow. "The power of love, indeed."

I couldn't help but smile. We were alive, and okay. That was a fucking win. I'd take it.

"What?" he asked, catching my smirk.

"I don't think I'm gonna get along with your mum."

"That makes both of us."

"Er, guys?" Gina called, leaning on the still intact part of rail. "We'd better leave now before the IRL show up and slap us all in cuffs."

I took a final look into the crater to make sure Jocelyn Kempthorne wasn't about to reappear. "You think she's gone?"

"From here, yes. But she'll be back."

We started up the slipway and emerged into a crowd of people eagerly filming us. I high-fived Cas. "Nice moves."

"Right?!" She tucked the book under her arm. It was hers now.

I was about to ask where my mum was when I saw the rental car parked across the road, engine idling, mum behind the wheel as our getaway driver. I threw her a wave. She grinned and threw one back.

Gina thumbed over her shoulder toward the car. "Let's go."

"To where though?" I asked Alex.

"Home," he said. "All roads lead to London."

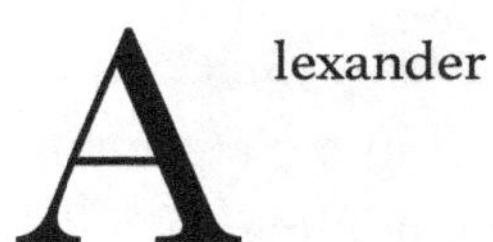

## 37

Alexander

John, Cas, and I squeezed into the back of the rental, Janine Domenici drove, and Gina rode in the front passenger seat. John dozed on my shoulder. His mum provided ample stories from John's colorful childhood, which was probably why he'd chosen to sleep through much of it, until we dropped her off a short walk from her house. John gave her a hug, they shared a few words, some of them no doubt regarding me, if his mother's glances were any indication, and they parted somewhat emotionally.

His relationship with his mother was wholesome and admirable. Whereas mine was... not. Even now, after everything we'd seen, a part of me ached for her approval. I hadn't been good enough, latent enough, clever enough. She was unhinged, but she was also my mother. I despised her. And loved her.

We returned to John's Shoreditch apartment by nightfall. Gina put the kettle on while I tidied the mess I'd made tearing down the murder wall. John helped by scooping up old documents. The right thing to do would be to ask if he was all right. He'd killed a man. A man he'd cared for. Such a thing would leave a mark, but his silence suggested he wasn't ready to discuss it.

I pinned a picture of Jocelyn Kempthorne to the middle of the wall and directed all the red threads back to her.

Montgomery, Wordsworth, the academy, Blackwater, even Olivia Barnes... it all filtered down to my mother—now we knew she was alive—and her meddling with the discovery of psychic resonance in the early 70s. The more I reassembled the wall around her, the more the pieces fit.

"We good?" John asked, rousing me from my reverie. He handed over a welcome cup of tea.

Gina had fallen asleep on the sofa while Cas tapped away on a laptop at the back of the lounge area.

"Thank you." I sipped the tea and side-eyed John.

He gulped his own drink, attacking it with gusto, and admired our new murder wall. We hadn't talked much since the beach. There was almost too much to say that knowing where to start was its own challenge. Cassie had saved us all by using a *clean* artifact, enhancing her latent trick enough to shock my mother into her shadow form, *disappearing* her. I hadn't known such a thing was possible.

The last few days had been full of surprises. The main one being that John remained by my side. "I feel as though I should apologize," I told him quietly. "For everything."

He frowned, and I loved him for that, among many other reasons. "You know none of this is your fault, right?" he said.

All of it felt as though it was my doing. If not my fault, then at least my mother's, so by extension, mine. I sighed.

John's frown tightened into a scowl. "Alex, you aren't like her."

I cleared my throat. "We need to get inside Blackwater's storage vaults at St Katharine Docks and shut it down." That seemed like the sort of thing he'd respond well to. I was still of the mind to hog-tie him and throw him on a plane to Australia, but *that* he would never forgive.

He sipped his tea and eyed the murder wall. "You think she's been at the vaults this whole time?"

"Considering she's part shadow, it seems likely she's been among the shadows."

"Here or... like... somewhere else? Is there a *Somewhere Else*?"

"The shadows must originate from somewhere."

He shook his head, likely finding all of this overwhelming. "This must be difficult for you? Learning she's still alive after all this time?"

Was it difficult? It didn't feel it. "I've never really grieved their passing. When I was told of their passing, I felt nothing. And with my sister's death, I didn't believe I had the right to grieve, because I'd killed her."

"Alex, you were a kid. Montgomery killed her. Not you. And your mother is a manipulative psycho. All those things Kage said about you, she's that. All of it." John sighed. "Maybe he was right, he just had the wrong Kempthorne, huh?" John attempted one of his cocky smiles, but it didn't linger, and his eyes turned sad. He faced the murder wall again, breaking eye contact.

"I'm sorry," I said. "About Kage."

"Yeah." He combed his fingers through his hair and cupped the back of his neck. "It shouldn't get easier, right? Killing?"

"Was it easy?" I asked.

His lips twisted around thoughts he couldn't say. "Yeah. Does that make me an arsehole?"

"No. You saw what needed to be done and you acted. We'd given him more chances than he deserved." His expression remained troubled. I set my tea down on the nearby table and slipped an arm around his waist. He leaned in and we fit together like two pieces of a puzzle, completing the picture of us. "I should have been able to kill him—"

"Stop blaming yourself for everyone else's fuckup," John interrupted with a stubborn growl. "I mean it. It's done. I should have done it when he executed that latent in the alleyway, months ago, right in front of me. I saw then what he was and ignored it."

"Because he was handsome?"

John snorted. "You were way out of my league and he was hot, so yeah."

"Also my fault then."

"Yeah," he mocked. "Because if you and me had

fucked from day one, none of this would've happened." He gestured wildly at the wall and the long history of latents, the academy, and Blackwater, stretching back decades. "You had nothing to do with any of it, besides the buying me part and trying to do some good."

I touched my forehead and tried to massage away the ache left over from absorbing too much trick. "What we did, on the beach, I think you had it right. We can absorb her power and send it back, right the wrong she did all those years ago. But I fear I'm not strong enough."

"You are." He pulled free of my arm and stood defiant between me and the wall. "She's in your head. Alex, I know. I've seen what she did to you. I was there—the knife showed me. I think that's what's holding you back."

"What about the book?" Cas said. The marriage registry book sat on the desk in front of her, its artifact thrum beating soft and warm. "Artifacts amplify a latent's power, yeah? This one—" She pointed at the book. "It's different, we all feel it. When I touched it, it didn't want to burn me up. What if you use it, Alex, when you're absorbing her? Maybe it'll give you the kick you need without, you know, killing you."

It was our only advantage. "Then we're to face her again, I suppose."

"And soon," John agreed. "While she's weakened. If we can figure out a way to get into the vaults." He approached the map and the pin holding in place the red thread over St Katharine Docks.

"The security is extreme," I added. "Keypad entries, steel doors, biometrics. Short of kidnapping McGovern, I'm at a loss as to how to breach the vaults."

"I know a way." Gina yawned into her hand, stretched, and shuffled up in the sofa's cushions. "The vents."

John snorted. "You want us to crawl inside the vents in the middle of a busy marina?"

"No, what?" She snorted. "Dom, no offense, but you'd never fit. We *block* the vents. Maintenance will come looking, we jump the guy—"

"Or girl," Cas added.

"Jump *them*. And we got ourselves a pass to get inside."

John shrugged. "Jump the non-binary maintenance person. Sounds like a plan."

"And if that doesn't work, we kidnap McGovern," I suggested. Again.

"You really don't like this McGovern guy, huh? What did he do to piss you off?"

I opened my mouth to explain how McGovern had likely been a large part of my mother's success, when Cas said, "He's like Kempthorne's evil doppelgänger."

John checked me for confirmation.

"An accurate description," I concurred.

"I gotta meet him." He chuckled. "Kidnap McGovern can be Plan B—"

The apartment lights flickered. Which would have been nothing, if London's background hum of source hadn't flickered too, withdrawing and then surging back in.

Cas shot from her chair. "You guys felt that, right?"

"What?" Gina asked.

I spread my hands at my sides, but John stood very, very still. He was the most sensitive when it came to the flow of trick beneath London. "You know how in the movies," he said, eyes going wide, "before the tsunami hits, all the water rushes away from the beaches?"

"Yeah?" Gina flung off her blanket.

"That just happened to my trick."

"Yeah," Cas agreed. "It feels... thin."

"Someone is drawing from it, absorbing it." And it wasn't me. But it was, in all likelihood, my mother. Or the origin.

John headed to the apartment's large windows and opened the blinds, revealing the twinkling, still dark view of London's skyline. Nothing appeared to be amiss. The Shard's angular top gleamed, its lights blinking against the black canvas of night sky.

Then a glow caught my eye, growing larger, not far from the Shard's base, close to where Renick had met his end near Tower Bridge. I leaned in. "Are those lights getting brighter?"

John leaned close too. "I dunno. Maybe?"

The growing light erupted in a mushroom from the ground upward, rolling over the nearby buildings, *consuming* them. John tackled me to the floor. A thunderous rumble poured over us, then roared. Glass shattered. John's weight smothered, and his breath sawed against my ear. If I could feel him, hear him, then we were both still alive. The onslaught only lasted a few seconds, but it felt as though hours had passed. The rumbling waned, and I lifted my head. Sirens and car alarms wailed outside. Cool, metallic-tasting air breezed in through the now shattered windows.

"Alex, you all right?" John's lips brushed my cheek, then he crawled off and took my hand.

"Yes. Fine."

John shook glass from his clothes. "Gina? Cas? You all right?"

"Yeah..." Gina straightened from behind the couch and Cas appeared from under the table.

I approached the gaping window. The skyline still stood, but it was in tatters, with paper raining from the Shard's broken windows. Beneath it, a golden glow throbbed. With each beat, shadows rippled, spilling like a flooded Thames between buildings, filling the streets.

The origin was no longer confined.

"You know, I reckon that's not good," John said, watching at my side.

No. It definitely wasn't. "Cassie, track down McGovern's home address."

"On it."

"There's no time for Plan A. We're going straight to B."

John smiled. "It's time McGovern met Candidate Thirty-Two."

## 38

D<sup>om</sup>

Fire trucks and police cars tore through London's streets, heading away from the quiet little leafy West London street I was lurking in. I shivered under a tree with my hood up and rubbed my hands together, trying not to look shifty. Alex's Kensington pad where we'd shared our first kiss was a short walk away. Things had changed a bit since then. I had his ring on my finger, for one.

It gleamed in the dark.

Technically, I was Mr Domenici-Kempthorne. Although, like the man, the name was a mouthful, so we'd agreed to keep our names unchanged. Also, technically, we weren't married. We weren't in *the book* yet, and were probably yet to be added to a database somewhere, since we'd trashed the registry office. But I didn't care. Registered or not, I was bloody married.

The mid-terrace's front door slammed and a tall, slim guy dressed way too smartly for 3 a.m. jogged down his shiny limestone steps, flicking his coat lapels into place. Dark hair, touched with a hint of grey, aged a mature but handsome late-forties, early-fifties face. Christ, I'd seen him before, but from a photo taken decades ago. He was one of the first Blackwater people. But he hadn't aged at all.

His sleek Jaguar's car alarm blipped as he reached for the door. Alex scooted out from behind the steps and slotted himself between McGovern and the car. "Good morning, Mr McGovern. Might I have a word?"

McGovern startled and the pair of them straightened. "Mr Kempthorne?"

Christ, it was like watching two well-dressed cockerels sizing each other up, right before they tore into each other. Cas had it right. McGovern was Kempthorne, but more evil and older. That made Blackwater Kempthorne & Co's evil twin. This was going to be interesting.

"I should have known you'd be behind this some-how," McGovern sneered. "What happened at the docks? What did you do?"

"What I should have done the first time," Alex lied. "Let's go for a little walk."

"No, I don't think so." McGovern peered down his nose. "Don't think I won't call the authorities—"

I stepped from the shadows, crossed the street, and with McGovern's focus on Alex, I laid my trick-simmering hand on McGovern's lower back. He jolted but froze.

"Easy now. We're all gonna get in your nice Jag or I'm gonna fry some nerves in your spine and make it so you can't get it up anymore."

McGovern tensed. I couldn't see his face, but I saw Alex's expression hint at that dark little streak he had, the one that believed murder to be an acceptable Plan B. "Open the door." McGovern obeyed. I nodded at Alex and he dashed around to the passenger side, climbing in. McGovern dropped behind the wheel and I slipped into the rear seat behind him.

"What is this?" McGovern seethed. "What do you expect to gain from this? I can't help you."

"We'll see." Alex fixed his belt in place. "You're going to take us inside Blackwater's vaults."

"Your mother..." McGovern caught sight of me in the rearview mirror and his eyes darted as his thoughts whirred. "You didn't do this. *She* did. The origin breached containment." McGovern gripped the steering wheel in both hands. "God help us all."

"I don't think God will be saving anyone," Alex said.

"I told her this would happen. I warned her." McGovern slumped in his seat.

"But *you* didn't stop her."

He dry-laughed. "Stop her? Have you met your mother, Alexander? She cannot be stopped."

"Drive, please," Alex urged.

McGovern started the engine and pulled the car from the curb. "Nobody stops Jocelyn. It was the same years ago, and she's only gotten worse."

Alex glanced back at me, then plowed on with his questioning. "How long have you known her?"

I leaned back in the seat, content to let them talk. McGovern wasn't resisting. In fact, he was pretty bloody chatty, suggesting he was scared.

"Since the beginning," he said. "We worked in Geneva on CERN, the particle collider." He side-eyed Alex, then me in the mirror. "If the origin has breached containment, then we don't have much time... I suppose I should begin at the beginning. Jocelyn discovered the sparks of trick, but CERN shut her down. She was removed due to ethical concerns but took a small number of the staff with her. Including me. Together, we continued her work. What we discovered... Trick. It opened the door to another world. A world beneath the surface of ours. A world we could draw power from, draw life itself."

"What happened?" Alex urged.

"We cut a lot of corners. Jocelyn was driven, dangerously so. She'd do anything to achieve the outcome she wanted. She experimented on herself, despite my advice. But she succeeded." He laughed. "She discovered the breakthrough of the century."

"What breakthrough, exactly?"

"Opened a fissure to the other side. She went through, and when she came back, she had... abilities. We initially thought she'd lost her mind, but then others in the team began to exhibit the same strange abilities. They spoke of items charged with more energy, an energy we couldn't see, but they could feel it, they could *use* it. It was the beginning of artifacts and trick. We, of course, didn't know we were on the cusp of changing the world."

That couldn't be all of it. They didn't just discover trick, or it would have been here all along. The origin had to have come from somewhere. "She brought something back with her?" I said.

"Yes. She didn't reveal it to anyone, until the thing had grown to almost double its size. An orb of power. We studied it, learned how it fed on historical psychic shocks and gave off an energy we could tap into. We thought we had it contained, but then there were rumors of children being born with the same abilities, and of course, we suspected it was the orb's influence. Jocelyn convinced the team to contain it, further study it, but even then, she was absorbing its resonance. It changed her, the way power often does." He sighed. "It changed all of us."

"Are there others left from that time?" Alex asked.

"Not anymore. Some took their own lives. The rest, she killed."

"Then it's just you and my mother left from those early days?" he asked.

"Just me. I do what she says, or I die. She can rip my shadow right out of me—the part of us that lives on after we die. I guess some might call it a soul, if you're religiously inclined."

I leaned forward. "Did nobody think fuckin' with nature was a bad idea?"

McGovern flicked his gaze to the rearview mirror. "Who *are* you?"

"Candidate Thirty-Two, John Domenici, nice to meet you."

That shut him up. He glanced at Alex in the passenger seat, then back at me. "What are you going to do?"

"Not kill you, if that's what you're thinking. Yet. So keep your knickers on. We want to end this."

"End it?" McGovern echoed.

"It's why I had you reactivate the candidates," Alex said. "Why I eventually bought John from the military, from Blackwater. I believe he can save every latent and stop my mother."

McGovern glanced again at me, clearly unconvinced the scruffy guy in the back seat was capable of anything besides bringing the muscle.

I frowned. "I have hidden skills."

"Jocelyn isn't just a latent," McGovern said. "She's extremely powerful."

"We know," I grumbled. "We met her dark half in Cornwall."

"Ah, that disturbance was you? And you repelled her? Impressive." McGovern even sounded like Alex. Were we sure Jocelyn hadn't had a fling with McGovern a few decades ago and oops, she's pregnant with her newest experiment, Alexander? They did kinda look like each other. But now wasn't the time to suggest it. I wasn't sure how much more emotional shit Alex could take. It wouldn't change anything anyway. Might even make things worse.

"She wields both trick and shadows," McGovern went on. "Exists in both worlds simultaneously."

"I can talk to shadows," I said, with more confidence than I had. I'd never really been sure what I could do with shadows, but everyone else seemed to think I had the ability to control them, so maybe I did. McGovern glanced again at me, less judgmental this time. "You made me," I said. "In a lab, right?"

"The candidate project was Jocelyn's brainchild. It was eventually shut down, but Alexander rebooted funding, at which point the surviving candidates were already out in the world, yourself included, John."

I didn't need to look at Alex to know he was blaming himself for that too. If he'd been enough, his mother wouldn't have had to go to the extremes of creating more trick-altered children she could tamper with. But she'd have done it anyway. He'd been just a kid back then. He couldn't have stopped her. But the grown-ups should have. McGovern could have.

Was he feeling that guilt now?

McGovern had pulled the car into traffic five minutes ago and we still hadn't moved. He finally pulled the car onto the curb and cut the engine. "It's gridlocked. We'll have to go on foot from here."

We left the car and walked a little ways ahead, to where a crowd had gathered on the pavements of a busy intersection near the tube station. Traffic lights blinked red, amber, and green, but the traffic was jammed. The people had left their cars and stood around what appeared to be a curtain of shimmering gold. It stretched high into the sky. And as we approached, my trick simmered, awakening. The curtain was trick. An aura of it that everyone could see, not just latents. Some stood inside, drifting along the pavement, gawking at the light. They were latents, their sparkling fingers giving them away. Were only latents able to pass through?

I reached out to touch the veil. It shivered over my

fingers, accepting me. I could pass through, but others around me glared with curious, some even envious, eyes.

"Dom! Hey, Dom!"

I yanked my hand back "Gina, hey."

Cas jogged behind her, clutching the book.

Gina shot McGovern a scathing snarl.

"I suggest we proceed quickly," McGovern said, stepping *through* the barrier.

"I can't, I tried." Gina pushed against the glowing curtain, but the veil flared, blocking her. It wouldn't let her pass.

"Here." Cas handed me the tingling book. "I reckon you're gonna need it."

"Come with us?"

"Nah... I er... I think I might be needed out here." She nodded at Gina, still trying to push at the barrier and silently freaking out beside her. "You and the boss man have got this."

Alex stepped through without so much as ruffling his already ruffled hair. A few gasps sailed around the crowd, and not all of them the good kind. Some of the crowd likely recognized us. It wouldn't take much for the gathering to turn vicious.

"Be careful," I told Cas and Gina.

Alex's outline rippled, distorted through the golden veil. "Tell the others..." he said, his voice warped too. "The Business latents. Get them all here. I suspect we're going to need them."

Cas nodded. "They probably already feel it. Latents are coming from all over London. But sure, boss. I'll tell 'em. They'll come."

"Come along," McGovern grumbled. "The longer we dally, the more powerful she becomes."

Alex arched his eyebrow and McGovern adjusted his shirt cuffs.

Gina glanced between them and frowned. "Yeah, I know…" I said. "It's weird. Stay classy, both of you." I took a breath and stepped through the veil. A tingle washed over me, like the pull of static electricity, and when I let out the breath I was holding, everything was the same, only now Gina and Cas and a whole lot of curious people watched from the other side of the shimmering veil.

"Latents only," I mumbled.

Shit was getting weird. And as Alex, McGovern, and me maneuvered around shattered glass and fallen debris from the damaged buildings, I had a feeling that whatever came next was going to be worse.

Alexander

"Do you have a plan?" McGovern asked. He led the way along quiet streets on the periphery of the Tower of London's vast stone walls. Cars had been abandoned on the roads, their doors open and occupants vanished. When the blast had struck, had the passengers fled or had the trick vanished them?

"We have our ways," I replied. We did not, in fact, have any kind of plan besides reaching my mother, subduing her, and sending her power and that of the origin back where it belonged, using John as a conduit. We were, as John would say, *winging it.*

A glance behind revealed John's concerned expression. He attempted a smile but it didn't make it to his eyes. We had to do this, we had to be here, but I couldn't shake the feeling the cost would be too great.

I couldn't lose him. Not even to save tens of thousands of lives.

We'd fought my mother once and narrowly survived. Now she was home, in her territory, with the origin close and her power growing. John was marvelous, powerful, endlessly optimistic, ruthless when he needed to be, but you could do everything right and still lose.

"I want to help," McGovern said. We crossed the road leading onto Tower Bridge, eerily deserted now, and McGovern swiped his card at the convenience store's door. We ventured inside, past the shelves, to the back wall. So far, he did appear to be aiding us. But he'd also covered for my mother for decades. "I realize you are unlikely to trust me," he said, noticing my keen attention.

He unlocked the rear door. We entered the storage closet and he eased back the shelving to reveal the thick steel security door. "But I've seen the damage we've done, and I want to make it right."

"Why the change of heart?" I asked.

The steel door opened. We stepped inside the elevator and down we went, beneath the Thames waterline, into cooler, thinner air.

"I didn't want this. I'm a man of science, of discovery for good. This wasn't what we wanted to create. And, frankly, I'm tired," McGovern said, sounding it. "It must end."

A chill lifted the fine hairs at the back of my neck. John stepped closer, likely having felt it too. What we were about to face would test us as latents, as people, and partners. We'd already been through so much, and it had all led us here. To my mother.

"It's the right thing," John said, referring to our mission or McGovern's words.

Of course it was, and hadn't I sponsored Candidate Thirty-Two for this exact reason, to right the wrongs and fix the mistakes? I hadn't known my own mother had been behind it all, but I'd wanted this to end. But I hadn't planned for John to be my heart in a world where I'd thought myself incapable of having one.

The elevator doors whispered open into a familiar unfinished steel-lined corridor, with its wet walls and thick lengths of wrapped cables all feeding like veins to the beating heart of all latent power. The hairs on my arms lifted now too, and the visceral chill seeped beneath my skin.

"Christ, are we under the Thames?" John asked, wandering forward. His boots clunked on the steel-grated walkway.

"Under the water table, yes." McGovern followed. "The Thames itself is a few hundred meters east, behind several thousand tons of Victorian-engineered dock walls."

"St Katharine's is reclaimed land," I added. "Long ago, this entire area would have been marshland." I hung back, my feet rooted to the spot.

John and I had discussed how London was a hotbed of historic trauma, stretching far back to Boudica's rebellion and the slaughter of tens of thousands of Londinium Romans. My mother was an authenticator like John, she could sense the ancient psychic burn, use it, and she could also absorb power, like me. She was the both of us, in one devastating vessel. She was an artifact, made flesh, and full of rage.

I wasn't ready for this, for her, for what we were about to face. I was a failure, I always had been. Not good enough, not powerful enough, not what I'd been made to be. *Disappointing. Limited.*

"Alex?"

John turned, lifting his gaze. Both men waited for me to exit the elevator.

"Yes. Right." I stepped out. The door closed behind me with an ominous hiss of pressurized air. The last time I'd been there, I'd learned my mother was alive and I hadn't stopped running since. Now I was back, having run in circles.

John didn't have his cards, but he did have the registry book. Was it enough to protect him?

I straightened my cuffs, pulling out the creases. "Let's get this done." I strode forward, passing both of them, and headed toward the central chamber. Momentum alone drove me on, until the origin's liquid light filled the opening ahead. I pushed through the fear and emerged into the enormous vaults. The origin had grown, devouring its bars. It filled its space, throbbing and writhing, so blinding it hurt to gaze upon.

"We're all seeing this, right?" John said.

"Yes."

"It's like my dream..." He drifted forward, hand shielding his eyes from the glare, his face lit by golden light. I grabbed his shoulder, but he smiled, as though he knew everything was going to be all right. "I've been here before," he said. "It won't hurt me."

Some might argue it had been hurting all of us our entire lives. But not John. His smile made everything reasonable. "It's not the origin I'm concerned about." But I released him and let him drift toward the light, so small against its brilliance.

My mother was here somewhere, replenishing herself from the origin. She didn't spiral, not like the rest of us. She absorbed, like a tumor on London's psychic heart. And she'd been here, feasting, for a very long time.

We had a book full of hope, John without his cards, an apparently immortal man whom I did not trust, and myself. It wasn't enough.

Panic turned my heart to ice. *Take John and run.* But he'd never allow it, and he saw through all my attempts to maneuver him onto the path I wanted. There was nothing I could do but stand in my mother's way, when the time came, and buy John time to win this battle.

"Sean." My mother's voice filled the chamber, so cold, like ice on a burn. "I see you brought them to me. Well done."

"Ma'am, I..." McGovern hung his head. "Yes, of course."

The ice encasing my heart shattered. I turned. She stood on a suspended metal gangway, peering down at us. Her aura writhed and twitched, like the origin, but was woven with threads of shadow. Life and death. Both dead and alive.

"Mother."

"Alexander." Her smile held no love. It was a predator's smile. I'd tried for years to be a son she *could* love, but the task had been an unobtainable one. I knew now, she wasn't capable.

John stood behind me, near the origin. As long as he was there, with me between them, he was safe.

"What you're doing is wrong." John approached. "Tens of thousands of lives you've altered." He flung a hand back, gesturing at the origin. "You brought it here, outside of its place, its time. It has to go back."

She smiled kindly, as though she cared. "No, my dear. What I did was change the course of history and gave power to those who had none."

"That's a lie," I said. "This isn't a crusade for good. It's collateral damage in your pursuit of immortality."

Her smile cracked. "It would have been easier to manipulate you if you weren't so bright, Alexander. You were always intelligent, but so lacking in my gift."

"'Gift'?" I laughed. "Latency is no gift, it's a curse."

She pushed from the gangway's rail and descended the metal stairs. She almost appeared normal, dressed in a cream pantsuit with her dark hair tumbling down her back. But her appearance was an echo. She was a *shadow*. Her appearance could not be trusted. Her heels clicked on the metal risers, and then she was on our level and approaching, moving like a snake in a pantsuit. Her eyes glowed golden with trick.

"This needs to end. You can stop this," John said.

Her gaze flicked to him but soon returned to me. "The boy who was made," she said. "They knew, my shadows. They knew you were mine, all along." Her pale hand lifted, reaching for my face. Her touch landed cool and hard, like ice. "Alexander, I had such high hopes for you."

Despite her methods, her abuse, her selfish crusade, she was my mother. I placed my hand over hers, on my cheek.

"You'll do as I say, won't you? And absorb the excess, rendering the origin stable. This was what you were made for."

"Yes." With my free hand, I reached backward, searching for John's warm fingers. They closed in mine. He was here, with me, we were together. I had been the boy who was made, the boy alone, tied down, begging to be loved, but I was no longer that boy. And sometimes the things we make, they don't quite finish in the way we'd hoped. The boy who was made was now the man who would stop her.

I had my hand over hers on my face, my other hand linked with John. The time had come. "Now!"

John's power surged. Mine dove deep, through my mother's touch, into the latent heart of her, and I drew her power, her light and her darkness, into me. Her mind screamed in mine. Trick blazed in her eyes and spread, setting her face ablaze, and all of that power, that heart, that rage, it poured through me. It would be too much. That had always been her plan. I was never meant to survive this. But I wasn't stabilizing the origin; I was stealing her trick to give to John, for him to return it all.

A psychic blast tore through me and rolled outward, washing over Mother. She screamed, although I didn't hear it. There was only a single noise, a heartbeat. Not mine. John's. And it was strong.

## 40

D<sup>om</sup>

Everything I'd survived, Wordsworth, the military, the LOA, Kage, my dad... I'd crawled away from each, bloody and broken, somehow alive. I'd thought them failures, but each one had made me stronger. I needed that strength now, because Alex's power was a thousand times brighter and hotter than anything I'd touched. He burned, lit by his mother's trick, combined with his own. And I had to funnel that monumental surge back to where it belonged. It was like trying to pour a liquid inferno into a tiny bottle. It wanted to escape, to overflow, to burn the world. I'd fucked this up before, and that power had been a fraction of what came at me now. I couldn't fuck it up again, or there might not be much left of London, and nothing left of me and Alex.

The registry book, its psychic burn full of hopeful light, blazed too, but its touch was cool, soothing, nothing like the madness of the dirty artifacts I'd authenticated before. And through all of this, I wasn't alone. Alex was here, the rings on our fingers sparking, becoming new artifacts. But more than all of that—more even than Alex's mother, whose power had become a monstrous thing—was the origin. Full of hunger and chaos and confusion. It wasn't conscious, it didn't think, it just *was*. And it teetered on the edge of spiraling, so close to imploding and taking London's nine million people with it.

But I couldn't bloody think about that, because if I thought about all those lives, resting on *me*…

My trick twitched, snapped.

Memories that weren't mine poured in. Alex bound to a table while his mother drew on his power, testing him, torturing him. His begging filled my head, along with the whispers from a million shadows, all swirling from the cracks and crevices of the world, bubbling to the surface, to us. *"The boy who was made."* It was all wrong, everything from the moment Alex's mother had breached the world of the dead and returned with the origin. The fall of the card castle began with her.

More memories swirled, of Jocelyn Kempthorne in these vaults, her eyes alight with possibility as she cradled the origin in her hands. Human beings were capable of amazing things, but we were also capable of fucking amazing things up.

Sean McGovern watched on, his face ghostlike outside of the warping, writhing trick. Blackwater's machines sparked and whirred behind him. It all had to go, not just the origin. Everything had to be destroyed, or this would happen again. I could do it. I could end it. I'd protected Alex from the explosion when the helicopter had gone down in the US and wiped that place off the map. I could do the same here; I knew it with startling clarity. The origin's veil had kept people out, not all, but most. There would be deaths, maybe our own, but the time was now.

*"Turn... the machines... off!"*

I wasn't sure if he'd heard, but then McGovern blinked and stared at me.

*"Now!"*

He bolted and began pressing buttons, flicking switches, pulling cables. Pulling out life support for the origin. It had to be unbound, it had to be free enough for me to *push it back,* but not too free or we'd lose control.

My vision blurred, my skin sizzled; if there was pain, I no longer felt it. I dropped the book and reached behind me, toward the origin. If I made the connection, if I completed the circuit, it would return to where it belonged, through me, down... down into the earth, into the memories of thousands of years, back to its own world.

In my mind, I reached outward, seeking the pinpricks of light, the latents who had gathered nearby, drawn to the veil like moths to a flame. So many, they glowed, each one with their hands up, alight with trick, holding their gift or curse up, like a beacon in the dark for me to find. I needed them. I couldn't bring the trick home without them.

Alex's trick stuttered. His hand—holding mine so fiercely—slipped.

His mother's laugh ricocheted through me, weakening my hold on the threads keeping everything together.

*"You were never strong enough!"*

Alex... She was talking to Alex.

*"Too weak, too pathetic. You can't stop me, Alexander."*

His fingers slipped from mine and our connection snapped, lashing back. I reeled, pulled away from him, pulled away from everything. The sensation of falling yanked me down... *Wait...* Alex fell to his knees. I reached out. Jocelyn's gaze pierced my soul and gave me a final, teetering shove that toppled me over an edge I hadn't seen.

Alex saw his mother's smile, the trajectory of her gaze, and twisted on his knees. "No!"

The light swallowed me whole while tearing Alex, the vaults, and everything else away. There was only boiling trick, a flood, a river, veins of golden light pulsing, everywhere. A tiny, fearful voice inside told me this was bad, that this was what the end looked like and I had no way out, nothing to hold on to.

A hand thrust into the storm, the wedding band shining its new artifact light. I grabbed it, locked my hand in his, and lurched from the golden light into a whole world of hurt. I choked on trick, trick danced off my skin, a million sparks of it scattered across the wet floor, steam drifting into the air like smoke, and Alex was there, his face furious. "Never... ever... do that again!"

Breathless, I gave him a thumbs-up, and all that rage vanished behind a touch of glittering humor in his eyes.

Alex's witch-mother ruined the moment by launching one of her trick-shadow-tentacle things toward us. Alex flung his own small whip of trick at her, smaller but no less accurate as he cracked it across her cheek, ripping her skin open. Shadow burst from the slit. "Wretched creature!" she screamed.

Alex caught my arm, hauled me to my feet, and together we lurched behind one of the banks of machines and monitors where McGovern already hid.

"Okay," I panted, still wresting my own consciousness to stick with me. "Nobody panic, but I think we're fucked."

Alex swooped in and kissed me on the mouth too quickly for me to respond. His warm fingers cradled the back of my head but his face was all stern disapproval. Or perhaps that was terror, masked by fury.

"Alexander," his mother called. "Darling boy, it's time you faced your destiny."

His hand dropped, and he pressed himself back against the consoles. "She is quite tiresome."

"I'm sorry," McGovern mumbled, similarly pressed against the consoles, his face whiter than before. "I'm so sorry. It's over. You can't stop her. The origin will spiral. We're all going to die here and it won't stop until everything is a world of shadow!"

"Oi, mate! Look at me." He did, his eyes like those of a rabbit's caught under a wolf's paw. "You know her better than any of us. She must have a weakness. Something?"

He shook his head. "She doesn't."

"For fuck's sake. Something? Anything?"

"The origin *is* her weakness. That's all she cares about, all she lives for. It's her life."

Then we were attacking the wrong thing. The argument was out as to whether there was any of Alex's mum left in that thing. If we took the origin away, she'd have no more fuel, no reason to exist.

"Forget your mum." I faced Alex. "We have to go straight for the origin."

"No, absolutely not. I just pulled you out of there."

"Alex, we don't have a choice."

Shadow and trick lashed against the console we hid behind, raining sparks and debris. Alex's mother cackled. "Come to me, darlings, come home... where you both belong."

On a scale of one to crazy, that woman was right up there. "I think I prefer Montgomery to your mother."

"I concur." He dropped his head back and squeezed his eyes closed. "I can't lose you."

"You won't." I wasn't sure, but I had to say it, right? "Listen, I can do this."

"No, John. I already—" The words caught in his throat. He opened his eyes. "I already lost you once before." Tears brimmed, stuttering my heart. I reached out, but he batted my hand away and bolted from cover.

"Wait!"

Too late. Alex dashed toward the origin. His mother —the shadow-witch she'd become—lashed a whip of shadow toward him. I flung out a hand and launched a bolt of trick. It blasted the tendril away, giving Alex the seconds he needed. He scooped up the shining book, whirled, with his back to the vastness of the origin, and raised his hand. "Mother!"

"What's he doing?" McGovern whispered at my shoulder.

"The same thing he always does." He was going to get himself killed by spiraling and taking his mother and the origin with him, hoping the registry book kept the blast contained. Hadn't he learned a bloody thing? We *were* always better together.

I spied a length of thick electric cable nearby. "Are those live?"

McGovern followed my gaze. "No. I turned off the main power switch when you said to shut it all down."

"Turn the power back on."

"The pumps are off. The water level is rising. If those electrics touch the water…"

The cables were close to multiple growing puddles. "Yeah, I get it, we're all fried. Just do it."

"Why?"

"Just turn it back on." With Jocelyn's attention on Alex, I scurried out from behind the console, grabbed the loose cable as thick as my forearm, and nodded at McGovern. He nodded back, dashed behind the bank of computers, and remerged on the other side next to the huge grey box on the wall with a shit-load of *Danger of Death* warning signs.

There were puddles all over, water dripping from the vaulted brick ceiling. Electricity and water did not mix. Whatever happened next, there would be fireworks.

"One little artifact cannot stop me," the shadow witch

was saying, her back to me, her black and gold liquid tentacles writhing.

Alex held the book out like a shield, his hand poised to slam against its bindings and draw the brilliant power from inside it. The whole place was a tinderbox of trick, waiting to blow.

I had the match.

I crept forward. McGovern flicked the power back on and the overhead lights flickered, but their glow was lost in the origin's blinding light. The cable buzzed in my grip. Now all I had to do was poke the shadow witch with it without setting myself on fire. Again. Unlike Alex's schemes, my plans were best *not* thought through. A leap of faith, a right hook, the flick of a wrist, draw the right card, a bit of luck... I'd lived that way my whole life. This was just one of those times.

"You cannot stop me, Alexander. Too much like your father, too weak-hearted."

She'd lifted herself up onto those shadow-tentacles. They pulsed either side of me as I approached, like thick black veins feeding into her.

Alex saw me, saw the cable, and he knew what I was about to do. He lifted his chin and faced his mum. "You should have stayed dead." He slammed his hand down onto the book, igniting a blast of white light.

I jabbed the power cable into the shadow limb and let go. Electric blue light danced up the tentacle, into and over her. Assaulted from the front and from behind, caught in the middle, she screamed. Her whole body arched, limbs contorting. Her scream reached its pitch and Alex's mother blasted into a million fragments of shadow. We'd done it! The bitch was dead. Then her fragments coalesced, turning to smoke, and the pieces of shadow flowed, like water, straight into the origin. The origin swelled, growing. Golden whips flung outward, latching onto the consoles, sinking veins into the machines.

"Turn it off!"

McGovern yanked the switch down. The power died, the lights blinked out, the origin shrunk, but not my much. Its feeders were still attached to the machines, still pulsing, feeding.

Alex dashed to me. "She's gone to the other side."

"The what?"

"Where the shadows reside."

I'd seen it, in my dreams. I'd been there, sort of, been a part of it. As I'd lain unconscious in a hospital bed, I'd slipped between worlds, stepped into the shadow realm. And if she'd fled there, then I had to go back.

"John? Don't think it."

I faced the origin. It had always been trying to pull me in. Even in Wordsworth, I'd heard it calling. I mean, fuck it, I was the messiah, right?

"John, no." Alex's face crumpled.

"The whole time, we've been trying to fix it from the wrong side."

"John, no. Don't. I will beg. Is that what you want?"

But Alex didn't reach for me. Because he knew it too. This had to happen.

"Kage said I had a hero complex," I said.

"Fuck Kage." Alex blocked my route to the origin. His whole aura glowed golden. "If you go in there, and you manage to draw the origin back to you, how will you get back?"

Was it better to break his heart now or later? "I don't think it's a return journey."

His face fell, taking my heart with it. I knew what this would do to him. I felt it too, the hurt of us breaking in two. I cupped his dirt-smudged face and brushed a thumb across his cheek. "I fuckin' love you, Alexander Kempthorne. More than anything. I don't have all the fancy words and shit, but you know it right? You can feel it?"

His mouth twisted, lips pinching together. "I won't let you do this."

I smiled. "Yeah, you will."

"John." He flung his arms around me, hauling me against his chest. Like this he was scared and vulnerable, and all I wanted to do was make it not hurt again for him. "Why does it have to be you?"

"Candidate Thirty-Two? It was always gonna be me. And you knew it. You've always known it." My voice skipped at the last words. I pushed from his arms and coughed away the emotional knot in my throat. McGovern had stumbled over, still wide-eyed and uncertain.

Alex reluctantly let me go. I couldn't meet his gaze, not when I saw how his eyes glittered with unshed tears and how his heart was breaking. "Okay, you guys," I told them both. "If it doesn't work and the origin stays, destroy the pumps and flood the place. That's like Plan F or something. At the least, Jocelyn won't be able to come back through if the vaults are underwater." I didn't know that for certain, but it sounded like it had a shot. "Alex, look after Gina."

I turned away before Alex's wrecked expression could drop me to my knees. I couldn't say goodbye, I just couldn't. Everyone he'd ever loved had left him, and shit, I knew I had to do this but... why'd it have to be me? Why couldn't we have a happy bloody ending? Hadn't we earned it?

I swiped at my cheek, wiping away a stray tear.

It was going to be okay. I squinted into the origin's light. Some shit just had to be done, and this was one of those moments. "Ain't no other idiot gonna save London."

## 41

Alexander

Every thought, every muscle, every piece of me screamed to stop him. The man I loved walked away, and there was nothing I could do, nothing he'd *allow* me to do to prevent him going. Because this was John, wasn't it? This was who he was. Better than me in a thousand different ways, better than most of us. He'd followed Kage Mitchell, a man of suspect motives, halfway around the world to try to rescue him. He'd pulled me back from the brink of chaos and death, countless times. He'd given me a reason to live. And was I really going to stand back and let him walk into some version of death alone?

The glow from the origin had almost swallowed him whole by the time I broke my inertia and began to move. My heart raced, my steps quickened into a run.

He had a connection to the source like no other latent. John was the link, he always had been, he could do this, but there was no guarantee I'd survive what happened next.

He stepped into the glow, most of him disappearing inside the origin. In the last, fateful second, I took a breath, closed my eyes, and caught his hand. He turned his head, met my gaze, and we both fell through.

*Cold.*

As though I'd plunged into a bath of ice water. I'd felt it before, lying near death on Montgomery's desk in Wordsworth and sprawled in the back of Trent's car in the US. I'd been close both times, close to... whatever this was. No living thing was supposed to cross into this realm.

"Alex, for fuck's sake." John staggered and whirled on me. "What the hell, you could have died!" His form wisped, like smoke, as though one strong gust of wind would scatter him.

I swallowed, his rage secondary as I took in our surroundings. We were in London, but not. The origin had brought us to the surface, probably above where we'd been battling my mother, alongside St Katharine Docks with Tower Bridge's recognizable silhouette behind John, its grand span stretching over a smoky Thames. I blinked, trying to clear my vision, but my focus still swam. There were no people here, no noise, just silence and smoke. A world of shadows.

John's wrath ebbed away as he realized where we stood. "Fuck me. Are we dead?"

"So eloquently put."

He wobbled. His hand went to his head, and I caught his arm, holding him firm.

"Shit, just... It's a lot. The psychic echoes are everywhere." Once he had his balance back under him, he smiled. John pulled on my hand, still in his. "You're an idiot, but thanks, Alex," he whispered.

I'd watched him die, and I'd be damned if I let it happen again. "Let's put this right *together*."

Now all we had to do was find my mother, finish her here, and drag the origin back where it belonged.

"We *aren't* dead though, right?" he asked.

"A halfway point, perhaps. Or just another realm, like ours, separated by psychic energy. We've been assuming the shadows are dead latents, but I suspect some part of them has been trapped here since my mother upset the resonance of all this. Death, shadows, ghosts, it's what we grasp at, given our frame of reference."

John almost laughed. He pulled away, curiosity driving him. "I love it when you talk dirty." His hand left mine and he took a few steps away, making my heart leap toward panic all over again. "So, where do you think the shadow witch is?"

A trail of burning embers wisped across Tower Bridge's barren road surface, the only other light in this world. "That way."

John glanced around, always alert, always assessing for threats. I just looked at *him*. His trick made him glow, highlighting him from the gloom.

We crossed onto the bridge with its vast Victorian-engineered twin towers and thick, ornate ironwork. The bridge was blue and silver in our realm, but its colors here had turned to shades of grey. The Thames beneath us was a river of fog, its passing as silent as the rest of the strange, insubstantial place.

John stopped at dead center of the bridge and leaned against the rail. Much of central London stretched before us, all of it grey and silent.

He swallowed and turned to me. "I can summon the origin back here, I know I can."

"All right."

"Just watch my back, okay? I don't think we're alone here."

"Always."

He shoved off the rail and backed toward the middle of the bridge's roadway, lowered his hands to his sides, and summoned his trick, making his hands glow. I triggered my own power, teasing it awake. In the corner of my eyes, shadows shifted, only to settle again when I tried to pin them down with a glance. We definitely weren't alone.

John's eyes closed; he dipped his chin and lifted his hands, summoning a veil of light.

A shadow shot from across the river, bolting straight toward him. I raised my hand, coiling my trick around my forearm, and... hesitated. He'd always had an affinity with the shadows. They spoke to him, and when he'd needed them in Wordsworth, they'd come. But if I didn't strike it down, and it hurt him... I couldn't take the risk.

*"Alexander... wait..."*

My sister's voice sent shivers racing down the back of my neck, halting my impulse to protect. The shadow whirled around John's veil but didn't attack. More spilled from the echo of nearby houses and streets, spiraling around John.

*"It's going to be okay."* Charlotte's featherlight touch landed on my shoulder. *"You're going to be okay."*

I turned my head to catch a glimpse of her face—knowing it would be my last—but she was already gone, drawn toward John with the others.

John's power grew, the veil shone, the shadows swirled, and it felt right, as though we might succeed. A blast bloomed from John, sending trick through the shadows, over me, rolling into Grey London. A pillar of light shot from him, pierced the sky, and tore open a jagged split between worlds.

So lost in admiring him and the maelstrom of trick and shadows he'd summoned, I almost missed the streak of sparking embers rushing through the Thames fog. This shadow was different, full of fury and callousness. My mother—or more accurately, the monstrous thing she'd become.

I flung out a whip of trick, slashing through the racing cloud of burning embers. They split apart but reformed seconds later, heading for John. She meant to harm him. Destroy him. Her hatred was so fierce a thing it tainted the air, thickening it. She knew John was bringing her reign to an end.

I flung a second and third whip, lighting up the darkness, but the embers split and spiraled and danced until they shot vertically, and then they dove down, toward John. I couldn't allow her through. I summoned a fan of trick, lashed it outward, and swept the embers away. They scattered, reformed again, and grew, rising high above the Thames's murky fog.

This creature my mother had become—whatever it was, whatever wicked energy had created it and fueled it —would not get past me. John was mine to protect. I'd die to keep him safe.

A face appeared among the embers, one I knew well. *"Dear boy..."* Thomas Montgomery. A latent, of course he'd be here. The face contorted, shifting, remade itself into that of my mother. *"Such a regrettable failure."*

Then this malevolent storm was all of them combined. "If this is the best you can do—"

Olivia Barnes appeared in the embers. *"We could have been gods."*

Ghosts, all from my past, memories from the times I'd failed.

*"Let us through!"*

I spread my stance, summoned all the trick I could muster, and gathered it under my skin until it was too much to contain. "Never!" And set it free.

## 42

D<sup>om</sup>

I had the origin, all of it so close I could taste the win. A fissure between worlds was open; the origin had answered my call to return to where it belonged, even as it burned and thrashed and fought to keep itself rooted in the living London.

The shadows were here, and more poured through. Not to attack, but to protect.

Alex's power slammed into me, tripping me off my stride. My grasp on the origin slipped, but I clung on, gasping, desperate. Alex? He needed me... He'd come with me, and he fought for me, and I was ready to die for London, for latents, but *he* didn't have to.

*"John, no..."* a voice cried close by, one I'd heard before.

The voice from the study. Charlotte's voice, her shadow. *"Alexander... must... do this."*

But I could help him. The origin twitched, sensing my determination wavering. I staggered, the veil shimmered, the shadows howled. No, if I lost control now, everything would be over. I couldn't... save him and everyone else. I had to choose.

I saw him then, through a storm of light and darkness, saw him standing against a monstrous cloud of fire, burning as brightly as a star, holding the fiery shadows back. He had this... He was in control, buying me time for the final push.

Charlotte's voice joined the others, a thousand voices and memories all churning as one, spiraling faster and faster. I squeezed my eyes closed, drew on the trick, drew every last drop of power I had, and pulled the source—the origin, all of it—through the fissure. Light flooded the world, washing away the grayness, turning every surface silver and sharp and bright. The shadows splashed away, vanished, like mist on a summer's morning. My trick spluttered, the veil collapsed, and I dropped. Spent. Numb. Cold. Empty. "Alex?" I croaked.

The origin's light blinded, it throbbed like a second sun on my back. We'd done it, we'd brought it home, but this world wasn't ours, we did not belong. Alex? Where was Alex? I couldn't see. Everything had bleached in the light, blurred together as one.

I reached for him inside, the link we shared, but my trick was gone.

"John!" Alex staggered into sight, dropped beside me, and hauled me against him. I wrapped my arms around him, holding him so bloody close, feeling his every breath and the beat of his heart. It was going to be all right. Even if we died here, it was okay. I wasn't alone. I had Alex. I crushed him close. His breath fluttered on my neck. His heart beat in time with mine. The light burned, brighter, colder, scorching and freezing all at once. It poured into my mouth, choked my throat, filled me, drowned and burned me in a blink.

And then, with a high-pitched screech, the light, the world, my place in it, shattered and reformed, leaving me spent and gasping on my knees, with Alex wrapped in my arms in the gloom of the St Katharine Dock vaults.

"John..." Alex grabbed my face in his trembling hands. "Are you all right? Can you hear me? Breathe..."

"No, yeah... I'm okay." He crushed me in a hug, mumbled a string of words, sounding pissed off, then held me back and glared into my eyes. "Hey," I said, and his glower softened. "See, we're alive, it's all good."

A cough nearby alerted me to the fact we weren't alone.

McGovern, wringing wet and still ghostly pale, loitered nearby. "We er... We should vacate the area. After the shockwaves, the structure has become unsound." He nodded toward the far walls where water poured through great cracks in the bricks. That couldn't be good. He'd said something about the Thames being held back but that was a hell of a lot of water pouring in.

"Quickly," he urged.

The origin had gone. Only half-melted steel bars remained. Alex and I staggered to our feet and sloshed through water up to our ankles. We needed to get out, to see the sky, people, reality. I needed to know this was real, that we weren't still trapped in Grey London. I needed to know it was truly over.

A rumble trembled through the ground.

Behind us, bricks splashed into the water. Something structural cracked above.

"Go, now!" McGovern shoved us both toward the rear tunnel door. "Hurry!"

"C'mon!" I waved him after us.

The far wall behind him collapsed in a hail of brick and roaring water. Alex's hand closed on my arm and yanked me after him, into a run. We bolted down the steel walkway, through a pressure door, and into the tunnel with the exit elevator at its end. "That elevator had better bloody have power!" Its lights glowed. But the water had risen up to our thighs and continued to lap higher.

Alex jabbed the elevator's call button. Water lapped at my crotch and roared behind us, out of sight but still pouring into the vaults. "Where the fuck is McGovern?"

Another almighty crack and rumbling shook the walls. A wave surged toward us and slammed me back against Alex, and him into the elevator doors as they split apart. We tumbled into the elevator car, washed inside.

Alex fought back to his feet. "Come on! Quickly!" He waved for McGovern.

I saw him then, trying to hold the tunnel door closed against the surge, but the water still poured through. He couldn't close it, not with that force.

"Go!" he yelled.

Once we closed the elevators doors, it was over for him.

"Go, Alex! I've lived long enough in her shadow!" McGovern smiled. "I'll die doing the right thing."

More water poured in, rising to our waists. The door behind McGovern shuddered. He heaved back, fighting against the force of the Thames trying to break through.

Alex jabbed the elevator button. The doors sealed and the car jolted, groaned, the lights flickered, but the car heaved and lifted. Almost instantly the water began to drain away.

I bent double, clutched my wet thighs, and *breathed*. "Fuck."

We'd just left a man to drown. We'd returned the origin. My trick had vanished. And it wasn't coming back, not this time. I was... normal? "Did we just cure all latents?"

"We'll see," Alex said in his stone-cold unimpressed tone that meant he was hiding a fuck-ton of emotion.

How the fuck were we even alive?

I launched at him, slammed him back against the elevator car wall, pinned him there, but kissed him gently, a brush of the lips, a tease of the tongue. He groaned, one hand twisted in my wet hair while his other clutched my arse and yanked me tight against his hard, shivering body.

Yes. Him and me. We were un-fucking-stoppable!

The elevator doors rumbled open. Water poured out into the corridor in a wave.

"IRL, step away from each other! Move! Move!"

They struck so bloody fast there was no time to react.

One guy tore me off Alex, threw me to my knees, and yanked my hands behind my back. Another had Alex pinned face-first to the elevator wall, cuffing his hands behind him.

"Under the Latent Registration Act of Nineteen-Seventy-Eight—"

"Hey, arseholes! We just saved you, you ungrateful dicks." Two men hauled me through the storage closet, through the convenience store, and onto the street where a trio of black vans waited along with a whole crowd of onlookers with their phones out, filming.

"Nothing bloody changes," I grumbled.

They threw me into a van and Alex into another so bloody fast I didn't get a chance to see him. "Typical. Save the bloody world, and the IRL ruins the afterglow."

## 43

One Month Later

Alexander

Sunlight glittered off the bobbing multi-million-dollar yachts berthed in the nearby Puerto Banús marina. The sounds of laughter, the smooth play of Spanish accents, and the *chink* of glasses sailed around the pretty marina's storefronts and eateries. I watched the turquoise water shimmer, almost too afraid to move, should the peace of the moment be shattered. Weeks of relentless questioning, latent tests, interviews, paperwork, and lawyers. Every aspect of my life had been turned upside down, rifled through, and exposed. I'd only escaped prison by the skin of my teeth.

"Hm, this view never gets old." John leaned down, kissed me unashamedly on the mouth, and thrust a hand down my shirt, lighting my heart and soul on fire. If we hadn't been surrounded by the bar's other customers, I'd have hauled him into my lap and made him finish what that heated kiss promised.

He breathed in with a hiss through his teeth and reluctantly pulled back, then sprawled into the opposite chair. He wore a short-sleeved shirt, casually unbuttoned at the neck. The strong Spanish sun had tanned his chest and arms, turning his skin a deep shade of bronze and his hair a lighter shade of chestnut. He even had a few startling freckles on his face. He spotted me admiring his body and those eyes turned hungry.

"Keep looking at me like that and you and me will have a date with a bathroom stall."

"That's not beyond the realm of possibility."

He laughed, grinned, and cast his gaze across the marina. "I don't know whose life this is, but it sure as shit ain't mine. I keep waiting for the next disaster to strike."

We'd spent the last two weeks on our yacht, having left England as soon as the IRL turned their backs. We weren't technically permitted to leave, but I doubted they'd come after us in Spain. They were too busy figuring out what role they had to play now latents appeared to be *cured*. The London Met, however, were another issue. In the eyes of the law and most of the public, I was still everyone's favorite bad billionaire, and John was still my accomplice. However, it did help that we'd given the police everything on the Business, bringing the organized crime gang to its knees. As for Kage Mitchell's death and his part in revealing my involvement in my sister's demise, the legal wranglings were ongoing, but considering John's abuse, we had a strong argument for self defense.

"It could be... Your life, I mean. *Our* life." My ring glinted on my finger when I reached for my wine glass. John's did the same in the sunlight.

"Live the high life on your posh boat, sipping cocktails?"

"Sail the world?"

He smirked, intrigued but unconvinced. "I kinda miss London, though. The weather's nice here, the people are hot, but you don't get called a wanker for crossing the road. It just ain't the same."

"Yes, I know." I chuckled. "We will return. Cecil Court will be reopened as a bookstore, I think. Rare editions. Gina and Cassie have suggested we repurpose Ravenscourt as a wedding venue."

"Hopefully with fewer executions than our Big Day?" He snorted.

"We have options. But for now, we deserve a break. Don't you agree?"

He learned forward, eyes full of mischief. "You ever skinny-dipped, Kempthorne?"

I stroked the stem of my glass and imagined John swimming naked in warm, sparkling waters. "Regrettably, I have not." His grin alone was temptation personified. "I know a place. A hidden bay, accessible only by boat. Extremely private."

He stole my glass from my fingers, downed the expensive wine in a few gulps, and handed the empty glass back with a grin. "Why aren't we already there?"

## 44

# D<sup>om</sup>

It still blew my mind that I was allowed on the yacht. As a London boy, I didn't do boats. Kage's canal boat was the closet I'd gotten to being on the water, so the floating palace that was Alex's superyacht was so far outside of my world that I kept wondering if I had died back in shadow-London.

We'd swum naked and fooled around, which wasn't easy while treading water. After climbing out, I'd disappeared below deck to grab the whiskey, also grabbing a shirt on the way, leaving it unbuttoned, forgetting pants altogether. When I returned with glasses and the bottle, Alex was lounged on the front deck, naked from head to toe, one leg drawn up, hands behind his head, eyes closed, basking in the sun. The sight stopped me dead. The location, the yacht, our messy lives, none of it mattered. Just him. So bloody powerful, so vulnerable, and mine. I had the ring to prove it.

We'd been close to losing.

A sharp knot caught in my throat. I cleared it with a cough and he squinted over, shielding his eyes with a smile.

"You brought ice?"

"Yeah, although it won't last in this heat." Sitting cross-legged beside him, I set down the whiskey and glasses and poured us both drinks.

Alex had a few scars. Those scars gleamed in the sun. One was next to his heart, where a bullet had almost taken him from me in the US. I reached out and skimmed my fingers over it, then through the few fine black hairs. After a minute of stroking, he caught my wrist, his face turning serious.

"This is too good," I told him. "This, right now. Something is gonna happen to fuck it up."

"I understand why you'd think that. But it won't." He lifted my hand, took my middle finger, and slipped it between his lips, then withdrew and said, "I'll make sure of it." His voice rumbled with heat.

"With what?" I teased. "Your billions of pounds and this ship's big dick energy?"

That got his lips twitching. "Blackwater's collapse wiped out fifty percent of Kempthorne Estates."

"Oh no." I braced an arm over his shoulder and stroked my damp finger along his bottom lip. "You'll have to rough it with me?"

"We still have a few billion to keep the lights on. Mostly in property and stocks. And this yacht."

"Hm, less money talk." I grabbed an ice cube from the whiskey, threw a knee over his hip and, straddling his thighs, encircled his right nipple with the ice. "More fucking."

His eyes flashed that brilliant spark of sharpness that came from being ordered. "That money is yours now, you realize?"

Yeah, but was it? We had the rings, but our marriage had been interrupted by his bat-shit crazy Shadow Witch mum.

He caught my hand again, making me look up. "We're married," he said. "Legally. I made sure of it. Everything that is mine, is yours. Including this—" He pressed my hand to his heart.

The soppy bastard. "Christ, what did you do?" I chuckled. "You didn't threaten the lovely registry office woman?"

"I may have called her."

"You *did* threaten her." I pushed upright onto my knees, leaving the ice cube melting on his abs. We were ignoring the fact we were both as hard as iron bars.

"No," he lied, but his mouth fought a smile. "I was... persuasive."

"'Persuasive'?" I laughed, and in that second I took my gaze off him, he hooked my leg under his, grabbed my arm, and flipped me onto my back. His hips rocked, his cock rubbed mine, his hand came down gently around my neck, and my laughter vanished behind a throaty moan. There wasn't much I liked more than Alex getting me on my back.

"You don't believe I can be persuasive *without* threatening?" Even now, his tone threatened, but in that growly way I loved.

"You goin' to show me?"

His grip tightened and his cock twitched against mine, chasing away all the sensible thoughts and replacing them with the raw need to have him inside.

He leaned close, his mouth almost brushing mine, but the grip on my neck held me down. "Will you beg me to finish you, John?"

"Persuade me an' I might."

His free hand dropped, his fingers wrapped my dick, and he stroked, stealing my self-control. If I'd had any intelligent thoughts, they were long gone. He grabbed a handful of ice and dumped it on my chest. Cold slapped my sunbaked skin. I yelped, tried to flick the ice off, and sent our drinks flying, soaking my shirt and me in cool whiskey.

Alex, the prick, rolled off, laughing so hard he clutched his stomach.

I lunged, pinned him, got a knee between his legs and a hand on his chest, and with my free hand, I skimmed his balls, cupping them in my palm. He choked on his last laugh, looked down his body at me, and on seeing my grin, his eyes widened.

"Want me to stop, tell me it's raining," I purred. And with that, I flicked my fingers though a pool of ice water and whiskey, probed between his arse cheeks, and eased inside. Alex gasped, let his head fall back and, naked on the deck of his insanely expensive boat, he surrendered. Mine for the taking.

I tweaked him until his breathing shuddered, his cock leaked, and his body gleamed with sweat, then stopped.

He lifted his head. "What are you doing?"

"Persuade me."

"Now?"

I shrugged. His muscles clamped around my two fingers. I didn't want to stop any more than he wanted me to, but the anticipation was worth it.

"I just..." He licked his lips. "Spare me a moment. I'm struggling to think."

"Why? It's not like I have my fingers up your arse... Oh wait." I stroked inside him and almost laughed when his eyes rolled and he dropped his head back again. His cock was right there, within sucking distance, precum gleaming. I wanted it between my lips, but there was something real special about having Alex at my mercy.

"Is it raining?" I asked.

He chuckled darkly. "You have five seconds before I switch this around and fuck you into this deck."

Heat rolled through me; my skin prickled and my cock throbbed. "That's not persuading, that's threatening. I was right. You don't know the difference."

He looked up, eyes dark and hungry. "It's not threatening, John, when you and I both know you want it."

Bugger it, he was right. I should have known not to try to win an argument with him. I stroked him to the point where his eyes rolled, gathered his cock in my free hand,

and sealed my lips around its warm, veined length. His moan was worth the wait. His hips twitched, aching to drive himself deep down my throat. I swallowed him, balls to my chin, then withdrew, lapping up his saltiness. His hand plunged into my hair, fingers gripping, urging me on, and for a while, there was just me and him, his cock and arse both mine.

"It's raining!"

I withdrew fast, fearing I'd gone too far, but then Alex was on his knees, my face in his hands, his expression panicked. "Shit. You all right?" I asked.

"Yes." His smile danced. "I just... I need to be in you, John. Right now. Before I come just thinking about it."

"All right then." The words had barely left my lips when he dropped his hands, grabbed my hips, flipped me around, spread my arse, splashed something cold and wet on my hole, and drove himself inside, so fucking fast and hard I almost swallowed my tongue. *"Fuck."*

"Too much?"

"No, just—" I chuckled. "A lot."

Hot hands gripped my shoulders and he slammed in. Blinding pleasure lashed up my back and down to my balls, making my dick leap. I must have fuckin' died, because there was no way John Domenici got railed by Alexander Kempthorne in some Mediterranean paradise. Or maybe I did finally get to take home the win. Maybe we did get a happy ever after, and this was it. It felt like one.

His fingers looped around my neck and he leaned over, his mouth at my ear, breaths racing. "I love you." The words shuddered into me with his every thrust.

"You're my whole world, the reason I breathe, the blood in my heart. You're mine, and I'd burn the world for you." The fingers of his free hand wrapped around my dick. I was all his. Just like he was mine.

Yeah, we deserved the win. This was our fucking time, and I was owning it.

 lexander

While John spoke with Gina on the phone, organizing when to pick her and Cassie up from Tangier's airport in a week's time, I rummaged through the kitchen drawer and removed a small, plain cardboard box. What it contained could ruin our honeymoon-mood, but I was long overdue giving it to him.

My phone pinged. Another message from Janine Domenici, this one a recipe for chicken and mushroom risotto. As John returned, I showed him the message.

"I'm sorry, she thinks you can cook."

His mother had been sending me recipes for weeks, one every few days. "And why does she think that?"

He winced. "I maybe told her you could?"

"I *had* a cook. Now I don't, and frankly, as I struggle

with preparing cereal, I don't believe you'd want to consume anything I dare attempt to make."

"I know, but she wants to help and it's her way." He waved a hand. "She likes you, or she'd be sending you death threats. Just go with it." His gaze snagged on the box. "That's ominous."

"Before we left England, these were returned to me, for you."

He took the box and flipped the lid open, revealing his half-burned, tattered, sand-scuffed deck of cards.

"Huh." He scratched his cheek and side-eyed them.

"I wasn't sure if you'd want them. They're no longer an artifact... obviously." Artifacts didn't exist, or if they did, nobody could sense, read, or use them anymore.

He set the box down, not touching the cards inside. The fact we both had lost our trick, along with countless other latents, was something we hadn't discussed. What was there to say? It was gone. A good thing, but... if John was anything like me, while our tricks were more trouble than they were worth, they had still been a part of our lives. The hole its absence had left might never be filled. And that was something every latent had to live with.

John replaced the lid, shutting the cards inside. "Thanks, but er... I don't think they fit me anymore." He sighed, his hand still resting on the box. "You think the trick is ever coming back?" he asked, letting go and leaning against the counter.

"Not if the origin and its realm are left well alone." A frown darkened his face. "We did a good thing," I said. "We did what had to be done."

"Yeah, I know. I just hope it's over." He took the box

and dropped it into the trashcan, then looped an arm around my waist and kissed me on the lips. "Come outside, the sun's setting. It's moody and dramatic, you'll fit right in."

What was he implying? "Go, I'll bring the drinks."

He cocked an eyebrow but a hint of uncertainty touched his smile. I let him leave and considered how different our future might be now. The sense of unease, of helplessness, came from losing the trick, but also from knowing Blackwater's research was likely still out there somewhere. Latency wasn't something that could be put back in a box and forgotten. My mother and her actions had changed everything. We all had to find our way in a new world. But at least we *had* a new world.

And if the trick did ever return, we'd be here, John and I. Together. And we'd do the right thing.

I retrieved the deck of cards and hid them back inside the drawer.

Well, *John* would do the right thing. I'd always found the right thing to be highly negotiable.


The End

# ABOUT THE AUTHOR

Born to wolves, Rainbow Award Winner Ariana Nash only ventures from the Cornish moors when the moon is fat and the night alive with myths and legends. She captures those myths in glass jars and returning home, weaves them into stories filled with forbidden desires, fantasy realms, and wicked delights.

Sign up to her newsletter and get a free ebook here: https://www.subscribepage.com/silk-steel